STAR TREK 10:
THE FINAL REFLECTION

STAR TREK NOVELS

STAR TREK GIANT NOVELS

A *STAR TREK*® NOVEL

THE FINAL REFLECTION

JOHN M. FORD

TITAN BOOKS

LONDON

STAR TREK: **THE FINAL REFLECTION**
ISBN 1 85286 064 2

Published by
Titan Books Ltd
42-44 Dolben Street
London SE1 0UP

First Titan Edition May 1988
10 9 8 7 6 5 4 3

British Library Cataloguing-in-Publication Data. A catalogue record for this book is available from the British Library.

Printed and bound in Great Britain by Cox and Wyman Ltd, Reading, Berkshire.

For J.B.
after fifteen years,
the genuine article.

Prologue

Enterprise, dormant for nearly a week now, was waking up.

Captain James Kirk had stayed aboard, while the crew took leave on Starbase 12: Dr. McCoy had given him a stern lecture on the perils of overwork, and Engineer Scott a milder talk on the pleasures Kirk would be missing. Even Spock had gone stationside; something to do with new materials for the ship's library computer.

But Kirk was all right. In fact, he felt wonderful. He had given himself a walking inspection tour of his ship, quite alone, at whatever pace he felt like at the moment. It was not work. It had been sheer play.

Now the crew was returning, making *Enterprise* ready for voyage, and that too was satisfactory. Kirk walked the corridors, giving salutes and greetings, feeling almost light-headed, as if he were present at a new creation.

Yeoman Janice Rand came up the corridor toward Kirk, still in a civilian tunic and loose trousers, travelling bag slung over her shoulder. Her hair was in a new, non-regulation style, upswept, quite striking and attractive; Kirk could not remember having seen the style before—

And then he knew he had seen it, once only: on Specialist Mara, the consort of the Klingon Captain Kang.

Kirk gave a clumsy gesture somewhere between a salute and a wave; Rand smiled and waved back.

She's still off duty, Kirk thought, she has the right to wear her hair any way she pleases—but why on earth . . . ? It surely hadn't been that long since the Organian Peace: Kirk wondered if it could *ever* be that long.

He shook his head and walked on. A little farther down the corridor, he heard a crewman use a few words in a foreign language. Kirk did not know the meaning, but knew from the harsh, consonantal sound that the language must be Klingonese. He also knew that only a half-dozen of the ship's complement spoke Klingonese, and this was not one of them.

Kirk went up a level to Sickbay. Inside, Dr. McCoy was unpacking a carrier marked MEDICAL SUPPLIES. Kirk's medical training was sufficient to identify Romulan ale, Saurian brandy in the trademark bottle, and a complete set of components for Argelian nine-layer cocktails.

"Expecting an epidemic, Bones?"

McCoy looked up. His expression was odd: slightly distant, slightly sour. "I hope to Lucius Beebe there is—" He stopped short, shook his head.

"Who?" Kirk said.

"Nothing. Something my granddaddy used to say when he got dry." McCoy reverently held up a bottle of

8

Jack Daniel's Black Label.

want, Jim."

Something in the way McC

Kirk hesitate. Bones was alwa

geon, but when he was really

pleasant company. "Later, Bon

now." Kirk smiled. "Promises

go . . ."

"Uh-huh." McCoy put the b

little forlorn.

"Bones," Kirk said quietly, "v

"Hm? *Oh.* 'Course, you don't know." He reached
down into the carrier, clinking bottles and cans, and
brought out a book. "Here you go. Read all about
it."

Kirk took the book. It was a bookstore edition, in
hard covers, not a computer offprint. *The Final Reflection,* the cover said, above a lurid painting showing a Klingon battle cruiser. He turned it over,
scanned the blurbs. "This is the one the Starfleet
memos were about, isn't it? The novel about the
Klingons."

"Novel, yeah," McCoy said. "About the Klingons."
His voice was just slightly less tense. "You might like
it . . . there's some good space-battle stuff."

"I'll get a print—"

"Take it," McCoy said, and at once his voice cleared,
as if there had never been anything wrong at all. "I'd
better get my office in order. I'm about to get four
hundred cases of station leave."

"All right, Bones. Hold that drink for me."

"Sure, Jim."

Kirk went on down the corridor, looking at the book,
half conscious that others were saluting him or dodging
out of his way. He tried to remember the texts of the
Starfleet memos about the novel: their substance
seemed to have been the routine disclaimers about
any book not Fully Approved by the Public Informa-

9

. . . a little more strongly worded than

. . . es, Bones had said. According to the
. . . y, the story was set not long after first
. . . with the Klingons, just before Kirk himself
. . . been born; back before dilithium, when the best
. . . pwrights in Starfleet thought Warp 4.8 was the
absolute limit. Before phasers. Before *Enterprise*
had gone on the drawing boards. That should be
interesting, Kirk thought, even if those days seemed
as far away as Captain Hornblower's sails and can-
non.

But then, Kirk had always liked Horatio Hornblower.

A name caught his eye: Dr. Emanuel Tagore. A
political scientist, Kirk recalled. He had died about a
year ago, aged 120 or so; Spock had mentioned it.
Spock. . . .

Kirk got into the next turbolift.

Spock was already back in duty uniform, though he
had not even unpacked. His small travelling case was
on the bed, still sealed; against the wall of the cabin
were two large carriers labeled COMPUTER DATA—
KEEP FROM ALL RADIATION.

"Captain. I am sorry I have not reported to the
Bridge. I was . . ."

"Spock. . . . Welcome back."

"Thank you, Captain, though I have not been gone
in any real sense." Spock looked down slightly, saw the
book in Kirk's hand. "I see you have . . . already
obtained a copy of that work."

"Yes. Bones gave it to me."

The eyebrow went up like a flag. "Indeed. I find
that . . . well. Perhaps not surprising."

"I wanted to ask you about it."

"It is a work of fiction, Captain. That is, I believe, all
that needs to be said."

It's some kind of strange new hangover, Kirk

10

thought, one leave and my whole crew goes crazy. "I was going to ask about Emanuel Tagore. Did you know him?"

"He was an acquaintance of my father's. When I was a student at the Makropyrios, we had . . . discussions, though I was never enrolled in his classes."

That said more than perhaps Spock had intended; there were over two million students at the Federation's finest university, too many for anyone to casually "have discussions" outside the classroom.

Kirk said, "So then you did know him."

"I believe that was what I said, Captain."

Kirk almost shook his head. "Analysis, Spock," he said, trying to sound as if he were joking. "Enhancement, please."

"Yes, Captain, I did know Dr. Emanuel Tagore. I admired him, as did my father the Ambassador, although in many ways Dr. Tagore was a most illogical man. But I knew him as a Human, not a character in a novel."

"I haven't read the book yet."

"Yes, I had just realized there was not time for you to have done so. Is that all you require from me at this time, Captain?" The tone was no cooler than any Vulcan might use. But this was not just any Vulcan.

"Yes, Spock," Kirk said, too puzzled to be really hurt. "See you on the Bridge." He looked at Spock, vaguely hoping the Science officer would recover as Dr. McCoy had.

But Spock did not. "Of course, Captain." Kirk went out.

The corridor was empty, silent except for the distant chiming of an annunciator. Kirk looked at the book again, at the Klingon ship. *The Final Reflection*. Reflection of what? he thought. He could remember times when he had seen himself reflected in books . . . in Mark Twain, in the Hornblower stories. Sometimes the

11

image was startling. But they were, after all, only stories.

Which was, sort of, what Spock had said.

Kirk went to his own quarters, changed from fatigues into duty uniform, put the book on the bedside table.

First *Enterprise,* he thought. Then McCoy's drink. Then we'll see what it has to say.

THE FINAL REFLECTION

Researcher's Note

"Be a storyteller, an embellisher, a liar; they'll
call you that and worse anyway. It hardly matters. The Tao which can be perceived is not the true
Tao."

—Dr. Emanuel Tagore, to the author

It has been sixty-five years since USS *Sentry* met
IKV *Devisor* in the UFP's first known contact with
the Klingon Empire. The final events of the story
which follows took place some forty years ago. Some
time back we celebrated ten years of *Pax Organia*
(of which more in a moment). There are many who
are convinced that "the Klingon Phase of Federation history is over." I first heard that phrase used
in a lecture at the Makropyrios. No one even
smiled.

So perhaps I may be excused a certain puzzlement at the curtains of silence that descended during the research for this work. UFP "Klingon authorities" were unavailable for extended periods, coinciding with my calls and visits. Official records of the "Dissolution Babel" are incomplete, containing little more than the "we kissed and made up" account found in children's books. Important persons have died or dropped from sight—neither rare events, but highly concentrated in this area. While my life was not threatened, my researcher's credentials and my computer's memory cores were. Only one person was willing to speak freely, and that one both warned me that his memory was fallible and gave me the advice quoted above. He was too modest about his memory. But his counsels were always wise.

Thus what follows is a novelist's reconstruction of events, rather than a history, let alone an exposé. (It would be embarrassing to admit the size of the fee I lost from *Insider Illustrated* for not rewriting to their specifications. Sample specification: **More details on Klingon torture please.**) My defenses are fictional license and absence of malice; perhaps if the Van Diemen Papers were not under DOUBLET REGAL classification (two steps higher than the Nova Weapons research files) my tale would be different.

I note in passing that I do not intend to disappear from public view in the immediate future.

An old Italian proverb runs *traduttore, traditore:* the translator is a traitor. And it is nowhere more true than when translating between races from different stars; still, I have tried to speak as little treason as possible. For clarity's sake, certain *klingonaase* technical terms have been translated as their Federation Standard equivalents: thus *warp drive, transporter, disruptor,* instead of the more literal

16

anticurve rider, particle displacer, vibratory destructor (most literally: the "shake-it-till-it-falls-apart-tool"). After usual practice, directly equivalent ranks and titles such as "Captain" or "Lieutenant" are given as such, while specifically Klingon titles are translated directly (Specialist, Force Leader) or by convention (Thought Admiral, Examiner).

The translation of *kuve* as *servitor* may raise eyebrows, especially among my Vulcan readers, but it is a growing belief among experts on the *Komerex Klingon* (or at least it was) that the usual translation as "slave" is not only inaccurate but inflammatory, much as the phrases "Centaurian lover" and "filthy Ghibelline" of Earth's past.

Anticipating another Vulcan response: I am not a geneticist, and I have documentation that the practice of *tharavul* still exists.

This book would not have been possible without the interest (and frequent forbearance) of two persons. Dr. Emanuel Tagore's notes were indispensable, but no more so than Dr. Tagore himself; the brief time I could spend with him was an education in culture and language, and not only Klingon culture and language. And it was Mimi Panitch, my editor, who first decided that the Federation was ready for this story, and then stayed on Earth while I bummed the warp routes to track it down.

Finally, the work is about more than what (may have) happened four decades ago, in the last Babel Conference to be held on Earth's surface. Inevitably I come back to Dr. Tagore: "The Organian Peace is a peace of the biggest guns: it neither requires nor creates any understanding among the parties. In the absence of that understanding, the most that can be said about the Organian Treaty is that it works.

"For the present."

Those were his last words to me before his death last year.

I still wonder what he had seen, that we have not.

—JMF/SD 8303.24

Tempt not the stars, young man; thou canst not play
With the severity of fate. . . . In thy aspect I note
A consequence of danger.

—from *The Broken Heart*

Contents

PART ONE

The Clouded Levels

If there are gods, they do not help, and justice belongs to the strong: but know that all things done before the naked stars are remembered.

—Klingon proverb

Chapter 1
Tactics

The children of the Empire were arming for the Game.

Vrenn was a Lancer. He tested the adhesion of his thick-soled boots, adjusted a strap and found them excellent. He flexed his shoulders within their padding —the armor was slightly stiff with newness; he would have to allow for that.

Vrenn's Lance still hung on its charge rack. He leaned into the wall cabinet, read full charge on the indicator, and carefully lifted the weapon out. The Lance was a cylinder of metal and crystal, as thick as his palm was wide. He rested its blank metal, Null end on the floor, and the glass Active tip just reached his shoulder. Then he hefted it, spun it, ran his fingers over the controls in the checkout sequence, watching flashes and listening to answering clicks. The crystal tip glowed blue with neutral charge.

It was a fine Lance, absolutely new like his armor.

Vrenn had never before had anything that was new. He wondered what would happen to these things, after they had won the game . . . if there would be prizes to the victors. He took a deep breath of the prep room's air, which was warm and deliciously moist; he lifted his Lance to shoulder-ready and turned around.

Across the room, Dezhe and Rokis were helping each other into Flier rigs, shiny metal harnesses and glossy boots with spurs. Rokis tightened her left hand inside the control gauntlet, and rose very rapidly, almost banging her green helmet on the dim ceiling. Dezhe snorted, grabbed one of Rokis's spurs and pretended to pull her back down.

"*G'daya* new stuff." That was Ragga, who was struggling his immense bulk into the even greater bulk of a Blockader's studded hide armor. "Not a *g'dayt* crease in it, can't *khest'n* move." He did a few squats-and-stretches, looked a little more satisfied, but not much.

"Who said you could move anyway?" Gelly said. Ragga swiped at her; she danced out of the way without the slightest difficulty. "You'd better not move. You might fall down, and I don't think the rest of us together could get you up again."

Ragga showed his teeth and arched his arms, roared like a stormwalker. Gelly skittered away, laughing. Ragga was laughing too, a sound not much different from his roar.

Gelly sealed up the front of her uniform, a coverall of shiny green mesh, with gloves and boots of finely jointed metal on her slender hands and feet. She was the best Swift of their House: the House Proctors said she might be the best Swift of all the Houses.

Others said other things, about her slimness, her smooth forehead, the lightness of her bones and flesh. Vrenn felt a little sorry for her: when they were younger, he had called her "Ugly, ugly!" with the others. But she couldn't help being ugly, and if it was

26

true that some of her genes were Vulcan or Romulan—
or even Human!—that was not her fault either. He did
not think she was part-Human, though. Vrenn had
killed a Human in the Year Games, when he was six,
his first intelligent kill, and Humans were slow, not
swift.

There had been the one who called Gelly *kuveleta:*
servitor's half-child. Zharn had killed that one, and
done it well. They had all killed, Zharn and Vrenn and
Ragga many different races, but Zharn was the best.

But they were all the best, Vrenn thought. Their
positions had not been randomly chosen, nor they
themselves: of the three hundred residents of House
Twenty-Four, they were the nine best at *klin zha kinta*,
the game with live pieces.

Now Zharn was sitting against the wall of the prep
room, in full Fencer's armor: smooth green plates and
helmet, slender metal staff across his knees. He was
humming "Undefeated," a favorite song of House
Gensa. Segon, a lightly armored Vanguard, was near
him, keeping time with his bootheel. A little farther
away, Graade and Voloh, the other Vanguards, held
hands and kept harmony.

Zharn began to sing aloud, and in a moment they
were all singing.

> *And though the cold brittles the flesh,*
> *The chain of duty cannot be broken,*
> *For the chain is forged in the heart's own fire*
> *Which cold cannot extinguish . . .*

The door opened. In the long corridor beyond, lit
greenly by small lamps on the walls, was their Senior
Proctor, old Khidri tai-Gensa. Khidri was nearly forty
years old, very wrinkled; he had been a full Commander in the Navy until vacuum crippled his lungs. Next to
him was a Naval officer, in black tunic and gold dress
sash and Commander's insignia, with medals for ships
taken.

Zharn was instantly on his feet. "Green Team, present!"

The players snapped to attention at once, wrists crossed in salute, weapons at ready-arms.

Khidri gave them a slight smile and one short nod. "This is a high day for the House *Gensa,*" he said. "We are chosen to play at the command of Thought Admiral Kethas epetai-Khemara."

Vrenn felt his chest tighten, but he did not move. None of the Team did. A planner for the entire Navy! he thought, and knew then that he was right: they were the very best . . . and others knew it.

Khidri said, "The Thought Admiral is of course a Grand Master of *klin zha* . . . this day we must be worthy of a Grand Master's play." In the last was the smallest hint of a threat, or perhaps a warning. Next to Khidri, the Navy officer stood impassive and rather grim.

"Zharn Gensa, is your Green Team ready?"

"Armed and prepared, Proctor Khidri."

"Then bring them," Khidri said, and as he turned around Vrenn thought he saw the Proctor's smile widen. Then Vrenn looked at Zharn. The Fencer was nine, a year older than the rest of them, and seemed the pure image of leadership.

"House Twenty-Four Green Team," Zharn said, "onward to the victory!"

The *klin zha* players filed out of the room, marching in step down the green corridor, singing.

Yet if my line should die,
It dies with its teeth in the enemy's throat,
It dies with its name on the enemy's tongue.
For just as mere life is not victory,
Mere death is not defeat;
And in the next world I shall kill the foe a thousand
    times,
Laughing,
Undefeated.

28

The Arena Gallery was a long, low-ceilinged room, furnished with large soft cushions and small wooden tables with trays of succulents. Servitors, moving silently in clean tan gowns of restrictive cut, replaced the trays when they became empty or messy. Fog hung at the ceiling, humidifier mist mixed with the personal incenses some of the officers present carried. One long wall of the room was entirely of dark glass.

There were slightly more than a dozen of high ranks present, Naval and Marine, and two civilian administrators with a reputation at *klin zha*. Also in the room were a few of the officers' consorts—two for Admiral Kezhke, who was never moderate—and three Vulcans, all *tharavul*.

"The spindles for first move, Thought Admiral?" General Margon sutai-Demma held out a pair of hexagonal rods, of polished white bone with numerals inlaid in gold on their faces. Margon gave them a small, rattling toss and caught them again. They showed double sixes. There was a mildly unpleasant look on Margon's face, but there usually was, and the scar at the side of his mouth only added to it.

Behind Margon, Force Leader Mabli vestai-Galann sat on a cushion, looking quite uncomfortable. One of Margon's *kuve* consorts was stroking Mabli's shoulders, which did not seem to relax him at all, though the female's claws were fully retracted. Mabli kept glancing at the other officers: every one outranked him. Worse, the administrators did as well. Mabli looked straight at his opponent.

Thought Admiral Kethas epetai-Khemara had deep wrinkles in his knobbed forehead, hair very white at his temples. He was fifty-two years old, an age at which Klingons of the Imperial Race should be dead by one means or another, yet his eyes were clear and sharp as naked stars. He smiled at Force Leader Mabli, then faced General Margon. "I grant the option." Kethas reached casually to one side, picked a glass of black brandy from a servitor's tray.

Mabli said "I take . . . " He broke off, looked around. Only the civilians looked especially disapproving. ". . . I *choose* first position."

Kethas nodded, drank. A side door opened with a whisper of air, and the Game Operator entered the Gallery.

The Operator was a Vulcan, *tharavul* like the others of his race present. He wore a green and gold gown of his homeworld's cut. In his hands was a flat black case; two chains and pendants hung around his neck. The upper pendant was the triangle-circle-gemstone of the IDIC; the lower was a large silver figure of a biped astride a quadruped—a piece of the Human game chess.

The players stood as the Operator entered. "Kethas," the Vulcan said, and gestured with spread fingers.

"Sudok. This is Mabli: he shall have Gold today, and chooses first position."

Sudok inclined his head to Mabli, but did not raise his hand. Then the Operator held the black case level, before the Gallery's glass wall. A metal pedestal rose from the floor to support it. Sudok opened the case. Illuminated controls shone within, flashing color from Sudok's jewelry. He touched a series of buttons; the officers and their consorts began moving toward the glass wall.

Beyond the panel, lights flared, revealing the Arena. It was fifty meters across and high, six-sided, long sides alternating with short; the walls sloped inward slightly, pierced with the windows of other viewing galleries, mostly dark now. This gallery was near the Arena ceiling, which was hung with a mazework of lighting, camera, and projection equipment.

The floor was painted with a triangular emblem of three crooked arms, gold on black. Operator Sudok touched another button, and the floor split into three pieces, panels retracting outward.

"T'tain," General Maida said to the *tharavul* behind him, "what was the price for the last shipment of gladiators to Triskelion?"

"Two point six million in crystals and fissionables," the Vulcan said, in a flat tone.

"That's down, isn't it?" a Naval officer said.

"Twenty percent," T'tain said, and started to say more, but was cut off by a sharp gesture from Maida. The General's mouth twisted, and then he said, "The *gagny* brains that rule the place get bored very quickly. Give 'em new races, they say, or the price will drop to nothing. So when are you going to find us some new *kuve?*"

"We're in a *g'daya* box!" the Admiral snapped back. "Federation one way, Romulans another, Kinshaya one more—where are the *kuve* supposed to breed?"

"You Navy have the grand master strategists—"

"Do it elsewhere," General Margon said. His hand was on his dress weapon, apparently casually. There was a long, silent moment; no one moved but Sudok, who continued to work his controls, looking straight out the Gallery window.

"It's done," Maida said finally, without having looked at Margon. Eyes turned back to the Arena.

The game grid was rising from below floor level: a three-sided pyramid of metal struts and transparent panels, a tetrahedral frame nine four-meter pyramids on each edge. Spectra flickered across its facets.

There was a metallic thump, more felt than heard, as the grid locked into place. Then doors opened at Arena floor level, and the Green and Gold pieces filed out: Fencer, Swift, Fliers, Lancer, Vanguards, and Blockader for each side. They executed sharp halts-and-turns and stood, looking upward toward the Gallery.

Kethas waved to the pieces. Mabli saluted his.

Sudok said, "If the players will take their positions." Another key pressed: at either end of the window-wall, small cubicles lit behind glass, one green, one gold. The

31

glass panels slid aside. Within were enveloping, deeply cushioned chairs, like a ship captain's command chair, set before holo displays already showing miniatures of the huge Arena grid.

"A shame this one will be Clouded," Kethas said to Mabli. "I prefer to watch my pieces through my own eyes, don't you?"

Mabli looked puzzled, said nothing.

"Only a thought," Kethas said, and laughed. "A Thought." Then he held out his brandy glass to Mabli. The Force Leader accepted it, took a swallow. A servitor appeared to carry the glass away.

Kethas and Mabli spread their arms, snarled and embraced, heads tilted back, throats exposed. The fury between them seemed to radiate; there were grunts of approval from the others.

The players separated, went to their cubicles. The spectators took up comfortable viewing positions, servitors moving cushions and tables to suit. A small, white-fleshed *kuve* folded its body to pillow the head of Margon's consort; she scratched it with a talon and purred. Finally only the four Vulcans and the serving *kuve* remained standing.

Sudok said clearly, "Gold to position first. The clouds descend." At the Arena ceiling, holo projectors came glowing to life.

Vrenn saw the Thought Admiral's wave. He thought, dimly, that it was an odd gesture, not at all like the Marine player's sharp salute, but in a moment it was past, and he was thinking about the game, and the victory. He felt the weight of his Lance, its good balance, the fine fit of his armor.

Prizes, he thought. The House had all the taped episodes of *Battlecruiser Vengeance,* and Vrenn had watched every one of them, and they all ended with the same line. Humans, Romulans, Kinshaya, servitors who had somehow managed to enter space, all of them asked their conqueror who he was, and the answer was always: "I am Captain Koth. Koth of the *Vengeance*. And this ship is my prize."

Not that Vrenn could ever have a ship—not ever a ship, not without a line-name or a line—but perhaps he could have the Lance. A prize of war, his entirely. And like Koth, he would use his prize—

The *klin zha* pyramid was glowing from within, clear panels turning opaque with holo images. Vrenn heard a slight escape of breath from Ragga, that said more than a mouthful of curses. The Clouded Game was hardest on a Blockader. It was not Vrenn's favorite, either. At least Gelly would be pleased, and the Fliers.

And Zharn, perhaps; it was hard to tell. Zharn was always leader-hard and leader-calm. No form of *klin zha* was easy for the Fencer.

On the other side of the Arena floor, the Gold team was moving, filing into the game grid. Green Team had second placement, then, and second move. Vrenn did not know how much advantage there was to second position, when the opponent's set-up was partly hidden; he did not like the Clouded game even when he controlled all the pieces. One could not see the enemy's pieces, or the enemy.

The Naval officer with Proctor Khidri spoke quietly; Khidri gestured, and Green Team entered the grid.

"Green player chooses the left-hand point," Sudok announced. The Gold pieces had been placed as Mabli chose; now the Green pieces occupied another point on the Grid's lowest level, leaving the third point empty.

"I can't *see* them all," Margon's consort said, annoyed. Margon grunted at her, a threatening sound. Sudok said nothing, and moved a control; the Gallery glass darkened, and the grid cleared as the obscuring holos were polarized out. Hazy shimmers remained, indicating which panels were blocked to the players' view.

"Drownfish's teeth, look at that," one of the civilians said to the other. "Old Khemara's got a Lancer Advanced opening. What do you say to doubled stakes?"

The other administrator looked doubtful, turned to his *tharavul*. "Sovin. Percentages of success for the Lancer Advanced?"

The Vulcan said at once, "Nine percent of such openings lead to victory. Adjusted for the three-dimensional game, Obscuration rules, four percent."

"Well . . . let's say redoubled—wait. Sovin, adjust for Grand Master play."

"Data base is small, Manager Akten."

"Coarse data, then."

"Coarse data indicate twenty-two percent success. I cannot correlate for Grand Masters versus Masters of Force Leader Mabli's rating."

"Double and that's all, then," Akten said, giving the *tharavul* a sidelong look. "Sometimes, Atro, you want to cut more out of their skulls than just their mind-snoop. . . ."

Sovin, of course, did not react. Operator Sudok said "Starting positions are chosen. Goals are being placed." He pushed two slides forward.

General Margon stroked his consort's arm, watched her claws involuntarily extend, and smiled.

Vrenn stood in a triangular cell of metal and light. The floor was a sheet of heavy clear stuff with darkness below, bounded by black metal strips, each with a slot along its length.

He knew he was in the right front space of the starting position. It was a bad place for a Lancer in flat-board *klin zha*, backed against an edge, but perhaps not in this game. They must follow the Grand Master's lead, he thought. And be worthy of his play, as Khidri had said.

Voloh, the Vanguard, was to Vrenn's left, and Graade Vanguard was behind Vrenn. A *very* unusual starting position. Just beyond Voloh stood Ragga, still tensing against his Blockader armor. In the center of the position was Zharn; that made sense at least. Vrenn could not see any of the others, nor any of the Gold Team.

There was a flicker of light in Zharn's space. A disk, half a meter across and a handbreadth thick, materialized in midair. Zharn caught it nimbly. The Goal was of polished green metal, heavy by the way Zharn held it. Vrenn hoped he would not have to find out. Zharn put the Goal gently on the floor of his space, put a boot up on it and stood tensed and ready.

The slots in the floor strips lit yellow. At once Vrenn leaned forward, shifting his balance for action; he dropped his Lance from parade to ready position, and moved fingers on the controls. The Lance hummed through his fingers, and the Active tip went from blue to green.

There was a movement before him. A large shape, golden: the enemy Blockader, passing through an unClouded space. Vrenn watched the yellow strip in front of him, waiting for it to change, but it did not.

Ragga's did, yellow to blue, and the Blockader moved, watching to all sides, and even above, though of course no pieces could yet be on the higher levels.

But that was not a bad caution. In non-combat *klin zha*, a Blockader could not be killed at all; but it was different in *klin zha kinta*, and Blocks who forgot that it was different learned again in hard fashion. Another strip turned blue, and Ragga moved on; he disappeared as he crossed the line, which went yellow again after him.

Segon Vanguard walked from a mist into Ragga's empty space. He did it too hastily, Vrenn thought, went through the Cloud panel too sure the space beyond would be empty. Segon turned slightly, to wave to Zharn Fencer.

The Golden Vanguard emerged from Cloud and slammed his fist into Segon's chest, all in one motion.

Segon staggered, sank down almost to kneeling—

35

then brought the heels of both hands up hard into the Gold player's chin. The Gold's head went back, and Segon's left gauntlet chopped into her throat. Almost too fast to see, the enemy kicked to the side of Segon's knee; they fell together. The bodies locked, and tensed for a long, long moment, and then there was the liquid-metal sound of a joint failing.

Segon stood up, shoulders pumping as he breathed. He took an unsteady step away from the fallen Vanguard. The Gold's body shimmered, vanished, transported away.

The panel beneath Vrenn's boots trembled, then began to rise, riding on the rails of the game grid. Vrenn returned Zharn's salute, gave one to Segon, who raised a shaking hand to acknowledge.

The panel stopped on the next level above. Vrenn was completely surrounded by Cloud panels. The Elevation move had been toward the grid center, so there was still a board edge to his right—safe to ignore that panel—but he was not in a corner. Two directions to cover—no, four. He looked up.

Spurs flashed by Vrenn's face. Vrenn swung the Null end of his Lance, caught the Flier in the thigh; the swooping Gold rolled in midair and landed on his back, spurred boots pointed at Vrenn. Vrenn reversed the Lance, touched the controls; the Active tip glowed yellow. The Flier twisted his control-gloved hand and was off the floor instantly; his bootheels struck the Lance's deflector shield, and the Gold spun in midair. His shoulder grazed a side panel of the cell, above a yellow floor strip; there was a blue flare and the Flier's jacket smoked, but the player made no sound. *"Kai,"* Vrenn said under his breath, at the same time dropping the shield and checking the Lance's charge counter. It was down by almost a sixth.

The Gold somersaulted forward. Vrenn raised his Lance horizontally, catching the gilded steel spurs against it. The Flier continued his roll. Before the enemy could vault over and land behind him, Vrenn fell forward, twisting to fall on his backside. The Flier whirled, just short of striking the far wall; swooped down again.

Vrenn touched his weapon controls. The crystal tip pulsed green.

The Flier was struck in the left ribs, knocked off course. Vrenn spun the Lance end-for-end, smashing the Null end at the Flier's control gauntlet. He connected. Small bones crunched, and wires. As if swept by an invisible hand, the Gold's harness flung him into the wall of the cell, and pressed him there, outlined in blue fire. The harness spent its charge. The Gold Flier hit the floor, moved just a little, then sparkled and vanished without a sound.

A floor strip turned blue. Vrenn walked through the holo into the space beyond.

Some of the Naval officers, and even one of the Marines, were slapping their thighs in approval. "Good play! Good play!"

Admiral Kezhke said, "Who's the Green Lancer?"

Operator Sudok pressed keys, and the closeup image was printed over with red letters.

"Vrenn," Kezhke read, "*Gensa*, good House . . . *Rustazh?*" Kezhke knocked aside the fruit one of his consorts was feeding him. There was a silence in the gallery.

General Maida had a just-lit incense stick in his fingers; he stopped halfway to the holder on his shoulder. "I thought the Rustazh line was extinct."

"So did I," Kezhke said. "I wonder if Kethas knows."

"Can such things be?" Margon said amiably, and gestured to remind Maida of his smoldering incense.

Kezhke said, "Sudok—"

"The Admiral Grand Master inspected his players' complete records some days ago."

Margon said, "You can hardly assume a Grand Master's play would be affected by his interest in one of the pieces."

"No," Kezhke said levelly, "not Kethas. But it's been . . . seven years since all the Rustazh died—"

"All but one, it would seem."

"It would seem." Kezhke stroked his stomach, turned to the cubicle at the end of the room.

Within it, Thought Admiral Kethas again moved his Lancer.

Vrenn had reached the sixth level of the grid, four cells to an edge. There were only a few Clouds here; about half the level was visible, and several spaces on the level above. Vrenn wondered briefly if the other Gold Flier was still in play, and almost without thinking checked his Lance. The indicator read four-tenths charge. The Fliers could not carry Goals, but surely that did not matter yet; surely they were not so close to endgame.

Behind Vrenn, a player was rising from below. He turned; it was Gelly, bouncing from toe to toe as if she were weightless. There was a film of blood on her metal gloves. She was smiling, like a shining light in her face. Vrenn nodded to her, and she spun round on the ball of one foot.

The other enemy Flier shot upward, through a space two away from Vrenn's, and was lost in the Clouds above.

Huge green-armored shoulders appeared near the far point of Vrenn's level: Ragga was coming up. There were creases now in his heavy leather, and a few rips. Vrenn wondered if he was happier now. He stood as if nothing had ever, could ever, touch him.

The Golden Lancer stepped out of Cloud, faced Ragga directly. Vrenn leaned forward slightly, eager to see.

The enemy's Lance flashed green. Ragga made no

38

attempt to dodge the bolt; he did not even grunt as it struck him. Then he swung.

The Lancer was at least smart enough not to bother with his shields. He reversed his weapon to the Null end. Vrenn smacked a hand on his thigh; it was a bold move. Not that it would save him, not against Ragga.

The Green Blocker's fist smashed at the Lance butt, knocking it down, almost out of the Gold's hands. The enemy staggered.

So did Ragga.

Vrenn stared as the best Blocker of all the Houses sank to his knees. The Lancer stepped back to recover. Ragga barely moved. The Null end struck him, and struck again, and again.

On the third stroke Vrenn heard the pop of a spark, and then he understood: the Lance butt was not Null. There was something hidden in it; a contact stunner, or an agonizer.

It must, he thought, it *must* be a rule he did not know—some handicap against a Grand Master, perhaps—Vrenn checked his controls, touched a finger to the Null of his own Lance; only the grip of training kept him from banging the blunt end against the floor or into one of the wall barriers. Vrenn looked up, toward the window where he had seen the players, but it was blocked now from his view.

An edge of Gelly's space went from yellow to blue. Vrenn turned, saw the path of blue lines leading to the Gold Lancer. Ragga was gone. Vrenn opened his mouth, to warn her. His jaw was tense enough to hurt, and before he could strain out any words Gelly Swift was across the spaces at warp speed.

The Gold brought up his weapon. Gelly danced around it, kicked the Lancer. He stumbled, started to turn. She kicked him again, punched him in the lower back. He seemed about to fall; she tumbled, did a handstand and struck his helmet with her bootheel.

The Lancer fell.

Gelly cartwheeled upright.

The Lancer stood and sent a bolt into her body.

Gelly doubled over. The Lancer hit her with the blunt non-Null steel, hit her twice. There was blood. Gelly's blood was a very dark color.

A snarl came up in Vrenn's throat; he swallowed it back.

Vrenn was Elevated again. When he reached the seventh level, the Goal disk was just being transported into his space; he caught it as it fell. The metal Goal was indeed quite heavy.

The space was opaque on two sides, above, and below; the clear side showed nothing. Where, Vrenn wanted to know, was Zharn? Moving the Fencer away from the Goal was the most dangerous gambit in *klin zha*.

He wanted to know as well if the Gold players were cheating, and if so how they expected to succeed; and if Ragga and Gelly had been transported alive; and he wanted a Gold player, to kill for his own.

"About those odds . . . " Manager Atro said.

Akten, without looking away from the windows, said, "Wagers cancelled, of course. No fault."

Atro waved a hand.

Kezhke had retrieved the fruit from his consort and was chewing furiously. "I don't know about that Lancer," he said, juice running down his chin.

"The Thought Admiral might then be distracted?" General Margon said calmly, reaching for a glass of brandy.

"Not the Green Lancer, the Gold," Kezhke said at once, then turned to face Margon. "I am not a Thought Admiral, and I do not pretend to understand fleet strategy; but even you, General, know epetai-Khemara's record."

"Oh, yes," Margon said lightly, and made a gesture with fingertips to forehead, indicating mild insanity. The Marine officers laughed. So did some of the

Navals. "Does anyone know what sort of fusion that Green Swift was? She was rather interesting, in a skinny sort of way." Margon's consort threw a grape at him.

"The Green Goal's unprotected," General Maida said. "He's sent his Fencer off . . . "

"Operator," Kezhke said slowly, "replay of the last kill by Gold Fencer."

Sudok touched a key, and a small holo was thrown on the glass.

"Lancer Elevated to Seven, covering Goal," one of the Managers said. "Gold Lancer to Seven."

Kezhke said "Operator, stop replay, and enlarge. . . . General Margon, will you look at this?"

"When I mentioned the Swift, I only had the epetai-Khemara in mind . . . he likes skinny. And green."

"Green Lancer, carrying Goal, up to Eight."

As Vrenn set the Goal disc down, the enemy Lancer rose into view. Now, Vrenn thought, and waited for the yellow space barrier to change. Instead, the floor began rising again. Vrenn put a foot up on the Goal, fingers tight on his Lance; the ache in his jaw was radiating to the side of his head.

From the Eighth level, only two spaces on an edge, he could see downward, see Zharn on the Seventh; now he thought he understood. Zharn would move from Cloud, on the Lancer.

Zharn did. He swung his thin staff in the widest possible arc; the tip struck the Gold Lancer's right arm and wrapped around it. Zharn twisted the polarizing grip and the metal went rigid. Vrenn had seen Zharn execute this kill a hundred times: as the enemy was pulled around, he would be carried directly into Zharn's knifing left hand, and the Gold's own body energy would help to drop him.

Then, impossibly, Zharn stumbled. The Fencer's hand twitched, depolarizing his staff; the Lancer spun in the wrong direction, and shoved the Active Lance-

41

point into Zharn's throat. Green light flashed on green armor.

Zharn's head went back, far back, too far back. His eyes, very wide, looked up into Vrenn's, and his lips moved, spasming—

No, not just a spasm. Vrenn read them, very clearly.

Get this one, Zharn said, and flickered silently out of existence.

"Do you see that flare?" Kezhke said. "Between the Lance and the Swift's body?"

"That's just a lens flare," someone said, without force.

"Assuming that it isn't," Margon said, interested, "what is it?"

Kezhke said, "You know more of personal weapons than I, General. You are an authority on them."

Margon sniffed his brandy. His other hand rested, relaxed, on the grip of his dress weapon. "Are you proposing, oh, anything, Admiral?"

A few of the others stepped quietly aside.

Kezhke waved both his consorts away. He had no weapon visible, but of course no Klingon of rank would be unarmed in public. "Perhaps that you should examine this image, General, and a few others."

"Operator Sudok," Margon said, "did you examine the equipment for this game?"

"I did, General," the Vulcan said.

"And there were no irregularities?"

"None."

Kezhke said nothing. No one would appear so foolish as to doubt a Vulcan's word.

Margon took his hand away from his sidearm, gestured toward Thought Admiral Kethas's cubicle. "If the Naval champion wishes to stop the game, we will naturally accept a draw."

"Kethas," one of the Administrators said, distracted and puzzled, "has *never* been drawn in tournament."

"There is that." Margon went back to the viewing

window. "And certainly never by a Marine Force Leader. All that, and the son of the Thought Admiral's good dead friend playing, and the invincible Gold opposing him . . . I do so enjoy *klin zha*; nothing short of living war is so stimulating."

"Gold Lancer Elevated, to Eight."

"There is always," Manager Akten said, "the *kome-rex zha.*"

"I do not acknowledge the existence of the Perpetual Game," Margon said without turning. "Society is society, war war. If they are games at all, surely they are not all the same game. I deny it."

"That is a favored tactic," Akten said.

"Green Lancer to Level Nine."

There was no Cloud at the highest level. Vrenn stood in a four-sided pyramid of clear, shimmering panels edged in black steel, and waited for the last move of the Game.

There could only be one move now. Vrenn had carried the Goal to the Ninth Level: the enemy had his next move only to capture the disc. And only the Lancer could reach this space in one. The other Gold Flier might, of course, if she were on an edge space and still alive . . . but Vrenn knew it would not be the Flier. The move would be too easy, not bold enough for a game between Masters.

He was right. A spindle of light, dazzling, soundless, appeared in a point of the space, and the Golden Lancer materialized.

Vrenn smashed his Lance against the Gold's almost before the transport was complete; he felt the displacement field push him back as it did the air. Then the effect died, and Vrenn shoved the enemy back, so that both the Gold's shoulders struck wall panels. Vrenn cursed; he had been expecting shock fields, but here there was only plain matter.

The Gold pushed back, and tried to turn his Lance crosswise to Vrenn's, get freedom to use the Active or false-Null tips. The two Lancers struggled for a dozen heartbeats; then Vrenn was pushed back, by incredible strength. Lances cracked against each other, and against yellow energy shields. Vrenn read his charge counter: one-fourth. He dropped the shield and used the Lance as if it were a plain metal fighting stick, striking sparks, connecting with blows to the enemy's limbs that seemed to have no effect at all. He would have howled, but there was no breath to spare.

He looked into the enemy's face. Their eyes met. The Gold was clearly full-Klingon, as much Imperial Race as was Vrenn; the broad dark face was scarred heavily, and there was a strange high tension in the look, like electricity in the yellow eyes.

Vrenn knew that it was desperation that he saw, and thought the Gold must see the same. They were images in a mirror, only the colors of their clothing different.

No, not only. The Gold had his dishonest Lance. And with his desperation, Vrenn *Gensa* Green had his rage.

Vrenn struck downward to disengage, then spun full circle on the ball of his foot, extending his Lance as Zharn had swung his slender staff. The startled enemy had blocked high, and the crystal tip of Vrenn's Lance caught him just below the right armpit.

Vrenn fingered his controls, and the whole remaining charge in his weapon went into a single green bolt.

The Gold player dropped his Lance. Vrenn kicked it aside, then threw away his own. And then he stopped still, and stared.

He had been wrong. There had been no hidden weapon in the Gold player's Lance. Not in his *Lance,* at all.

The Gold's right arm lay on the floor, twitching, its fingers spasming one-two-three-four. Above it stood its former owner, wobbling on his feet. From his right shoulder, wires dangled and sparked, and coolant and fluidic oil dripped from broken tubes.

Vrenn drove a fist into the enemy's body, then

another. He felt tissue give beneath: only part-robot, then. Good. Very good. The enemy fell back, against a wall panel.

"Kai!" Vrenn shouted, only half meaning it as mockery, leaped and drove both feet into the Gold-thing's midsection.

Plastic splintered outward, and the cyborg Lancer went out and down, down fifty meters, and hit with a sound neither fleshly or mechanical. Blood and oil ran together.

"Gensa, the victory!" Vrenn shouted from the apex of the grid, out the open panel. He looked at the officers watching from their gallery, across space and a little below him now. *"Gensa,* a thousand times, undefeated!"

He wondered if any of them were listening.

"What an extraordinary endgame," Manager Akten said. General Maida coughed and snuffed out his incense. One of Admiral Kezhke's consorts turned and was sick; a servitor caught it in the hem of its robe. Kezhke said "I should call it more than—"

"Yes," Margon said, and his pistol was out. Consorts and officers went for cover.

"Tokhe straav'!" Margon shouted: *Willing slave,* the vilest name Klingon could call Klingon, an insult only death could redeem. Then Margon fired, a bolt of actinic blue light that starred the glass door of Force Leader Mabli's cubicle. Mabli had just turned when the second shot blasted the panel apart, showering the player with fragments of crystal. The third shot tore apart his chest. Margon's pistol was holstered before the last shard of glass had struck the floor. The mist overhead swirled, and there was the sharp smell of ozone. Kezhke's left hand was tense on his leveled right forearm; slowly, he relaxed.

Margon raised the brandy glass he still held. *"Kai,* Thought Admiral. Another victory with your many."

Kethas stood in the open door of his cubicle. "Yes."

He looked past Margon. Servitors were already sweeping up the fragments. "And for every victory, a loss, Margon?"

"There was nothing else for him," Margon said plainly. "Certainly not life. What could be accepted as truth from one who would commit fraud at *klin zha?* I would suspect that, when the plodders of Security finish with this *straav*'s record, it will be found full of lies as well."

"I would not doubt that," Kezhke said, without sarcasm.

"But the corruption ends here," said General Maida.

Kethas was looking out the window, at the figure on the top of the pyramid. The Green Lancer had arms upraised, and was shouting something the glass filtered out. It was barely possible that Mabli had heard Margon's challenge, before his glass was broken; but it hardly mattered.

Kethas said, "There is a last thing, sutai-Demma. . . ."

Margon said, "Epetai-Khemara?"

"A pleasing game. My compliments to a worthy opponent."

Margon nodded. Kethas turned away. "Manager Akten," he said, "I should like to discuss a matter with you. An adoption from one of the Houses of Lineless Youth."

Akten gestured to his *tharavul.* "I took that to be the context of your message, and Sovin has a set of—" Akten stopped short. "You said an *adoption?* Not just a transfer of residence?"

Kethas gave the faintest of smiles. "You are a good player, Akten . . . but even I did not know in advance how the game would end."

Chapter 2
Strategies

Vrenn was in his sleeping room of the House Twenty-Four, alone. The six beds were all neat; the other occupants were at a morning instruction. Vrenn had a sudden, deep flash of wishing he wcre with them. But he was no longer Gensa, but Khemara. Shortly a transport would be here, to take him away to his destiny.

Vrenn crouched on the edge of the bed that he had slept in all his life, leaned forward, slipped his fingers beneath it, feeling out of sight of the room monitors for the slot between metal frames.

He found nothing.

His jaw tensed, and his lips curled back from his teeth. So the one thing he would have kept was gone as well. He thought that it was not right for the Proctors to take it; it did not really belong to the House. If he found Khidri, Vrenn wondered, could he convince him to give Vrenn that one thing? Or if he could not take it away, at least give it to a Housemate. . . .

That would be a poor strategy, Vrenn knew at once. It had been old Khi' who had cautioned Vrenn not to demand privileges too soon in the name of Khemara, not to call a victory what was not.

Let the House have the envelope, then. Let them burn it. And he would see it again, in the next life, when he captained a ship of the Black Fleet.

Vrenn left the room. The halls were very quiet; the walls were of smooth castrock, hung with a few machine-copy tapestries, good traps for sound.

"Khemara."

It was the sound that made Vrenn turn, not the name. Proctor Muros was standing not far away, hands folded. His control wand swung at his side: Vrenn could not think when the wand had seemed both less of a threat, and more.

"Are you lost, Khemara? Guests of this House are normally provided with guides. I will guide you if you wish, honored and exalted guest." *Epetai-zana*: an honorific so high it became absurd, an insult.

"I am not lost, Proctor," Vrenn said firmly, then hardened his neck muscles and said, "You may go about your duties."

Muros smiled faintly, showing points of teeth. "Of course, *epetai-zana*." He nodded politely, turned and walked silently away. Vrenn felt his liver relax.

Newcomers to the House often thought Muros was demanding their deference, and gave it. It was the wrong answer. "Are you *straave?*" he would snarl, and use the wand.

When Muros snaps, snap back: it was one of many secret rules of the House. When one arrived, one's five roommates, and only they, could tell the rules. Or not tell, as they chose. Usually they would tell a part, leave a part to be found out at the end of a wand. Zharn had warned Vrenn of Muros, and it was said he had ordered

48

Gelly's mates to warn her, which for her strangeness they might not have done.

Zharn and Gelly had not returned, after the *klin zha kinta*. The others game-killed had, including Ragga, but Ragga was sullen and distant now, hardly speaking even to curse.

Vrenn came into the front common room. The light was lower here, the air moister; there were plants and a shallow dark pool for meditations. Panels of colored glass in the ceiling formed a large Imperial trefoil, the *komerex stela,* glowing with angular morning sun. A *klin zha* table was idle near the wall; Vrenn went toward it.

"You are Vrenn Khemara." Again, it was the sound of someone speaking, not the name he was called, that made Vrenn turn: and this voice was not Klingon, though the language was *klingonaase*.

A tall, very thin figure was approaching: he wore a black and gold Navy uniform, without insignia. Vrenn did not know the race. A little behind him was Proctor Khidri, carrying a folded pile of dark cloth.

"My name is Tirian," the tall male said. He had an extremely angular face, very broad shoulders, a narrow waist. "I am Transporteer to Thought Admiral Kethas. I am now honored to serve you as well."

Khidri held out the bundle. "Epetai-Khemara has sent clothing for you."

Vrenn took the clothes. There was a long, loose tunic and trousers of deep blue fabric, very soft. Vrenn tugged open the seams of his gray House uniform and began changing on the spot; Khidri was after all a House Proctor, and Tirian, whatever his exact race, was obviously *kuve.* He had spoken of serving—and more telling, Khidri had said epetai-Khemara sent the clothes, not that Tirian brought them.

A thought occurred as Vrenn was dressing. "These are like Cadet's clothes, aren't they? Navy Cadet's?"

Tirian said, "Somewhat. A Cadet's tunic is less long or full, so that it does not balloon in no-weight."

Vrenn moved his shoulders. He had never touched cloth so soft. He picked up his discarded uniform, folding it automatically, and gave it to Khidri. "When do we depart, Transporteer?" he said, feeling his voice tremble just a bit as he tried for the sound of command.

"At your convenience, *zan* Vrenn. Do you have baggage?"

"No . . . nothing, Transporteer."

"If you wish, call me Tirian. *Kuvesa tokhesa.*" *I serve willingly,* the alien said, and yet Vrenn knew it for an instruction. "Then you shall call me Vrenn," he answered, a request.

They went into the House forecourt. There was a small flier parked there, short-winged and graceful, green-backed and white-bellied. The viewports had armored shutters ready to drop, and under the wings were mounted disruptors and missile pods. Vrenn knew it from the recognition books as a Teska-2: not just an armed transport but a real combat craft, able to meet a spaceship in orbit.

Around the flier, admiring it from a careful distance, were the residents of the House Gensa; at Kidri's appearance all turned, and fell neatly into ranks.

They sang "The *Vengeance* Flies at Morning," the theme from Vrenn's favorite tape series: "Undefeated" was the House favorite, but it was about facing enemies and death. This was a better song for today.

> *The guns are hot, the hull is ringing,*
> *The engines sing the sound of triumph;*
> *And every one aboard awaits*
> *A prize upon the high horizon.*
> *Hand and weapon! Heart and power!*
> *Cry it with the voice of Empire!*
> *Victory and prize and plunder!*
> Vengeance *flies at morning!*

It was the perfect song for today, and Vrenn's neck hurt with holding his jaw steady and his lips tight shut . . . but Zharn was not here to sing it, nor Gelly.

Rokis stepped forward, limping a bit; she had hurt her leg in the *klin zha kinta,* making a grand swooping kill. She held out her hands to Vrenn: in them was a brown paper envelope. "A gift from us," she said. "Some things to remember."

Vrenn almost smiled. So that was why he had not found it beneath his bed.

A hand intruded, and Vrenn stopped as he reached for the envelope; a Proctor passed a device over the package and withdrew again without touching it.

Vrenn took the package, held it as tightly as he could without wrinkling it. "This is . . . an honorable House," he said, and looked up, but of course sunlight and clouds clothed the stars.

Then the crowd parted, and Vrenn and Tirian went to the flier; the Transporteer touched controls on a wrist device, and the door opened and stairs swung down. Tirian gestured, and Vrenn went aboard.

Vrenn had seen pictures and tapes of ships' interiors, but he was not at all ready for this. He was in a tunnel, barely wider than his shoulders and not much higher than his head, lined with equipment of metal and plastic and rubber, alive with small lights and noises.

"Go on forward," Tirian said, turning his wide shoulders to follow. Vrenn emerged into a slightly larger space, fronted with thick tinted glass. There were two large padded chairs, each caged by equipment. Small displays flickered, and ducted air rushed by.

Tirian said, "You're left seat. That's—"

"Gunner's seat," Vrenn said.

Tirian clicked his teeth together. "Sure, you'd know that. Can you get belted in?"

Vrenn climbed into the seat, pulled the parts of the harness together and locked them over his chest.

"Fine job. Can you get out now?"

Vrenn slapped at the knob on the harness buckle.

51

Nothing happened. He slapped again, hard enough to hurt. Nothing.

Tirian reached across. "Turn, then push." He demonstrated, then relocked the harness. "Anything could bump open those old locks they show on the tapes. This is safer, and just as fast." He leaned against his chair, tapped his thin, pale fingers on his knee. "Now. I'm your Transporteer. Do you know what that means?"

Vrenn struggled with himself. Could this really be a servitor? Or was Vrenn's new status not what he had believed? He looked at Tirian, who waited, no expression on his bony face. Vrenn knew he must answer, and he would not lie. "No. Will you tell me?"

Tirian nodded gravely. "Of course, *zan* Vrenn. My duty is to keep you safe, while you are aboard any vehicle. If you travel by particle transporter, I will set the controls, that you may be properly reassembled. It may also become my duty to inform you of desirable or undesirable actions while in transit; as my master you must decide how to act on this information. Is this explanation sufficient?"

"Yes, Trans—Tirian." It was more than sufficient. A Captain lent his life to the one he trusted as transporter operator, each time he used the machine: the one chosen must be of special quality. It was reasonable that an Admiral should have a special officer for the purpose—and a *kuve* one, who could have no ambitions.

Now Vrenn realized he had insulted one he must trust. He was not sure how to correct the error; surely he should not express error, not to a servitor. He simply had no experience of *kuve;* on tapes they were so easily dealt with . . .

Finally Vrenn said, "I seem to have misunderstood you at first."

Tirian said, "I regret that this is common. I am a Withiki—" more a whistle than a word—"and I do not speak well." He got into his seat, fastened his harness, began bringing the flier to life.

Vrenn looked at him, wondering at what he had just heard. He had seen Withiki, real ones, at the Year Games, and Tirian could not possibly be of that race.

The flier began to lift. Through the windshield Vrenn could see his once-Housemates waving, and he waved back, though realizing they could not see him through the dark glass.

He waited until Tirian had brought them to cruising altitude, then said, "Could you provide me with some information on this equipment?"

Again Tirian's teeth clicked; Vrenn supposed it was his race's form of polite laughter, but he was not offended. "The weapons are indeed loaded, Vrenn, but are all on safety. However, you might enjoy the view through the gunsights. A moment to get us on guide-beam, and I'll show you how it works."

The Khemara linehold was almost a quarter of the world away; it took half a day airborne, beam-guided around reserved airspaces, military and private. Had they intruded, they would have vanished from the sky in an instant.

The Teska had a tiny, unenclosed waste facility, and a food locker stuffed with cold meat and fish and fruit nectars. Vrenn took a swallow and was astonished at the taste: the juice was real.

They swung near mist-cloaked hills and low over green lakes, crossing the Northwest Sea as the sun was setting. The clouds broke for a moment and showed the star, a white pinpoint; Vrenn shielded his eyes at once. Then the light was gone, and they were over the Kartade Forest. Tirian was dozing in his chair, breath whistling. Vrenn had no notion of sleep. He switched the gunsight to night vision and scanned the forest; the intertwined trees showed up in startling clarity, and now and then an animal streaked by, burning bright on the infrared screen.

A beep from the communications board woke Tirian instantly. He touched a switch, and a web of light was

53

projected on the windshield: the image of a landing grid that lay, invisible, on the ground ahead. Tirian hung an audio pickup behind his ear. "Center Space, this is Flier 04 . . . Aboard, affirm . . . My password is Tail-feather. What is your password? Affirm, off beam and landing now."

They touched down very gently. Outside the flier, a pathway lit up; then lights came on behind large windows. Tirian said,"You're to go on inside. My duty's here."

Vrenn nodded. "It was a good trip," he said, sure it was not too much praise.

Tirian did not click his teeth. He said, "Thank you, master Vrenn," with clear satisfaction. And he had said *master,* not the neutral *zan.* He indicated the brown envelope: "May I bring your package?"

"No . . . I'll take that."

Vrenn went down the steps, holding the envelope. The path wound out before him through a garden, with shrubs and pools, and knotted-trunked trees as grew in the Kartade. There was a heavy scent of flower perfumes.

The house was quite high, at least three stories, with a V-shaped roof: the huge front windows seemed a little like angled eyes looking down on Vrenn. Behind the windows was what appeared to be one large room, with red light flickering within.

Without any pause at all, Vrenn went inside.

There was indeed one vast, high-ceilinged room, with wooden beams cutting across the space overhead, and iron-railed stairs to balconies on either side. In the center was a broad, black pillar, open at the base: a fire, fed by wood, burned within. Around the fireplace were cushions, and tables topped with wood inlay and black glass.

A figure stood, silhouetted by the fire. "Welcome, Vrenn. Be welcome in your house."

"Thought Admiral . . . " Vrenn said, and saw the tilt of Kethas's head. ". . . Father."

54

Kethas nodded, took Vrenn's free hand in both of his and drew him into the firelight. "Sit, if you like, though I suppose you've been sitting too long already. Are you hungry? Thirsty? We need a glass of something to talk over . . . you're nine, aren't you?"

"Nearly nine."

"Yes. Do they have strong drinks, in the Houses? I really don't know that much about them."

"I drink ale."

"Dark ale, then, that's the best when you're tired. Not the scorch of a distillate and less risky than brandy." Almost before Kethas finished speaking, a servitor had appeared with a tray.

Vrenn had never much cared for ale, but it was all he had experience of: this drink, however, was wonderful, as much as the fruit nectar had been. Vrenn began to wonder if he would simply have to relearn eating and drinking.

Another being, a female, came into view. She wore a long gown of some pale stuff that shimmered. Her skin was quite dark, and Vrenn thought for a moment she was Klingon, but then a white ceiling light showed the green cast to her complexion. Light gleamed on fingernails like polished green opals.

And then Vrenn felt something very strange, like an invisible hand squeezing inside his chest. It was not painful . . . not quite. He spilled a little of his drink.

"Pheromonal shock," Kethas said. "At your age, the rush of hormones could be deadly." Vrenn had no idea what Kethas was talking about. He knew from the female's color what she must be: half the ships Koth of the *Vengeance* captured had an Orion female aboard, all green, all beautiful past imagining . . . but Vrenn realized now that they were all just Klingon females in makeup. And compared to this one, they were all dead things.

"This is Rogaine," Kethas said. Vrenn forced himself to listen. "She is my sole consort. Rogaine, this is Vrenn, whom we have taken into the line."

Vrenn bowed. Rogaine returned it, and sank with an impossibly smooth motion onto a cushion by the fire. "Please don't stare," she said, in a fluid voice, one not at all suited to *klingonaase*. "It makes me feel that I have committed an error."

Kethas sat next to Rogaine, covered her hand with his. "In this House you are infallible," he said, and then said something in a language as ill-suited to his tongue as *klingonaase* was to hers. Rogaine laughed, a sound that melted in the air.

Kethas said, "Sit down, Vrenn. This isn't an examination."

Vrenn sat, very carefully. "Thought Admiral, a question."

"Of course; the first of many, I'm sure."

"Why am I here?"

"A fair enough opening," Kethas said. "You do not know your parents, do you? Your actual parents, not us."

"No . . . I do not remember anything but the House. We were told that was better."

"I cannot disagree. But listen now. Your line was Rustazh, your father Squadron Leader Kovar sutai-Rustazh."

"*I have a line?*" Vrenn burst out. "I—that is—"

"An understandable response. But the Rustazh line is extinct. Your once-father was leading a convoy of colonization; the line had received an Imperial grant of space. But the ships were ambushed, by Romulans. Kovar fought well, but there were problems . . . colony ships are a handicap in combat. There were no survivors, as one expects of Romulans."

"How do I . . . then live?"

"I don't know. Kovar's youngest son was named Vrenn, and he would be your age . . . and I see some resemblance, for whatever that's worth. But how you came to be in the House Twenty-four . . . that is a mystery. Records have been lost, or altered, enough to buy at least one death, could we find the actors."

Kethas drank his ale, and Vrenn did likewise. Kethas spoke again, in a very serious tone. "But you asked why you were here, and I have not answered yet. Under me, Kovar served Empire well, and because of certain things he did in that time I am disposed to do a thing for him."

Vrenn said, "I am—" Kethas cut him off with a raised finger.

The Thought Admiral said, "I have had eight children, which ought to be enough to preserve a line. But seven of them are dead in seven parts of space; and the eighth has changed his name to begin a line of his own, and when his last brother died it was too late to reverse this course. And I have spent many years in space, on the old thin-hulled ships, when the power came from isotopes, and I have taken too much radiation; my children now are monsters, that bubble and die."

Rogaine turned sharply away. Kethas touched her hand, but did not turn toward her. He said, "For Kovar's sake I took you out of the Lineless' House; one life was my debt to him. But for my sake I will make you heritor of the line Khemara, and to this linehold and all its property; and the price is that you will be Khemara and forget that you ever were Rustazh."

Vrenn felt slightly dizzy, but he had heard every word clearly, and there was no Cloud in his mind. He said, "I was never Rustazh until now . . . but now I am already Khemara. And so I will stay."

Kethas stood, put both hands on Vrenn's shoulders. "In you the *klin* lives, this is certain! Odise." A servitor appeared. "Take Vrenn Khemara to his rooms." He gave Vrenn's shoulder a squeeze, then let go.

Vrenn stood, retrieving his envelope. Kethas said, "What's that? Discharge papers?" He held out his hand.

"*No* . . . these are . . . just some things of mine."

Kethas nodded. "We'll talk again tomorrow, then. And . . . I saw you on the board; do you play *klin zha*, when you are not a piece?"

"Yes, Grand Master." Vrenn supposed the title was appropriate now.

Kethas smiled slightly. "Then we will do that." He went back to Rogaine, who sat very still by the fire; he spoke to her in her own language.

The servitor Odise bowed crookedly to Vrenn. It was a small being, a little over half Vrenn's height, with spindly legs and arms and a turret head, covered all over with smooth black fur. It turned, and Vrenn followed it, up stairs to a corridor above.

The *kuve* opened a door, handed the key to Vrenn, then gestured for him to enter the dark doorway. As Vrenn did, lights came on.

The chambers inside were fully the equal of a Captain's quarters. There was a study the size of Vrenn's shared room at the house, with a library screen and books on shelves; an equally large bedroom beyond that; a private wash-and-waste. Odise demonstrated some of the controls—silently; it apparently did not speak—bowed and went out, closing the door.

Vrenn wandered around the rooms for several minutes. The similarity to a Captain's cabin was not just superficial, he realized. He had seen pictures of ships showing the same furnishings: the cylindrical closets, the angular desks and chairs, the tracked spotlamps. The bed even had a concave surface, though there was no restraint web. There was a meal slot in the wall, with programming buttons. And the walls were covered with clearprints of stars and planets, lit from behind, exactly like viewports to Space beyond.

Vrenn sat down on the lumpless bed, weighted down with too many enormities for one day.

On a small table next to the bed was a *klin zha* set. The pieces were of heavy green and amber stone—jade and quartz, Vrenn guessed, having heard of those materials. The board was black enamel, with inlaid brass strips marking off the spaces. Vrenn looked at it for a long while, not touching it, then opened his brown envelope and slid its contents out onto the table: a triangular piece of heavy card, and some discs of soft wood.

Vrenn had found the board on the ground next to a recycling bin, and inked the triangular grid with another piece of scrap for a straightedge. The discs were hole-punchings from some packing material, scrounged in the same way. Vrenn had engraved the symbols for the pieces into the soft grain with a writing stylus. They were Green and Black, since he had no yellow ink.

Vrenn set up his pieces to match the stone set. He made a few moves, then looked up at the corners of his room. There was nothing overtly a monitor visible. He felt the key in his pocket, thought about getting up to lock the door, but did not.

Finally he scooped the paper board and pieces into their envelope, reached beneath his bed, and found a slot where the package would fit.

Morning light filtered through skylights, vines, and fog into the house's indoor garden. Vrenn felt the warm, wet air like a solid substance around him. Fog parted as he moved.

Kethas was armpit-deep in a sponge-tiled pool, watching text flicker by on a small viewer at the water's edge. "Come in, Vrenn," he said, and touched the display off.

Vrenn approached. His tunic and trousers were damp, impeding him. He stood on the edge of the water, on which bright plants were floating, giving off a sweet scent.

"Well, come *in*," Kethas said, smiling.

After a moment, Vrenn undressed and slipped into the water. It was an oddly neutral sensation, not cool, not hot, just . . . enveloping, and very comfortable.

"Now we're civilized," Kethas said. "Have you eaten?"

"I . . . just a little." The meal slot in his room served nine flavors of fruit nectar, and he had gone through a large glass of each. But they had not stayed with him.

59

And he had soon been more interested by the library screen, which also served as a starship action simulator.

"Two meals," Kethas said, to the apparently inert monitor. "You were up early."

Vrenn wondered then if his room was watched. "We always woke before sunrise, at the House."

"There's no such rule here. It would never work. I live midmorning to midnight, and Rogaine needs many little sleeptimes, and Tirian sleeps when it's convenient, like a Vulcan. If you like mornings, fine, but find the time you're best at and live there. That's the payoff strategy. The most efficient, that is to say."

That was exactly the opposite of what the House Proctors called efficiency, but Vrenn was already thinking of something else. "Are there Vulcans here?"

"No, I do not have a *tharavul*. Can you use a library unit?"

Watched or not? Vrenn thought, and said, "Yes."

"Then you have no need for *tharavul*. Here's food."

There were light fried anemones and crisp salt fish, sweet gel pastries (Vrenn was careful to take only two) and a hot dark drink he thought at first was heated ale, but which was something harsh and incredibly bitter. Vrenn nearly choked.

"Human *kafei*," Kethas said, laughing. "They bring it to me in course; I should have warned you. Awful, yes, but you learn to drink it. Some years back, I was on a deep mission, taking supply by forage, and for half the voyage we had nothing to drink but a case of that stuff taken as prize . . . that and the white fire the Engineer brewed up. They're not bad together, too." Kethas drained his cup. "*And* it has a mind-clearing effect, which you're going to need."

The Thought Admiral reached to the display unit again. As he rose slightly from the water, Vrenn could see rippled scars on Kethas's flank. He had watched enough tapes of battles to know that only delta rays left marks like that: Kethas had been burned by either an unshielded warpdrive, or Romulan lasers.

"Bring down my green tunic," Kethas said to the unit, "and for Vrenn, the gold."

Vrenn and Kethas walked around the fireplace in the large front room. Along the walls were boards and pieces for every game Vrenn had ever heard of, and even more than he had not. For *klin zha* there were many sets, for all the variations.

"I've seen you in the Clouded Game," Kethas said. "Do you know the Ablative form?" He gestured to a board that was elevated on posts, pressed a finger on one of the spaces; the triangular tile fell out, into a tray below.

"Yes. And Blind, too." Vrenn wore a long coat of gold brocade, with the multicolored crest of a forest lizard sewn across the shoulders. Kethas's coat was of thick green cloth, with an Admiral's haloed stars on the sleeve.

Vrenn thought about his clothes; both the wardrobes in his rooms had been filled. This gown was too new to have been the Admiral's; it must have belonged to one of Kethas's children. Vrenn put the question away to ask later, if at all.

Kethas pointed at boards marked in squares instead of triangles. One was square overall, spaces alternately black and white; the other was rectangular, a tan color with gold lines.

"The *human zha*, *chess*. And the *rom zha*, which the Romulans call *latrunculo*. They are both fine games, though not so interesting or varied as *klin zha*."

"Do all races have a game?"

Kethas smiled, evidently pleased with the question. "Kinshaya have no stylized game, though they are excellent at small-war with model soldiers. Vulcans find games 'illogical,' though they create computer simulations that amount to the same thing, and labor at other races' games for some reason of the Vulcan sort. Do you know the saying, 'less pleasant than torturing Vulcans'?"

Vrenn laughed, which was enough answer. Kethas said "Among Masters of the Game it goes '. . . than *klin zha* against a Vulcan.'"

"And the *kuve?*"

"The *kuve* do not. They have games, yes, and some of them are worth a little study—I will show you, another time—but no *kuve zha* can be truly great."

"That is only sensible," Vrenn said, embarrassed. "I should have understood it."

"An obvious question is better than obvious ignorance," Kethas said. "In this house questions may always be asked. Only in the larger universe must one be cautious not to show one's blindness."

Vrenn nodded, silently resolving to be more cautious at once. He said "What variant is this?" realizing he was showing more ignorance.

The board and pieces before them were of *klin zha* pattern, but there was only one set of pieces, colored green and gold combined.

"That is for the Reflective Game. It is the highest form of *klin zha,* and the most difficult. Barring of course the *komerex zha*—or do you deny the Perpetual Game?" Kethas shook his head, smiling; evidently a joke was intended. "Come here; I'll show you."

Kethas picked up the Reflective set, carried it to one of the tables by the fireplace. He punched up a cushion and sat against it, then swept the single set of two-colored pieces to the side of the board.

Vrenn sat, folding his tunic beneath himself, and waited.

"In the Reflective Game," Kethas said, "there is a single group of pieces which either player may move in turn. All pieces move in the fashion of the normal, Open Game."

"How does one win?"

"In the same fashion as the Open Game: by making it impossible for the opponent to move legally. . . . We begin by setting up. Choose a piece and place it: any piece, anywhere. Then I shall do so, and so on, alternating."

Without hesitation, Vrenn reached for the Fencer, placing it in the corner of the board nearest himself. He watched Kethas: but suddenly nothing at all, not even a smile, was readable from the Grand Master's face. Kethas selected a Vanguard, placed it some distance from Vrenn's Fencer.

When all the pieces were placed, in what seemed to Vrenn a totally random fashion, Kethas said, "I move first. This is a disadvantage." He shifted a Vanguard. "Now, your move."

"Any piece? And I may kill as well?"

"Of course. *Remember only,*" he said, still without expression, that you may not voluntarily put your Goal in danger of attack. Even though it is *also* my Goal."

Suddenly Vrenn began to understand. He examined the board, realizing that most of the moves he had thought were possible actually endangered the Goal disc. If he even moved the Fencer off the Goal, it would then become the enemy's Fencer, and give the enemy an instant victory.

The game lasted only three moves after that.

Kethas sat back. "A pleasing game," he said. "My compliments to a worthy opponent."

Vrenn felt frustrated, angry. He felt he had been used, to win a cheap and honorless victory. Controlling his voice, he said, "I am a good player, at the forms of *klin zha* which I know, but I do not know this one, and I could not play well against you."

Kethas answered in a voice that seemed to reach out and physically take hold of Vrenn. "I am an undrawn Grand Master of the Game, and you cannot *lose* well against me, no matter the form. But as with all my children, I will play this game or another against you every day that you are here, and in time you will learn to lose well, and you may even learn to lose brilliantly."

Vrenn held his hands below the table, keeping them

63

from clawing into fists, kept his lips from curling back. He wanted to understand, but was not sure at all that he did, or ever would. "And if in time I learn to win . . . however badly?"

"Kai Kassai, Klingon!" Kethas said, laughing, and slapped Vrenn's shoulder. "Then I will make you a Thought Admiral in my place, and retire to my consort and my garden pool forever!"

That night, after a long and useless assault on sleep, Vrenn touched on the bedside lamp and stared at the stonecut *klin zha* set in the pool of light. Then he reached beneath the bed, took out the envelope, shook its contents onto the table and set up a game.

It was an afternoon deep in the cold season, and the perpetual fireplace was stoked high; there had been a trace of real white frost on the garden outside, just at dawn, and Vrenn had watched until the day reclaimed it. He had never been so far north, and found the change of seasons amazing. He had been Khemara now for two-thirds of a year.

Kethas had been away from the house for ten days, at a meeting of the Imperial Council, in the Throne City on the other side of the world. Today, the morning's message said, he would be returning.

Tirian had at once gone to check the working of the house's transporter station; he seemed satisfied, and now sat in the front room reading a printed book, while Vrenn experimented with *klin zha* positions on a computer grid. Music drifted down from a balcony: Rogaine was playing the harp in her chambers. The sound was pleasing, but it was not like Klingon music; there could be no words to it, and it did not inspire.

The harp fell silent. A moment later, Tirian's belt annunciator chimed. He tucked his book away inside his clothing. Vrenn blanked the game display and followed Tirian out of the house.

Beyond the formal garden and the flier landing, all to itself, was a small hexagonal pavilion, much newer than the main house. The particle transporter had been safe for Klingon use for less than thirty years; only very recently had anyone, even an Admiral, the luxury of a home station.

Inside the small building, Tirian unlocked two banks of controls. On the first, he dilated an opening in the deflector shield covering the estate, set to scramble any unauthorized attempt to beam in. Then he went to the second console and began setting to receive.

There were three discs on the floor before the control consoles, matching three on the ceiling. Between one pair a column of sparkling golden light appeared, entirely without sound.

Kethas epetai-Khemara, in black silk tunic and full-formal gold vest heavy with medals, stepped off the disc, and sighed. The grooves in his face and forehead stood out very darkly. Vrenn could not remember seeing him look so tired, or old.

"Well done, Tirian," Kethas said. "The war continues, on every space of the board." He nodded to Vrenn, and went out of the transporter pavilion, toward the house.

Tirian began locking up the console. Vrenn thought of what he had wanted to ask the servitor, for a long time now: suddenly, perhaps because of the quiet of the mood, or their distance from the life of the house, it seemed the right time to ask. "Tirian, do you believe in the Black Fleet?"

"My people mostly believe in a next life," Tirian said, without looking from his work, "though there are not starships in it. But we evolved separately, and if one world's idea is true, I suppose all must be."

It was much more answer than Vrenn had expected, but he took it as affirmation. "When my father has gone to command there . . . will you then be his Transporteer?"

"What," Tirian said quietly, "does the Empire's hold extend so far as that?"

"Any race may reach—"

"I know. Kethas has told me. I will have a place on his Black Ship. Even if I do not want it."

"You are Withiki," Vrenn said. "You would have wings again."

Tirian turned. His skull face was drawn, pure white. "So my younger master is a strategist as well," he said flatly. "The Thought Admiral will be pleased.

"But I wonder if you are right, Master Vrenn. I had fine wings once, blue-feathered, if you know what that means, and of spread twice my height. But such broad wings are awkward in the corridors of a starship. So a Force Leader of Imperial Race told me, when he had his Marines pull my wings from their sockets. Do you think that officer is also in the Black Fleet, waiting to maim me a thousand times? Laughing?

"*Kuvesa tokhesa*. Your father. While I live." Tirian walked out of the room, toward the flier hangars, not the house.

After a little while, Vrenn went back to the house, thinking that he had in fact won a victory, gotten the information he wanted. But it did not have the taste of victory.

The female Rogaine was seated among the web ferns of the indoor garden, playing her harp. There was no light from above, and she was no more than a dark shape outlined in light, almost one with the reflections on the pool beyond. Thick mist floated, glowing, diffuse.

Rogaine turned, playing a complex chord, and Vrenn could see that the mist was all that covered her. He felt a stitch in his side, as if his air was short. It was not quite pain, and then it was something worse than any pain Vrenn had ever known. Rogaine's long nails stroked the strings, and Vrenn heard himself groan.

Then a cold hand touched him, and all his nerves cried out at once.

Vrenn lay on his back, in his bed. Above him, touching Vrenn's shoulder, was Kethas, wearing his dress uniform. Only the bedside lamp was on; it seemed to be still the middle of the night, when Kethas slept.

"Get up, and dress," the Thought Admiral said. "It is a night for decisions. Meet me in the garden outside." He went away.

Vrenn lay still a moment longer, not entirely certain he had not simply slipped from one dream into another. But his senses told him otherwise; surely, he thought, the relics he felt of his last dream would not carry over to this one. So he rose, and put on his adoption-day clothes that were like a Cadet's, and went outside.

The night air was very cold, and Vrenn's breath misted. The sky was very dark. . . .

The sky, Vrenn saw, was cloudless. Overhead were stars, hard and white, all the thousand stars of the world's sky standing naked, as they did on less than one night in a hundred.

So whatever Vrenn and Kethas said here, whatever they did, would be remembered for all time to come.

"Shortly you will be ten years old," Kethas said, a figure of gold and darkness—but no dream, Vrenn knew. "It will be time for you to choose what you will be. Have you thought on this?"

"The Navy," Vrenn said instantly.

Kethas did not smile. "You know that I do not require this of you? That you may, as you wish, be a scientist, or an administrator—or even a Marine?"

"I know, father. And I would not be anything else."

Then the Thought Admiral smiled. "And so you should not. You captain the machine like you were made for it. I am pleased to find you wise as well as skillful."

Vrenn said, "Was my father sutai-Rustazh a great captain?"

Kethas tilted his head. "You have no father but myself." After a moment he added, "Though it is true I once knew one called sutai-Rustazh, who was great."

Vrenn bowed his head, ashamed at the stupidity of

the question. And still Kethas—indeed his only father, his whole line—had answered it; Vrenn wondered what this strategy was.

Kethas said, "There are assistances I can provide. You will be assigned directly to the Academy, of course, and the Path of Command. A cruise can be arranged at the earliest—"

"I would make my own path, Father."

Kethas's hand slashed crosswise. "Don't talk like a Romulan! What, do you think you are the only son of an Admiral who will attend the Academy? Half your mates will be Admirals' sons; and some of them will be *kuvekhestat* unfit to *serve* aboard a ship, and those especially will use every advantage their lines can win them. You are still not a good enough player to give your enemies odds." He paused, said more gently, "And surely you do not deny the Perpetual Game?"

Vrenn stood entirely still, feeling his jaw clench, his lips pulling apart. He knew then that he must have a ship, a command, and he would have them, and he would never know shame again. He looked at the stars, stark burning naked, and knew the oath was sealed.

"Let's go inside," Kethas said, his manner easy again. "We'll play *klin zha.*"

They went into the house. The fire was uncommonly welcome after the cold of the night. Vrenn sat at the game table, reached to turn it on.

"Not that set," Kethas said. "The one in your room. The one beneath your bed."

Vrenn felt his eyes twitch with staring. Kethas's look was bland. Vrenn went to his room, brought back the envelope with the set of wood and card.

"There is never time to teach everything, so the important things must take precedence," Kethas said, as they played through a standard opening. "And example works quickest . . . you do know the proverb: If you do not wish a thing heard—"

"Do not say it."

"Yes. This will always be true; it will be so if you are

68

a Captain, or an Admiral, or the Emperor. You will be watched, so live as if you are watched. Beds are a terrible place for secrets . . . you are about to lose your Vanguard." And Kethas moved, killing it. He picked up the dead piece, turned the disc over in his fingers. "You know that there is a form of *klin zha* we have not yet played."

"What is that, Father?"

"It is the form least often taught, less even than the Reflective, but in a way it is the most important of all to a Captain. I think we should play it now." Kethas flicked his fingers, and the wooden Vanguard sailed through the air, into the fireplace, where the flames absorbed it with the smallest of whispers.

It had happened faster than Vrenn could think, and now he did not know what to think. He wondered if Kethas had flipped the piece through the fire, and out the other side, but he did not believe that.

Finally the Thought Admiral said, "Your move."

Vrenn looked around the room, and the gameboards along the walls. He started to rise. "And which set will the Thought Admiral risk?"

Kethas waved a finger at Vrenn's seat cushion. It looked like a casual gesture. It was not. Vrenn sat.

Kethas said, "You are not ready to count your enemy's losses until you have learned to count your own. And remember that some enemies will never have learned to count."

Vrenn looked at the board and pieces that he had made so carefully, kept so long; he tried to see them as nothing but scraps of fiber, bits of waste saved from the bin, and he could not. "What happens, then, when I kill a piece of your side?"

"Keep it," Kethas said. "Eventually there will be only one set left. And then we will play the Reflective Game."

Vrenn moved his Fencer and Goal, feeling the wood very warm and fragile against his fingers, like a living thing.

Chapter 3
Gambits

Romulan plasma hit Klingon shields: power leaked through in second and third harmonics, and the target cruiser shook.

"Damage?" said the officer in the command chair.

Vrenn Khemara ran his finger down a screen, bright in the red-lit Bridge; a schematic of the cruiser *Blue Fire* flashed into view, yellow blocks marking areas hit. Vrenn read off the reports in a few short phrases of Battle Language.

Below Vrenn, the Commander spat an acknowledgement and turned back to the main display. Vrenn looked up: across the Bridge, another cadet flashed a hand at him, fingers spread. The gesture symbolized a Captain's starburst of rank: in words it would come out approximately as "You'll have a command by morning!"

Blue Fire rolled to starboard. She was pulling Warp 3, and the floorplates whined and the bulkheads groaned; a cadet grabbed a strut to steady himself under the shifting gravity. The commander caught sight of it. "Environmental?" he said, tone deadly even, eyes like disruptors.

The unbalanced cadet strained toward his board. "Point eight six two, nominal," he said.

The commander acknowledged, turned back to the main view. All the cadets understood very well: fall down, fall asleep, do as you like, as long as you've got the Captain's answers when he wants them.

It was not the Captain of *Blue Fire* in the Chair. Squadron Leader Kodon was five decks above, in the Primary Bridge. Commander Kev, the Executive officer, sat with the cadets in the Auxiliary Bridge, calling for situation reports and helm responses exactly as if he were Kodon, and the cadets worked their locked-off consoles just as if they controlled the ship.

Only the the data were real.

There was a flash in the corner of the display as the cruiser rolled; Vrenn's instruments picked up the wave of energy as a plasma bolt passed less than forty meters below their ship's port wing. It had not been fired when Kodon started the maneuver: he had somehow foreseen the enemy action. Vrenn watched, and tried to learn.

The Klingons were outnumbered, five to three; but the Klingon D4 cruisers were individually much more powerful than the Romulan Warbirds. "So we win, on numbers," Kodon had told them, before the raid began, "but there's a few things the numbers don't count."

Two Fingers, the portside ship of Kodon's Squadron, had picked up three of the Warbirds, which swarmed around it, firing plasma in continuous cycle, two ships' tubes cooling while one blazed, trying to batter their victim's shields down from all directions at once.

"One thing," Kodon said, "is that ships *move.* Tactics are real, and if you don't move right, you die."

Blue Fire was now turned perpendicular to *Two Fingers.* Commander Kev gave a firing order, and the cadets on Weapons followed just as the officers above

71

them. Six disruptors fired, making two pyramids of blue light whose points were Romulan ships. Romulan hulls buckled, as the forces holding their molecules together were suppressed and restored ninety times a second. That was disruption: or, as the big ships' batteries were nicknamed, the Sound of Destruction.

Two Warbirds lurched out of their loops, and *Two Fingers* went to work on the third. *Blue Fire* came about again, to find a prey of its own.

There was a sudden swelling spot of white light in the forward display: the screen darkened, and it was still too bright to look at. Then the flash faded, and was gone. Stars came back on in the display. Ahead, the other ship of the squadron, *Death Hand,* had turned into the blast, to take it against her strong forward shields.

"The other thing," the Squadron Leader had told them all, "Is that Roms have some pretty odd ideas about dying."

Kev said, "Communications, signal Code KATEN to Squadron. Helm, when KATEN is acknowledged executed, I want Warp 4 at once."

The Cadets tensed, almost as a unit. There would be no boarding this time, no prizes, not even a creditable kill they could stripe on their sashes. But this was only the first skirmish of the raid, as Kodon had outlined it to them all. Their goal was farther into the Rom-ulan sphere. Vrenn certainly understood; it was not an elaborate strategy, even for the frontier squadrons.

Still, he wanted a kill as much as the rest of them.

Perhaps more.

Both enemy squadrons were trying to regroup, to disentangle from each other's ships. The Klingon cruisers had more power, which counted most in large-ship maneuvers; *Death Hand* was able to bounce a Rom off its shields like a small animal off a groundcar's fender.

Formation lights flared on displays, drifting toward marked target positions: the three D4s moved, silently as all things in space, into a triskele formation, port engines inward. A Rom fired, the bolt glancing from *Blue Fire*'s shields.

"You may give him one for vengeance, *zan* Tatell," Kev said, and as Helm counted toward formation lock-on Weapons trued his crosshairs and his firing keys. Blue light reached out to the Rom, to the bronze raptor painted on its belly.

The bird was cut open from wing to drumstick.

Lights met their targets. "Warp 4," the Helmsman remembered to say, and the Romulans—what was left of them—streaked by and were gone, as Kodon's squadron pierced yet deeper into the space the Roms claimed as theirs, three times faster than their ships could follow.

Commander Kev stood, inspected the Cadets. He touched the phone in his ear that had sent him all of the actual Captain's orders. "A good engagement," he said, "damage done, no ships lost, only minor injuries to crewmen and none to officers . . . " Kev looked at Zhoka, the Cadet who had almost lost more than just his balance.

Kev paused, eyes narrowed, apparently getting some message through his earphone. "I am instructed to tell you that, by consensus of the Squadron Captains, *Blue Fire* is to be credited with one Romulan kill. May this be a favorable sign."

Kev stood silent then, watching. The cadets did not move. Vrenn thought the collar of his blue tunic must surely be contracting, but kept his hands firmly on his console.

Finally the Commander decided they had had enough. "Alert over. Stand down to cruise stations." And he saluted. "Blue Fire, the victory!"

"The victory!"

* * *

Vrenn and his roommate, an Engineering cadet named Ruzhe Avell, were playing Open *klin zha* in quarters. Vrenn had not played *klin zha* against a live opponent since halfway through his Academy year; until Ruzhe, everyone had too much minded losing.

Maybe Ruzhe didn't mind because he didn't pay attention anyway. "I still say it's better in Engineering. We get to work on the real ship, not dead controls."

"If something happened to the main Bridge, it'd be real enough."

"And you know how long we'd last after that? You know, you can still get off that Command Path, and do something with honest metal and current."

Vrenn felt a little annoyance at the word "honest," but only a little. It was only another game between them, and he could hardly fault Ruzhe for being better at it than at *klin zha*. "I think I'll stay up front in the pod. Away from the radiation."

"There's no radiation back there! We just keep the Drell design because it works!"

"All right, up front away from the Marines."

Ruzhe growled, stared at the board. "You're going to win again."

It was true enough. Vrenn said, "Maybe you'll get lucky, and the Roms will attack." He moved a Flier. "After all, we got lucky enough to get assigned to a raid, on our first full cruise."

Ruzhe said, "I heard one of the Lieutenants say everyone gets assigned to a raid, unless they're just so hopeless they have to put 'em on garbage scows or runs to Vulcan."

"Why?" Vrenn said, He had heard rumors like that, but only from superior-sounding cadets. Never officers.

"Same reason all the frontier captains go privateer: if you *khest* it, it's your fault, not the Academy's."

Vrenn knew that was true. "So I guess we better not *khest* it?"

Ruzhe laughed. "Sure you don't want to work aft?"

He bumped the board. Pieces tipped over. *"Gday't,* I lose."

"Well, you *khest't* it." Vrenn picked up a fallen piece. "Want to *khest* it again?"

"I'd like to *khest* just once on this trip," Ruzhe said. "Got an Orion female in your closet?"

The piece slipped out of Vrenn's fingers, bounced on the floor.

Kodon's Squadron had been inside Romulan claims for seventy-eight days. There had been two more skirmishes, early on, and a kill for *Death Hand* and another for *Blue Fire,* but nothing, not even a contact, for over fifty days now. They were eating salvage from the third battle, Romulan rations, solid enough food but dull on the tongue. Vrenn at last understood his father's story about Human *kafei,* and found it actually made the alien stuff more edible; but the trick didn't work for the other cadets. Some of those from old Navy lines had been given sealed parcels of food, with vague warnings about not opening them too soon; now anyone who had obeyed the warning had power, of a sort. Vrenn rather quickly saw the limitations of a fruitcake-based economy, and knew why Kethas had not so supplied him.

Still, it could be hard to be a strategist.

Vrenn was in the Junior Officers' Mess, chewing determinedly at a piece of vacuum-dried sausage, when the sounds of a discussion floated in his direction. There were three ensigns at a table across the room, and they had gotten on the subject of Orions, and (inevitably) Orion females. One of them, the Helmsman Kotkhe, was insisting he had actually been with one, prize of a cadet cruise. "I admit I was lucky—"

"Nobody gets that lucky on a cadet cruise," said an Ensign with Medical insignia.

"I suppose you two think I care if you believe me."

"Suppose we do." That was Merzhan, the youngest Security officer on the ship. He kept to himself less than the other Security crew, and he showed a nasty sense of humor on all occasions. "You wouldn't have some evidence? A lock of her hair, tied up with a green ribbon?"

"Well, I—" Kotkhe's hand stopped on the way to his pocket. Merzhan's smile was thin as the edge of a knife, and the other ensign looked nervous. Vrenn dumped his tray down the disposal slot, started for the door. He had seen the souvenirs you could buy in a leave port, knew how easily the green dye rubbed off. And he had heard, easily thirty times in his first Academy term, the tale of exotic delights that Kotkhe was now clumsily telling again. He'd have done better, Vrenn thought, to just quote some text from a volume of *Tales of the Privateers;* every other book in the series had the same scene in it.

"But there's a thing they never tell you in the books," Kotkhe said. "And that's the place, the only one place, where an Orion female's *not* green."

Vrenn paused. He wondered where it would be, this time.

Merzhan's eyes flickered over. "Well," he said, "you've got *something* convinced."

"I was just leaving," Vrenn said, and knew at once it was the wrong response: he should have just gone out the door. *Ensigns love cadets,* he had been warned at the Academy, *like you love jelly pastry. They won't talk to the crew and there's nobody else they can damage.*

"Don't go yet," the Security officer said. "You'll miss the best part."

Vrenn took a step toward the door.

"I said, *don't go,* Cadet."

Vrenn stopped. It was a legitimate order.

Merzhan said, "Well, 'Khe, we've got something here to educate. Finish the story."

Kotkhe seemed pleased; baiting cadets was much safer than whatever game Merzhan had been playing. He went on to detail exactly where Orion females were not green. It was the usual version. "Now, Pathfinder, have you learned something to help you walk?" The title and the phrase referred to the Path of Command: the statement was thoroughly insulting without containing any explicit insult.

Vrenn said suddenly, "No, Ensign."

Kotkhe's jaw opened, snapped shut. "Say that again, Pathfinder. For the record this time."

"If I hadn't wanted it heard I wouldn't have said it." Vrenn had not realized just how angry he was. they had, without realizing it, pushed him into an area of his mind he had very carefully walled off. Now Vrenn wondered how much his strategic blindness would cost him.

There was a coldness in the room, the ensigns still not quite believing what they had heard. *Sometimes to show teeth is enough,* Vrenn thought, *but if you bite, bite deep.* "What was there to learn? The lesson's wrong. There's no place they don't have a little green. No place at all."

"Kahlesste kaase," the surgeon's aide said, "he's right."

It was no improvement, though Vrenn wondered if anything short of a Romulan attack could be. Now not only was Ensign Kotkhe made out a liar, his boast of conquest had been upstaged—by a cadet.

"I guess it is true," Kotkhe said, sounding almost desperate; "they *will* open to anything—"

Vrenn leaped, knocking Kotkhe from his chair, taking both of them to the deck. Kotkhe was unready, and Vrenn gave him no chance: Vrenn punched four times rapidly to nerve junctions. Kotkhe went rigid. Vrenn struck once crosswise, neatly dislocating the ensign's jaw. Then he stopped—and realized the medical ensign was holding his arm in a wrestler's pinch above the elbow, shaking his head *no, no.* There were more Klingons in the room now, Security enforcers in duty armor, shock clubs out and ready. Merzhan was tucking away his communicator with his left hand; his right held a pistol casually level.

The look on the Security officer's face was that of one starving, suddenly offered a banquet.

Squadron Leader Kodon vestai-Karum sat behind his desk. Commander Kev sat a little distance to Kodon's right. Vrenn Khemara stood, in the crossfire between them.

"And that was when you assaulted the Ensign?" Kodon said, in a completely disinterested tone.

"Just then, Squadron Leader."

Kodon reached to the tape player in his desk, took out the cassette with the ensigns' and Vrenn's testimony. "I know the epetai-Khemara somewhat," he said, not quite offhand. "Is the one well?"

"At my last hearing, Squadron Leader."

"And his consort?"

Vrenn hesitated, only an instant. "And the one, Squadron Leader."

Kodon nodded. "The line Khemara is not to be insulted, even ignorantly by ignorant youth. Do you wish to enter a claim of line honor?"

"No, Squadron Leader." Vrenn was suddenly thinking of Ensign Merzhan's look, and his words, and wondering if complete ignorance had really been there.

"That seems best. As much as we need diversion, the duel circle does not seem right, just now. And I do not know Ensign Kotkhe's father; there are so many Admirals. . . . " Kodon sat back, turning the tape over in his hands. "The ensign didn't even scratch you, Cadet. How do you account for that?"

"I had the advantage of surprise, Squadron Leader."

Kodon laughed. "Ah. Well, I can hardly assume that the other ensigns held him down for you." He leaned over his desk again, held up the cassette as if weighing it. "Brawling aboard a ship under cruise is a violation of regulations, as is striking a superior office . . . but injuries sustained during a lesson in personal combat are of course not actionable."

"Combat lessons are usually given in the Officers' Gym," Kev said.

"It was occupied," Kodon said. "*I* was using it."

Kev said, "Of course, Captain."

Kodon dropped the cassette. It struck a pair of doors on the desktop, which opened to swallow it, and closed on the flash of destroying light. "It simplifies matters enormously when honor claims are absent."

Vrenn waited.

"Still, a disturbance was created, and Security was dispatched without cause. Commander Kev, I think you know what punishment is appropriate." Kodon stood, and Kev. Salutes were exchanged, and the Squadron Leader disappeared into his inner cabin.

Kev, a portable terminal under his arm, walked to the desk. He brought the black panel up to working position, pressed keys. Green light flashed in his yellow eyes. "The Surgeon reports that Ensign Kotkhe will be unfit for duty for several days. Given your responsibility for this, your punishment detail will be to assume his duties aboard."

"The Helm, Commander?"

"That is *zan* Kotkhe's current duty."

At times like this, Vrenn came close to denying the *komerex zha:* for the universe to be a game implied that it had knowable rules.

Kev looked at Vrenn. The look was very cool, very sharp. Vrenn had realized some time ago that Kev used his eyes as needles; he liked to watch others writhe, impaled on their points.

Finally the Executive said, "You seem to realize that you haven't won anything. That's good. It was necessary that the *g'dayt*-livered Kotkhe be replaced. You forced the Captain's hand; don't think he likes that. Just remember: he's made you a Helmsman. He can make you raw protein if he wants." Kev pushed more keys on his console. In a quieter but no less threatening voice, he said "You'll be breveted Ensign for the rest of the cruise . . . or as long as you last. Don't go changing your name yet. . . . "

"I understand, Commander."

Kev looked up sharply. In a wholly changed tone he said, "Yes . . . it's just possible that you do. But if you did plan this, Khemara, do not ever let anyone know it. *Dismissed.*"

Kodon's Squadron hid, literally, behind a rock. The three cruisers, in Spearhead formation, hung behind a two-kilometer planetoid, shadowed from enemy sensing. A drone, too small to register at this range, orbited the rock, relaying image and data to the D4s.

"Keep the guns cold until I call for them," Kodon said, not for the first time but without audible annoyance. *"Zan* Vrenn, watch the shadow."

Vrenn's console display showed a yellow-gridded sphere, the planetoid, and a larger blue arc, the electronic penumbra. "Margin seventy meters, firm," Vrenn said.

"That's good," said the Captain. It was only acknowledgement, not approval. But it was good work, Vrenn knew: he was successfully holding the cruiser to a mark less than a third of its length away. Ensign Kotkhe had been out of Sickbay for ten days now, but this was the climax of the raid, and Ensign Vrenn had the helm.

The Communications Officer gestured. The drone operator touched a control, adjusting the satellite's orbit: on the main display, a planet came into sharp focus, blue and brown and cloud-streaked. Keys were pressed, and data lines overlaid the visual, with a bright three-armed crosshair over the site of the Romulan groundport.

Tiny flecks appeared near the planet's edge, and were annotated at once: "Cargo tugs," the sensor operator announced. Then: "Shuttle launches confirmed."

Kodon watched the main board, scanned the repeater displays near the foot of his chair. "Helm signal 0.2 Warp," he said, in the short syllables of Battle Language.

"0.2 Warp read," Vrenn said.

"Show mag 8," said the Captain.

The picture on the screen swelled, sparkling as the sensors reached their limit of resolution. The image still clearly showed the Romulan shuttles rolling over, to dock with warp-drive tugs already in orbit above the port.

The schematic display drew in four yellow crescents: Warbirds moving into convoy positions.

Kodon said, "Helm, action. Affirm, action."

"Acting," Vrenn said, and pushed for thrust. The planetoid fell away, the target world dawning above it.

"Weapons preheat," Kodon ordered. "Shields attack standard." Each command was no longer than a single word, the acknowledgements just snaps of the tongue.

"Warp 0.2," Vrenn said.

"Squadron—" Kodon said, on relay to all the ships, and his next word was the same in plain or Battle language: *"Kill!"*

They fell on the Warbirds from ahead and above, out of the danger cone from their plasma guns. Rom lasers, warp-accelerated into the delta frequencies, stabbed up, to detune against shields. Triplet disruptors knifed down, blue light sweeping across the enemy ships' wings. *Two Fingers* severed a Romulan warp engine neatly; its other fire missed by meters. *Death Hand* cut almost entirely through a Warbird's wing, and tore its spine open, splashing fire and debris.

"Precision fire," Kodon said. "Helm, coordinate."

"Affirm," the Weapons officer said. "Affirm," Vrenn said, eyes on three different data displays at once. There was no vision to spare for the controls: now his hands had to know the task.

They did. *Blue Fire* scraped by a Warbird barely twice its length away, and cut both warp nacelles away in a stroke. The flat Rom hull, unable to maneuver or even self-destruct, wavered and began to tumble.

"Stern tractors," said the Squadron Leader.

"Locked." The beams pulled the crippled Rom away from the planet, slinging it on a slow curve toward deep space; the prize would still be there when they were ready to claim it.

"Five more coming, Squadron Leader," the sensor operator said, then, in a tighter voice, "Correction, ten more." He dropped out of Battle Language. "They must have been hiding in—"

"Show it," Kodon said.

Finger-fives of Warbirds were swinging into high strike-fractionals above the planet's east and west horizons. The Klingons were caught between.

Vrenn thought suddenly of white and black pieces on a square-gridded board: but this was no time for the image, and he shoved it away.

"Helm, Warp 0.3. Keep us well sublight, this close to the planet. Vector." Kodon stroked a finger on his armrest controls, drawing the path he wanted on Vrenn's display. It was not an escape vector. "Weapons, free fire," the Squadron Leader said, then, *"Zan* Kandel, reopen the Captains' Link."

Blue Fire caught plasma to starboard, and shook as the harmonics leaked through; Vrenn drifted off Kodon's line, by a hair, for a moment, then brought the ship back again. It was not responding normally: Vrenn scanned his readouts, found the power graphs dropping.

"Engineer—"

"You'll have to share with the deflectors," the Engineer said, as another bolt hit the cruiser. Power fell again. The Engineer turned. "Squadron Leader, commit?"

"Power to shields and weapons," Kodon said, clipped and very calm. "We still fight."

82

When Koth of the *Vengeance* said something like that, his Bridge crew usually raised a cheer. No one started one now.

Three Warbirds were in a precise, right-angled formation just below *Blue Fire.* Disruptors tore one open: trailing hot junk, it slid narrowly past another and dipped into air. There was a cometary flash. The remaining Romulans kept their formation.

"This admiral is an idiot," Kodon said. "He's got the ships, and he must have had a warning, but he is still an idiot."

On the screen ahead, Romulan ships were bracketing *Death Hand,* ahead, on the wings, behind. *Death Hand* fired back and did not miss—it was hardly possible at such ranges—but the number of Roms tipped the balance. A plasma bolt struck the Klingon cruiser's hangar deck from the rear, and detonated inside: there was a jet of incandescent gas from the dorsal vent.

Kandel on Communications said, "Squadron Leader, the Force Leader wants to know if you intend to land his Marines."

"Can't he see we're *expected?*" Kodon stared at *Death Hand* ahead, dying. "What shield shall I drop to transport him down?" Kodon's teeth showed. "Just tell him we are engaged, and that he is to stand by."

Death Hand killed one of her harriers. "Weapons, *that* one," Kodon said, stabbing a finger, and *Blue Fire* poured its namesake into another Rom. "Flat-thinker!" Kodon snarled, and as the Rom blew up there was finally a cheer on the Bridge.

The word closed the circuit in Vrenn's mind. It explained the lockstep formations, the flat-plane attacks, the way *Death Hand* had been surrounded. Now, if there was time to make any use of the knowledge—

"Squadron Leader, a thought," Vrenn said.

"Squadron Leader," Ensign Kandel cut in, *"Death Hand* sends intent to abandon and destruct."

There was a pause. A Captain did not abandon until the gravest extreme.

But not yet, Vrenn thought, not just yet—

"Affirmed," Kodon said. "Only a fool fights in a burning house." Then, with what seemed to Vrenn an infinite slowness, Kodon turned to him. "Proceed, *zan* Vrenn."

"Squadron Leader, I know the *rom zha, latrunculo*—"

"He wants to play games," the drone operator said.

Vrenn did not stop. "—which is played on squares, on a flat board. Pieces kill by pinning enemies between themselves—" Vrenn knew there was no time to explain the game, the thoughts behind it; Kodon must *see.* Vrenn pointed at the main display: the alignments of Warbirds and D4s were as clear to him as the naked stars around them all. If there were some way to show square references upon the triangular grid of the display . . . perhaps Kandel could. . . .

Kodon turned away. Vrenn felt eyes on him from all directions, felt the shame he had sworn under naked stars he would never know again, felt death in his liver.

"I know of the game," Kodon said. "It is a fair observation. . . . So, if this is the sort of idiot the Rom Admiral is, Thought Ensign Vrenn, what shall we do to him?"

"There is a single piece in *latrunculo*," Vrenn said, speaking almost faster than thought, "with the ability to leap over others, like a Flier of *klin zha.* Other pieces must be concentrated against the Centurion. . . . "

Kodon laughed loudly. "Signal to *Death Hand,* priority! Drop shields and transport, and separate, I say once more separate; *hold destruct.*"

"Helmsman—" A line appeared on Vrenn's display. Vrenn took *Blue Fire* to Warp 0.5 and skimmed the cruiser over a Warbird, almost close enough to touch.

The Rom moved.

"Number 3 shield down."

"Troop transporters energized to receive," the engineer said, and the power graphs dove as a wave of *Death Hand*'s Marines were beamed aboard *Blue Fire.*

Blue Fire jumped two more Warbirds, taking only token shots at them. Then, as Warbirds turned in place, a shudder went through *Death Hand* at the center of the enemy cluster: there was a brilliant ring of light at the junction of the cruiser's narrow forward boom with her broad main wing. The two structures parted, and the boom began to crawl forward on impulse drive.

The Roms hesitated, turned again inward.

"Number 4 shield down, 5 up."

"Transients in the signal," the Engineer said, his hands running over controls. Power curves spiked, and warnings flashed yellow. He said "We've got some scramble cases."

"Affirm," Kodon said.

Marine no-ranks did not have personal transporter operators watching for them.

Blue Fire glided on toward *Death Hand,* directly toward it. Vrenn watched as his boards showed tighter and tighter tolerances, less maneuver power as the mass transports stole it from engines.

"Transport arc's changing again," the Weapons officer said. "5 shield down, 6 up."

"Transients clearing from the signal," the Engineer said, as the two ships closed.

"Signal to *Death Hand,*" Kodon said. "Invitation to Naval officers aboard."

Moments later the main display lit with a picture of *Death Hand*'s bridge. Smoke obscured the scene. The Captain's left arm was tucked inside his sash. Behind him, someone was lying dead across a sparking console.

"Your invitation received," the Captain said. "My Ensigns are transporting now. I hope they find much glory with you."

"I am certain," Kodon said.

For the first time since the battle began, Vrenn thought about the damage to *Blue Fire:* who might be dead on the lower decks. But he had less time for such thoughts by the second. The two cruisers were less than a thousand meters apart, on collision course. An alarm screamed; Vrenn snapped it off.

He shifted power between port and starboard engines: *Blue Fire* began to roll.

Kodon said to the other Captain, "And your Executive?"

"Dead," *Death Hand*'s Captain said. "And I, of course . . . "

"This need not be said," said Kodon. "Kill Roms, with your Black Ship, Kadi."

The other Captain grinned. "Not these Roms. They're too stupid. After this death, no more for them. . . . " His lips pulled back from his teeth, and his arm spasmed; blood soaked through the sash. The picture broke up.

Blue Fire slipped sidewise through the gap between the parts of *Death Hand*. Roms still surrounded them, some still firing into the dead ship's hulk.

"Naval officers aboard," the Engineer said. "Ready to receive second Marine unit."

"Squadron Leader," Communications said, "They're breaking formation."

Vrenn heard, registered, ignored: He *was* the ship now, seeking out the one gap in the formation of Roms they never would have thought to cover: how can two ships be in the same place at once?

Kodon looked up from his foot repeaters. "So, not all their Captains are such fools as their Admiral. . . . Cancel transport. Signal Code TAZHAT. Action!"

"Acting," said all voices on the bridge.

The planet whirled over on the display as Vrenn, clear at last of *Death Hand,* brought the ship about. Yellow lines cut across his displays, then green ones, then a blue. Vrenn pushed for thrust, the first set of levers, then the second.

Blue Fire engaged warp drive, and the stars blazed violet, and black, and were past.

"Flash wave aft," said the Communications officer.

"Shield 6—" said Weapons, and a rumble through the decks finished the statement for her.

"*Power*," Vrenn said, and the Engineer gave it to him. *Blue Fire* reached Warp 2, and the rumble died away: the ship had just outrun the sphere of photons and debris that was everything left of *Death Hand*. And of the Roms around it.

"*Kai!*" Kodon cried out. Vrenn felt proud, then embarrassed: it surely must be Captain Kadi that the Squadron leader hailed.

Then Kodon said, "Navigator, course for the nearest outpost. Dronesman, trail one to flash. Communications, have *Two Fingers* home on the drone signal."

Kandel said, "Sir, the cargo ships—"

"Dust, like all good Roms," Kodon said, quiet but intense. "I am not now interested in prizes. I want an answer, and I do not think it is to be found back there."

"Squadron Leader, shall I signal to the Fleet—"

"Signal them *anything* and I'll have your throat out!"

So that, Vrenn thought, is what a *real* threat from Kodon sounds like.

After a moment, Kodon spoke again, in his normal tone. "Engineer, raise the heat and moisture on quarters decks; we're going to be hungry but we might as well be comfortable. And I want Warp 4 power as soon as possible." He got out of his chair. "Kurrozh, you have the conn. Vrenn, you will come with me."

Vrenn stood, not knowing what to think and so trying to think nothing. It was an old trick to threaten the one and punish the other: this had an intensified effect on both subjects. He could not think of what he had done wrong, but knew far better than to be reassured by that.

And then he knew too well what he had done: he had suggested a strategy to a Squadron Leader during battle, and worse, the strategy had worked.

But then, as Vrenn followed Kodon to the lift, he saw one of the Bridge crew flash him the spread fingers of the Captain's Star, and then another, and another. And he knew, then, that he would have his ship, even if it flew in the Black Fleet.

The ensign's tunic was torn, and smelled of smoke. He slung his bag on to the empty bed, sat down hard, and saluted with a bandaged hand. "Kelag, *Death Hand*," he said.

"*Kai Death Hand*," Vrenn said. "Vrenn—" He paused. "Brevet Lieutenant."

"Vrenn. . . ?" Kelag looked at Vrenn's rank badges. "But you're an ensign?"

"Brevet Ensign."

Kelag shook his head. His eyelids were drooping. "I don't understand. What'd you . . . "

"I was *Blue Fire*'s helmsman. I am, I mean."

"*Oh*," said Ensign Kelag, awake at once. "*Kai* Vrenn. *Kai Blue Fire*."

Vrenn nodded. "That was Ruzhe's bed," he said. "He was aft, in Engineering."

"Bad battle."

"He got through the battle all right . . . but when they were working on getting the power back up, some tubes blew. It was intercooler gas. Almost plasma, they said. Anyway, there hasn't been time to clear out his things."

Kelag was contemplating the floor. After a moment, Vrenn realized he was asleep sitting up. Vrenn stood, took a step, meaning to stretch the ensign out flat on the bed, but then he stopped. He did not look up. Security did not like any signs that one knew they were watching. They were much more likely to find something wrong with what they saw.

Vrenn turned out the lights—let them watch by infrared—and went to bed himself. He was instantly asleep.

Security had a Rom in the cube. It was running live on ship's entertainment channel, and in the Inspirational Theatres. Most of the newer officers had traded duty to watch, but Vrenn had stayed on the helm. Kodon laughed; "You've gotten to like the conn quick enough. I know what that's like."

The Weapons officer had the Examination picture on her repeater screen, sound too low for Vrenn to hear. If he looked that way, he could see it clearly enough. The right side of the screen showed the information display: a green outline of the Rom's body, with blue traces of major nerves and yellow crosses where the agonizers were focused. On the left, the Romulan sat in the chair—very firmly so; *Blue Fire*'s Specialist Examiner had set the booth foci so the Rom's muscles shoved her down and back into the seat cushions, leaving all the restraint straps slack. It was the work of a real expert, showing off just a little.

Vrenn supposed his view was really no worse than that in the Examining Room itself: the agonizer cubes were supposed to be entirely soundproof, with phones for the interested observer to listen at any chosen volume.

There had been three Romulans at the Imperial outpost where Kodon's Squadron stopped. They claimed diplomatic protection; Kodon was hardly interested, and the outpost commander was only too happy to stay out of the Squadron Leader's way—especially after the Executive made clear that *he* was next in line for cube time.

The Ambassador cut her own throat, by Romulan ritual and admirably well. The Romulan Naval Attaché tried to be a great hero by overloading his pistol, but mis-set the controls. Kodon gave him to the surviving Marines from *Death Hand*. That left the Mission Clerk, who was in the cube, while the Security analysts did similar electronic things to the coded recordings she had carried. Security was pleased with their catch: clerks often knew more useful things than the bureaucrats they served.

The Rom slumped over. The Weapons Officer yawned and turned away; on the screen behind her, the agonizer foci shifted to new nerves, and the clerk's head snapped up again. "So hey, Krenn," the Gunner said, "how long before we get someplace with thick air? I hate these little outposts, flatulent rocks."

Vrenn was getting used to the officers ennobling his name, though it couldn't be final until the Navy made his promotions official. Which might, he knew, never happen. Not everything a privateer captain did, lasted. But for now, it made the conversations easier. "Three days to Aviskie, Lieutenant, if the Squadron Leader wants Warp 4."

"He will. Got any plans?"

The Romulan was bleeding a thin green trickle from the corner of her mouth.

"I hadn't," Vrenn said.

"I think you do now."

Vrenn tried not to laugh, but did anyway. The two other Lieutenants on the bridge were carefully watching their boards.

"So what am I supposed to make of that?" the Gunner said. "There may be too much Cadet fuzz on your ears to know it, but you're on the warp route, Thought Ensign." Kodon's half-mocking title for him had spread. "Ever hear of the Warp 4 Club?"

"I *have* got duty."

"You can't conn the ship for three *khest'n* days."

Vrenn grinned. The Gunner had no serious faults he could see—except, perhaps, the rank badges on her vest: Vrenn wondered if he ought to wait, just until his Lieutenancy came through in cold metal.

But then he wouldn't be a full member of the Club.

The Romulan began to convulse, then went rigid: her lips moved, forming words. The Gunner turned up the sound: it was barely understandable as a string of Romulan numbers.

"Here come the code keys," the Communications Officer said, slapping his thigh.

"You see?" the Gunner said to Vrenn, laughing. "I hope your timing's *always* this good."

The rental room in Aviskie Column Five was dark, and finally quiet, and damp with room fog and perspiration. The incense in the bedside holder had burned out a little while ago.

Light lanced in, and cold outside air. Vrenn rolled off the bed, fingers arched to claw: on the other side, the Gunner had been just a little faster, and was already saluting.

"Come with us, *Lieutenant*," Ensign Merzhan said. Behind him were a Navy Commander with a silver Detached Service sash, and two armed enforcers, from the port complement, not *Blue Fire*'s.

Vrenn saluted: it did not occur to him to disagree. "I'll dress—"

"Why?" said Merzhan. The Commander made a tiny gesture, and Merzhan's face froze. The officer said, "Go ahead."

Vrenn pulled on trousers and boots and tunic, and finally his vest and sash, waiting for someone to stop him donning the rank marks. No one did. The gunner stood at parade rest.

"Let's go," the Detached Commander said, in a voice with less character than a ship's computer's. He looked at the Gunner, eyes not so much appraising as measuring her. "We weren't here."

"Nobody was," she said, and as Vrenn was led out he thought that she did not sound frightened at all: just rueful.

Vrenn sat in a bare conference room, windowless, with three Naval officers: Koll, the Commander who had come to his rental room, Commander Kev of *Blue Fire,* and Captain Kessum of *Two Fingers*. Vrenn had not seen Kodon. All the Security men had gone, so they were certainly watching by other means.

"This is not a tribunal," Koll said, "nor any other sort of official meeting. In fact, this meeting is not taking place, and never will have taken place. Is this understood?"

"Perfectly," Vrenn said.

Kev nodded. Koll put a rectangular object on the table; an antenna rose from it, and several small lights began to flicker. Vrenn realized that the Detached officer, whatever he was, was quite serious about the nature of the meeting: now, not even Security would be listening.

Commander Koll said, "As a result of certain Romulan decrypts, we have learned of a series of secret negotiations between the *Komerex Romulan* and a faction within the *Komerex Klingon*. Had these discussions resulted in a treaty, a neutral zone would have been established between the *Komerexi*, supposedly inviolable by either side. While such a treaty has often been proposed in the Imperial Council, and discarded, this group might have been able to enforce the support of an agreement presented as an accomplished fact. . . ."

Vrenn felt his liver shift in his chest. He knew one proponent of Rom Neutral Space, only one. The idea was related to the principle of center control in the game called *chess*.

". . . an excuse for destruction of Klingon frontier vessels on charting or colonization missions, having no effect at all on Romulan incursionary forces—"

"Commander," Kev said, "that's background." Kev looked at Vrenn, with his impaling eyes; Vrenn tried to puzzle out what the look said.

"Yes, correct," Koll said. "The point is that now the treaty conspirators have been identified. Among them is Thought Admiral Kethas epetai-Khemara." Koll gave Vrenn his mechanical, measuring look. Kessum tapped a hand on the table, the two-fingered right hand that gave his ship its name.

Kev said abruptly, "The point is this. Squadron

Leader Kodon thinks that you are not involved in this conspiracy, and are too good an officer to be disposed of for the sake of mere caution. I agree with both points. Now, we have worked very fast, faster than Security can follow, *we think,* so listen carefully. There's an independent command waiting for you, if you want it. A small frontier scout, but it's Navy, and it doesn't have to be a *khesterex thath* if you stay as clever as you've been."

Vrenn sat very still. He wondered if the stars above this world were clothed or naked now. Here was his ship, then; here too was its price.

"If the one hesitates," Captain Kessum said formally, "for the breaking of the chain of duty, let certain terms of the negotiation be stated."

Kev said, "The Roms wanted some proofs of the negotiators' intent. They wanted information on the next frontier raid. They got it."

Vrenn said, "Did the one—"

"The one knew," said Commander Koll. "The one verified it."

So there was only the *komerex zha,* Vrenn thought, and the pieces of the game were only bits of wood in the fire. "The Navy honors me," he said, "and where I am commanded, there I shall go."

"*Kai kassai,*" Kev said softly, but his look was still steel needles.

Vrenn said, "If I might take formal leave of Squadron Leader Kodon—"

Captain Kessum said stiffly, "This one is here for Kodon."

Yes, of course, Vrenn thought. *Blue Fire* lived, but *Death Hand* was dust. And there was the question of strategy, that least Klingon of sciences, whose practitioners made strange things happen; as Kev had said once before, *if you did plan this, do not let it be known.*

". . . it is of course understood that you will not operate in this part of the frontier."

"This need not be said," Vrenn said.

"Then it's done," Koll said, and reached for his sensor jammer.

Commander Kev said, "You'll have to change your name now."

Scout Captain Krenn was eighty days out on an exploratory cruise when the recordings arrived, scrambled with Krenn's personal cipher; there was no originating label.

He watched the taped deaths of Kethas and Rogaine twice through. They were competent kills, as the law of assassination specified: that indeed was the reason for taping at all.

Krenn was pleased to see that Rogaine fought very well, stabbing one assassin, blinding another with her nails after her body had hypnotized him. It served the fool right for such carelessness.

Kethas fell near his gameboards, firing back as he collapsed, upsetting the Reflective Game set that had been his favorite. Kethas's hand closed on the green-gold Lancer, and then did not move. The camera swung away. On the second play, Krenn stopped the image, enlarged it; he realized that the epetai-Khemara had not been reaching for the game piece, but toward his consort's body.

Krenn stopped the tape again, thinking to rewind and watch for Kethas's look, exactly as Rogaine died; but he did not do so.

The record covered only two of the house *kuve*. Little black-furred Odise was shot from a balcony, fell, landing in a wet and messy heap. Tirian they stunned, and agonized for a time, then carried aloft in a flier. His tunic was slit down the back, and the scars of his wings shown to the camera. Then they flung him out, perhaps twelve hundred meters above the dark twisted mass of the Kartade Forest. Vrenn did not rerun that scene.

He burned the cassette, thinking *It simplifies things enormously when honor claims are absent.*

Krenn stepped out onto the Bridge. The Helmsman

saluted, not too sharply, and the Sciences officer turned. They were enough Bridge crew; it was a small ship. But a Navy ship, and perhaps not a dead command.

"Anything of interest?" Krenn asked Sciences.

"Dust and smaller dust," Specialist Akhil said. "Your message?"

"Some bureaucratic housecleaning."

Akhil laughed. Then he said, "Is this a good time to ask a question, Captain?"

"As good as any."

"My oldest uncle was on a ship under a Captain of the Rustazh line. Are you any—"

"They're all gone," said Krenn tai-Rustazh. "The name was free for use."

"So you *are* starting a line," the Helmsman said.

"Why else would anyone be out here?" Krenn said. "To play the Perpetual Game?"

Then he laughed, and the Scientist and the Helmsman joined in.

PART TWO
The Naked Stars

Negotiation may cost far less than war, or infinitely more: for war cannot cost more than one's life.
—Klingon proverb

Chapter 4
Spaces

"We've got the ship on tractors, Captain."

"Pull it in. *Zan* Kafter, keep the guns hot: one through the command pod if her energy readings change."

"Affirm, Captain." The crew of Imperial Klingon Cruiser *Fencer* went to work, towing in the depowered but intact Willall starship: it was their twelfth such prize, and they knew the drill.

Captain Krenn vestai-Rustazh sat back in the Command Chair, folded his hands and rested his chin on them. The Willall vessel showed up magnified in the forward display: a boxy thing, without a hint of warp physics in the design. Willall ships all looked like outdoor toilets with warpdrive nacelles wired on. But those ridiculous-looking ships had made a very serious dent in Imperial space.

They didn't have any strategy, beyond just raiding

the next planet they stumbled across. They didn't know any tactics, either, other than shooting and swooping. *Willall* was shorthand *klingonaase* for their name for themselves, which fully translated said in much more grandiose fashion that they were the race which would command all the possible realities.

But they fought like—"like drunken Romulans" was a popular expression, here on the other side of Empire from Romulan claims. And their junk ships could absorb a lot of fire, and put out a respectable volume.

Still, even determined shooting and swooping only did so much. "Tactics are *real*," Krenn told his crew. *Fencer* had proven it, destroying Willall until Krenn was bored with that.

He and his Engineer had put on environment suits and gone probing through one of the Willall wrecks. They found a couple of weak structural points, where low-intensity disruptor shots would break the main superconducting lines to the warp engines, sever the Agaan Tubes. So now they didn't destroy Willall; they wrapped them up and sent them to the Emperor.

"Got her readings, Captain," Akhil said from the Sciences board. "Life, armed, all small weapons. No ship's systems above emergency levels."

"Transporter clear?"

"No spikes, no transients. Safe enough for the Emperor."

Krenn nodded. "Communications, open to the prize's bridge."

The image was fuzzy, made up of scan lines: Willall vision technology was no superior to the rest of it. Half-a-dozen aliens were looking up at the monitor. They always reminded Krenn of unbaked dough, or putty sculptures; soft and colorless. *Kuve.*

"I am Krenn of the *Fencer*," he said, slowly enough for the translation program to keep up. "I have destroyed your ability to resist the Empire. If you attempt any further hostility, I will destroy you. Is this understood?"

The Willall spoke, a sound like bubbles in stew. Several of them were talking at once; they had some kind of group command structure, and the Security analysts had not decided which of them did what. The cube was worthless: agonizers made Willall nerves fall literally to pieces.

"It is understood," the translator finally said. "The group is in isolation. It ceases." The aliens put their hand weapons in a pile on the deck.

Kuve, Krenn thought again. Yet they were correct, of course; had they not disarmed . . . well. There were several things he had done, in the course of a dozen captures.

This game was beginning to bore him as well, he knew.

"I will put Klingons aboard your ship. Some of these will repair the damage to your engines. When this is done, your ship will proceed to a world of the Empire, and there surrender.

"You may, as you choose, pilot the ship yourselves. However, there will be Klingons aboard to prevent errors in navigation, and others to protect the navigators and engineers. You will interfere with none of these, and aid them as you can."

The Willall crew flooped agreement. Krenn broke the link.

He went aft to the transporter room, for a last word with the prize crew. They were in a high enough mood: it would be easy duty, with a good welcome waiting for them when they turned the ship in.

"Ensign Kian," Krenn said.

"Captain?" Kian looked like he had just won a banner in the Year Games. He would, however briefly, have full charge of a starship: never mind that it was not a Navy ship, or even a Klingon ship.

Krenn indicated the portable computer Kian carried. "Don't use that unless you have to. You'll be in command; *command.*"

"Of course, Captain."

The small computer contained a special set of navigational routines, in the event that the Willall refused to cooperate. They had never yet done so, at least, not as far as anyone knew. Two of Krenn's prizes had never arrived, but many things could have happened, and in tin-plate ships like the Willall, who could tell?

Klingons would have found a way to attack their captors. Romulans or Andorians would have, even if they were all certain to die. Humans and Kinshaya were almost too devious to leave alive as prisoners. Even Vulcans, Krenn supposed, would use all their logic to find a flaw in the terms of surrender.

But these Willall just obeyed. Like any servitors. Perhaps the geneticists were right, and something in the *kuve* blood and flesh made *kuve*.

Krenn thought that was a stupid idea, but it was a private thought.

Akhil stepped out of the lift, went to the transporter controls; the petty officer there stepped aside at once. The prize crew straightened up to full attention: the Captain's own transporter operator made this an authentic heroes' sendoff.

"Ready to transport," Akhil said.

"*Zan* Kian," Krenn said.

"Captain?"

"Take care of our ship." He had chosen the possessive very carefully.

"This need not be said, Captain."

Krenn nodded. "Energize," he said, and Akhil pushed the control levers. The crewmen and Marines dissolved into spindles of light and were gone.

Krenn stroked his forehead ridge, his jaw. "I'll be in quarters, 'Khil."

"I've still got some of that Saurian brandy," Akhil said.

"Not this time." Krenn got into the lift car. "If I'm still there when Kian calls, ring me. Won't do to give formal leave from the bath."

Akhil said, not at all lightly, "You're thinking too much again, Thought Ensign."

Krenn grimaced as the lift door closed. He'd never found out where Akhil had heard of that title. But the Executive was careful never to use it except when they were alone. Just Krenn and Akhil and Security's monitors.

It was just possible, Krenn thought, as he undressed and slid into hot salt water, that he did think too much. Could a scientist believe that? Even a Klingon scientist?

Of course, he thought, as his senses began to dim. He had only known one Klingon who trusted all in thought. And the epetai-Khemara was dust six years.

Chiming woke Krenn. "I'm awake, 'Khil, I'm awake," he lied, stumbling out of the bath; he remembered to suppress vision before turning the intercom on.

It was not Akhil, but Kalitta, the Communications Officer. "Captain, I have a yellow-2 priority from Navy Command. It's an immediate recall of *Fencer*. To Klinzhai, Captain."

"Yellow priority," Krenn said. It was not a question: he could see the lights on Kalitta's board. Yellow-2 didn't mean the galaxy was exploding, but it was close enough. And to the *homeworld?* "Open link to Ensign Kian, aboard the prize."

"Acting." The picture stuttered and blanked: Kian appeared, through Willall scan lines. "Acknowledging *Fencer,*" he said, looking slightly puzzled.

"Stand by, *zan* Kian." Krenn grabbed a gown and tossed it on, then switched on his vision pickup.

"Captain?"

"We've been called home, Ensign. Warp 4 plus. No more time to spend on that thing, and we can't drag it along; prepare to transport and we'll cut it loose."

Kian looked startled, and angry. Krenn thought that

103

was reasonable; he felt the same way. The Ensign said, "We've got less than a third of a shift's work left, Captain. Zero problems so far."

"This is a priority recall, Ensign. We don't have a third of a shift to wait."

Kian stared up at the screen. Krenn saw him chew his tongue. Then he said, "A moment, Captain. We've got some transmission problems." He reached for his portable computer. "You're breaking up very badly, Captain. I don't know if it's safe to transport—"

Krenn almost laughed. "That's a good try, Kian, but you're perfectly clear to me."

Kian stopped with his hand on the black case. "Yes, Captain," he said calmly, "I suppose I am."

Krenn did laugh then.

Kian said, "Leave us behind, Captain."

"You're still depowered. Suppose you can't start the engines? This is the frontier; you might eat each other, but you can't breathe vacuum."

"We'll get power. I'll take responsibility."

Krenn's smile froze. Even bold young ensigns did not say that very often. Not and mean it, and Krenn could see Kian meant it. "And the rest of your crew? What about them?"

"It's my command, Captain Krenn."

Krenn looked into the hot yellow eyes on the sketchy screen, wondering if he had really looked like that, when Kodon first gave him *Blue Fire*'s conn. When he became a full member of the club.

"Yes, Ensign," Krenn said finally. "Your command. Bring home glory. The *klin* is already in you."

"Captain." Kian saluted, and then broke the link on his superior officer: Krenn had to grin. He wouldn't have given the old starburst time to rethink, either.

Krenn killed vision again, hit the Call key. "Captain to Bridge. Prepare to cut tractors and get under way. Tell Engineering Warp 4 is expected, 4.5 would be better."

104

Akhil's voice said, "Transport signal's clear."

"No one's transporting. The prize goes as she is."

"Affirm," Akhil said, sounding cheerful, or satisfied, or both. Krenn wondered if Kalitta had left the link open, on the Bridge . . . well, if he hadn't wanted it heard, he wouldn't have said it.

Kalitta said, "Statement to the crew, Captain?"

"Just tell them we're ordered to travel. Krenn out." He snapped the link, said to the air, "Unless you know something I don't?"

Just this once, he hoped Security was listening.

It took *Fencer* 112 days to reach the Klingon home-world: she had been far enough on the fringe of the spiral arm that Warp 4.85 was possible for the first twenty-plus days, and the Engineer was muttering about a record. The officers and crew were talking too: not many had visited Klinzhai itself, and fewer still had lived there: to them it was the ultimate of leave worlds, paradise with hotel service.

So the three-cruiser escort waiting for them in high orbit was a surprise to most of *Fencer*'s complement. So was the strict warning about leaving the escort's "protection"—that is, their cones of fire—or launching shuttles, or transporting down. Only one aboard was authorized to leave the ship—and Krenn was not surprised, not really. He was in fact rather pleased to be beaming down alone; it meant his crew was safe, for now.

He was met at the discs by a Security team in dress armor, wearing light weapons; they were polite, which did not at all mean that Krenn was not under arrest. He did not waste effort asking the team leader questions.

Krenn was taken through empty corridors to a room that might have been in one of the Throne City's better hotels. But its door would not open after the Security team departed. The communicator and the computer screen were both *khex*. There were no windows.

The meal slot did function: Krenn punched for pastry and fruit juice, and sat contemplating a clearprint on the wall of a D4 cutting up a Kinshaya supercarrier.

The thing he liked least about particle transporters, Krenn thought, was that the signal could be relayed: one could not really know where one was going. He *might* be in the Throne City, or someplace very different. Even aboard a ship: but he felt the gravity and doubted that.

The door opened, and three Klingons came in, and Krenn got his first real surprise.

One of them was Koll, the Commander who had come for him six years ago. He still wore the silver sash of Detached Service, but now had a Captain's stars. There was a heavyset Admiral with a parcel under his arm, and a tall, powerfully built Security officer without badges of specific rank—which meant, very high rank.

"Captain Krenn, I am Captain Koll."

Of course, Krenn thought; *we've never met.* Krenn was a little glad, in a backhand way, to have the Security supergrade there: whatever this meeting was, at least it would exist.

"Captain Koll. Honored."

"This is Admiral Kezhke zantai-Adion . . . and Operations Master Meth of Imperial Intelligence."

Intelligence? Krenn thought, feeling muscles tense. He knew Navy officers who feared Imperial Intelligence as they did not fear to die cowards; he had heard that Security feared them. And high rank indeed. Meth would be answerable to no one but the Emperor . . . and if II functioned as Krenn supposed it must, perhaps not the Emperor.

Admiral Kezhke had his package on a table and was unwrapping it; he set out four spherical glasses and a bottle of Saurian brandy. "Pleased to finally meet you, Captain Krenn," Kezhke said as he worked at the brandy stopper. "You've got a stormwalker's dinner of a record, you know." The plug came out. "Drinks?"

Only Koll declined. Krenn took a very small sip, on

the small chance that it was genuine Saurian. It was. Krenn felt as if he had been kicked in the liver. But (as Akhil said, over glasses of the reasonable fake he kept in his desk) it was a *wonderful* kick in the liver.

Kezhke stoppered the bottle again. "Only one of those to a meeting," he said. He smiled at Krenn, a bland look that might cover anything.

"Good rule," Meth of Intelligence said, and put down his half-emptied glass. He was not smiling, but his voice was pleasant enough.

Krenn felt his own voice coming back. "May the one ask the reason for urgent recall?" he said, perhaps a little too quickly.

"That much formality isn't necessary," Meth said. His expression was very still—not empty like Kezhke's or frozen like Koll's, but literally immobile. As Meth spoke, Krenn realized that most of his facial flesh was cosmetic plastic—whether a prosthetic, or a disguise, Krenn could not tell.

"The Admiral mentioned your record," Meth said. "It is rather extraordinary. No one, within my knowledge, has a similar rate of captures of intact ships."

"There are several with more captures," Koll said, not a correction but a machine annotation. "But none in so short a time. And none with a single ship."

"It's a talent," Meth said, "which shouldn't be wasted."

Krenn looked at Koll, but if the phrase registered in the Detached officer's mind, there was no sign. Not for the first time, Krenn wondered if the Aviskie meeting really had been nonexistent: if only he remembered it at all.

"We have a mission for you, Captain," Meth said, still echoing. "It's rather particular in its requirements, and no one seems better qualified than you."

Krenn squeezed another sip of the brandy down his throat. He knew perfectly well—and these officers must know that he knew—how often *best qualified* for a special mission meant *most expendable*.

107

If that were the case now, then if he refused, they would simply expend him and call the next name on the list. *So, bite deep.* "I am honored," Krenn said. "What is the mission?"

Meth touched his glass, but did not lift it. His hands were also surfaced with plastic. "We need one brought to this world. It will be a rather long cruise."

"On the frontier all cruises are long," Krenn said.

"This one will exceed a year, at Warp 4 speed."

"In each direction?"

"In each direction."

That meant it was to somewhere outside Klingon holdings. Krenn had a sudden thought of just how they might have chosen to expend him. "To Romulan space?"

"Not the Roms," Admiral Kezhke said. "The Federation." He gave the brandy bottle a hard look. "They want to send us an . . . *ambassador.* A ship must travel, under peace signals, to bring the one."

"Peace signals," Krenn said.

Captain Koll said, "The Imperial Council has, for the situation, agreed to the Federation idea that a ship bearing an Ambassador must not have combat."

"But this calls for a squadron," Krenn said, trying to think moves ahead in the game. Why would the Council consent to disarming a ship, and how could they expect to find a Captain for it? "With escorts, who may use their weapons—"

"One battlecruiser," Kezhke said. There was an authentic-sounding distress in his voice.

"And if we are attacked by . . . perhaps, Romulans?" Meth looked at him, and Krenn was suddenly afraid to even think what he never would have said: *Or, perhaps, Klingons.* Imperial Intelligence was said to know things they could not know by any natural means; they were said to know thoughts. Krenn did not believe this, and still he was afraid.

"A Romulan attack would be a diplomatic incident

between the three Empires," Koll was saying. "By the *komerex federazhon* law, an act of war."

Krenn wondered if that were the strategy. He imagined it would please certain of the Imperial Council very greatly if the son of Kethas, who had died trying to make peace with the Romulans, were to die igniting a war with them.

Meth said, "Are you declining the mission, Captain Krenn?"

"I am questioning it," Krenn said. "Only a servitor goes blindly to the death: I serve the Empire, but I am not the Empire's servitor."

"Kai, klingon," Kezhke said, with something like relief.

"We do not think it is the death," Operations Master Meth said. His tone was almost conciliatory. "The Federation has strong ideas about its own laws." He picked up the brandy glass. "But the mission is not commanded. Only offered."

"I would take *Fencer* and my crew?"

"Fencer and any crew you like," Kezhke said.

"But time is short," Meth said. "Some of your crew will doubtless need leave and rest; they may need replacement from the pools."

Of course Intelligence would put its people aboard; if Krenn tried to fight that, II would still get them aboard, and Krenn would have even less idea who they were. "I'll need my Sciences Officer; he's also my Executive."

"You'll get him," Kezhke said, before Meth could speak.

Meth said, "You accept the duty, then."

"I accept."

Meth nodded. Koll reached into his tunic, brought out several computer cassettes. "Your navigational tapes. A message of introduction from the Council. And a dream-learning tape of the Federation language."

Meth said, "If you would rather take the language by

109

RNA transfer, it can be arranged. We have a native *fedegonaase* speaker, freshly spun down."

"This will be adequate," Krenn said, taking the cassettes.

Kezhke said, "There's a dock space waiting for your ship, and priority orders. She's in good order?"

"Yes."

The Admiral smiled. "I knew she would be. Tune and trim, then. Image will matter, this cruise."

Meth said, "Tell your crew that leave has been arranged for them, at the Throne City port. At Imperial expense, naturally."

"They will be pleased."

Meth gave his unreal, dead-faced smile. It was impossible to tell if irony was meant. "Then hail the mission and its success." He drank the rest of his brandy. "We'll let you return to your ship, then. There's a lot to do, in a little time."

The door opened for the officers. The Security team leader was standing in the hall, without his team; Krenn had not seen anyone summon him.

Krenn was taken back to the transporter room. Just before the underofficer energized the disc, Admiral Kezhke came into the room. "Leave us for a moment," the Admiral said.

The Security man looked unhappy, but obeyed.

Kezhke motioned for Krenn to step off the transport stage. After he had, the Admiral pushed the transport levers halfway up. The discs flickered.

"Loose energy *khests* the monitors," Kezhke said. He looked straight at Krenn. "I knew the great of your line, vestai-Rustazh." He held out the bottle of brandy.

"This is a misapprehension I often find," Krenn said. "The name was—"

Kezhke was shaking his head. "No error, Captain. I knew *both* your fathers."

Krenn accepted the bottle, took a swallow.

"Listen to me, vestai-Rustazh, Khemara. You must bring the Federation Ambassador here, and you must

110

bring him alive, and without any incident. No matter what you are told, or *think* you are ordered, you must do this."

Krenn felt he was listening from light-years away. If this one was close to the sutai-Rustazh and the epetai-Khemara, then what was he doing alive, speaking to the one with the secret of both lines?

Krenn began to wonder if a Rom war would be such a bad thing to die for. Kahless, the greatest of all Emperors, had died so, and Kahless was known as The One Who Is Remembered.

What Krenn said was, "I understand the mission, Admiral. I do not mean to fail in it."

"I hope so," Kezhke said. "I hope you understand."

Krenn held out the bottle. "Keep it," Kezhke said, and went to the door; he let the Security transport operator in, then stood in the doorway. "Much glory, Captain Krenn," he said, which was the last thing Krenn had expected him to say.

The homeworld faded out.

Fencer faded in.

"Did you meet the Emperor?" Akhil said, smiling.

"Not unless he goes around in clever plastic disguises."

"*What?*" The Specialist's look fell on the object in Krenn's hands. "That *isn't* really—"

"Have some," Krenn said. "Let's both have some, right now, 'Khil. And then I'll *really* make your head spin."

The air turned to fire above the diamond grid of the cargo transporter, and a crate materialized, displacing a small breeze. *Fencer*'s Cargomaster ran a coding wand over its invoice plate and registered the load on his portable computer.

"What's that one, Keppa?" Krenn asked.

"More whitefang steaks," the Cargomaster said, with something close to awe. "Well, if we're captured, we can just eat ourselves to death."

"It's a two-year cruise, with no stops to forage."

"That wasn't a complaint, Captain," Keppa said quickly. "Any time they want to load meat instead of Marines, I'll clear the space."

Krenn laughed. "I know how you'd do it, too. But decompression's hard on the hull." Akhil was approaching, making notes on a small scribe panel. "Keep the steaks coming, Keppa."

"Affirm, Captain." The cargo module was lifted on antigravs; Krenn turned away.

"Keppa says another quarter-day to load stores," Krenn said to Akhil. "How are the other preparations?"

"The weapon interlocks are installed," Akhil said.

Krenn pointed a finger, and he and Akhil passed, quite casually, between two cargo modules. Krenn said quietly "My way or theirs?"

"Yours. Any time outbound, your personal cipher will get us disruptors."

"Good."

"And I got these last night." Akhil handed Krenn a pair of cassettes.

"Where did you get them?"

"A friend in the Institutes of Research for Language. That's their latest revision of Federation Standard, set up for dream-learning. And that's *all* that's on them."

Krenn took the black plastic boxes. "They offered me an RNA drip, too."

Akhil tapped his scribe on the board. "Human?"

"That's what Meth said."

"Do you really think they were planning to program you?"

"I *know* they meant to program me," Krenn said. "I don't know if there was anything clever on the dream-tapes."

Akhil nodded. They came out from between the crates, turned a corner; Akhil pressed for a lift car. The two Klingons got in. "Bridge," Krenn said, and they started the long ride from the cruiser's lowest tail deck, up the shaft of the boom to the command pod forward.

"And the crew?" Krenn said.

"They enjoyed themselves, but nobody's dead," Akhil said dryly. "Koplo and Aghi put in for long-term leave; they were entitled, and you said—"

"It's all right. This trip, everyone's a volunteer. They were replaced?"

"I've got the pool files on all the new crew. Krenn . . . there are a couple of things you're not going to like."

"Only a couple? What a relief."

"Kalitta was beaten up, outside a bar. The port patrols say they ran off some Marines—"

"But no one was caught, and it was very, very dark."

"As the void, Captain."

"I suppose we were fortunate, and an experienced Communications officer was available?"

"Blue lights, Captain."

"How's Kalitta doing?"

"That's the other thing you won't like."

Krenn growled deep in his throat. "They never take chances, do they." He said suddenly, "What about Maktai?"

"He checked aboard this morning, all lights blue."

Krenn thought about that. Imperial Intelligence could have just ordered the Security Commander replaced, and no one, least of all Mak, could have said anything. That they had not meant . . .

Nothing. Either Maktai belonged to II, or he did not, but they had someone else aboard. Someone unsuspected.

Someone in a good position to communicate his reports.

Krenn found himself staring at Akhil.

The Exec did not seem to notice. "I've got a hospital address for Kalitta, if you want to send her a tape."

"Tape?" Krenn said absently.

113

"They said she'd be conscious in a few days."

"*G'dayt,*" Krenn spat. "Yes, let's do that. Let's do it from the Bridge, and get everyone's face on it. And let's do it now, before the gossip link figures out what happened to her." The lift car slowed. "Besides, we can see our new Communications expert in action."

The car doors opened on *Fencer*'s Bridge. All stations were occupied, as the crew checked the ship down for cruise. Akhil and Krenn went to the Communications board.

"Captain, presenting—"

Krenn looked up, and disbelieved.

"Lieutenant Kelly, Electronics, Communications," Akhil said, and saw Krenn's face, and took a step backward.

"Captain Krenn," Gelly *Gensa* Swift said—though of course she was no longer any of those things—and rose from her chair, a smooth motion, and saluted. The movement of her arm was somehow wrong, and Krenn could see in his mind the steel Lance coming down, and the dark-colored blood.

"Welcome aboard *Fencer*, Lieutenant," Krenn said. "It has been quite some time."

Kelly nodded slightly. Krenn thought she relaxed, but he was not certain; he had never seen her when she was not dancing with energy—except for the one time, with the blood.

"You know each other?" Akhil said, more curious than surprised. All around the Bridge, work stopped, heads turned.

"Yes," Krenn said, wondering if it was the truth.

"But Zharn was alive after they transported you off the grid?" Krenn said. He and Kelly were alone in the Officers' Mess, talking, over warm black ale and plain pastry with pale butter.

"Alive, yes," she said. "His neck was broken, and of course he couldn't move . . . they put him into a frame and took him away. I was wrapped all up in

114

something . . . " She touched her arm. "I remember not liking being wrapped. But the care was really very good. It took two years." She straightened her elbow, lifted her arm; her shoulder swiveled, stopped, swiveled.

"Metal implant?" Krenn said.

Kelly nodded. "There weren't any grafts to match my fusion, so it had to be metal. You know, before that, I used to think I was half-Romulan. But they have lots of material for Klingon-Rom fusions, since they use so many on the border now."

Krenn had heard of that development, though of course he had been nowhere near that space.

Kelly said, "And they took samples, but . . . I still don't know what I am, really. I suppose I never will."

She drank some ale. There was still an astonishing grace to all her movements—even of her rebuilt arm— and Krenn found himself wondering if the medical geneticists had matched her against an Orion template.

He pulled back from the thought. She had been sent here, he knew, and those who sent her might have planned on exactly that reaction from him.

She said, "And you? How did you come to have a line, and a ship?"

She said she had not returned to the House, after the hospital released her, but had gone straight to Naval Technical School. She knew nothing of what had happened to him. She said.

"I was adopted out," Krenn said. "But I took another linename, to start new."

"Oh. You have consorts, then."

"No."

"Oh."

She stood up. No, Krenn thought, she was not Swift any longer: there was a deliberation that she had never shown before. It was not the calculated, mind-blinding stimulation of an Orion female, either.

Though Krenn could not deny that she affected him.

"Permission to retire, Captain?"

"Muros's *nose,* Kelly. . . . "

She nodded, trying either to force or restrain a smile. "Pleasant rest, Krenn."

"Pleasant rest, Kelly."

Early in the following dayshift, Akhil said to Krenn, "Do you think Imperial Intelligence sent her?"

"If they did," Krenn said, a rumble in his voice, "would we know it so soon?"

Krenn staggered out of his bed, almost falling over the loose restraint web. He felt his way to the washroom, turned on the sink, then ignored it, tumbled into the bath and hit the fill lever. Water flowed over him; his arms twitched at the stimulus, throwing water across the room.

"Is," he said, "are, was, were, be, been, am. Excuse me, citizen, but where may currency be exchanged? Pozhalasta prishl'yiti bagazh."

He started to sink, into the dreams that were mutually exclusive with dream-learning, into the hot water. Both felt good.

I am drowning, he thought, in Federation Standard. *Please inform the UFP Consulate.*

Eventually he noticed that the communicator was chiming, and managed to answer in *klingonaase* with only a slight Federation accent.

"Disputed Zone coming up, Captain."

"Strategic," Krenn said, using Battle Language automatically. The main display showed the area of space ahead in large scale, the Disputed Zone—what the Federation wanted to call a "border"—marked in white.

A set of yellow symbols appeared on the far side of the Zone: five ships in echelon.

"Kagga's crown, *Roms,*" the Weapons officer said, and reached for his board; his hands hovered, shaking, above the sealed-off controls.

They were only off, not sealed, but the Gunner didn't

116

know that. "Not Roms," Krenn said. "All but the *kuve* have five fingers. Akhil?"

Sensor schematics flashed on the display: four ships with flattened-sphere hulls, mounting warp tubes directly aft; and one that was a saucer connected to an oblong block, the warp engines in stand-off nacelles.

"Federation cruisers," the Science officer said, watching his sensor telltales, calling recognition data to the displays. "Two types . . . four *Mann* class, one unknown."

"*Human* class?" Krenn said.

"Different spelling, a Human proper name, probably. Imperial codename НОКОТ." But Akhil was smiling; Krenn had not been the only one to give up many nights' dreaming.

Nor just the two of them. "Signal from the lead ship, Captain, the unknown one," Kelly said. "They're asking our name and intentions."

"Open the link."

The display showed a bridge of the circular Federation design. In the Command Chair at its center sat a broadly built Human, with red-brown skin and very black hair. His face seemed to be cut from rock.

Krenn said, "I am Krenn, Captain of IKV *Fencer*. My intention is to enter your space, on a prearranged diplomatic mission."

The Human's eyes narrowed slightly; he looked for just a moment at an Andorian Krenn supposed was the Communications officer. Then the Human said, "This is Admiral Luther Whitetree, commanding Task Force K, aboard USS *Glasgow*. Do you have proof of your identity?"

"I have authorizations from the Klingon Imperial Council. Shall I transport them?"

"Launch anything and we'll *burn* it," said Admiral Luther—no, Krenn thought, Admiral Whitetree. Krenn wondered what in Keth's hundred years the Human meant. Then the Admiral said, "Play your tapes."

117

Krenn gestured to Kelly; she plugged the cassette into her board.

"Five *khest'n* cruisers," Security Commander Maktai said. "Are they cowards of such *great* degree?"

On the display, Whitetree's head snapped up; Kelly at once broke the Bridge-to-Bridge link. "Captain, I—"

"No fault, Lieutenant," Krenn said. "I'm pleased they heard it." He turned to Maktai, who stood rigid with embarrassment. Krenn did wonder at a Security officer who was so careless of who might be listening, but that was Mak's way. "I don't think they're cowards, Mak. Cautious, yes, but . . ." He turned back to the display, where the Human Admiral was again watching the Council's message. Krenn said, "I think that one would make a good Klingon, don't you?"

Kelly warned them of the end of tape in time for the laughter to fade away.

"If you are ready, Captain Krenn," Admiral Whitetree said, less challenging than before but no less hard, "we will escort you to Starbase 6."

The disc-and-block starship, *Glasgow,* came about, flashing formation lights; the four spheroid ships moved apart, to surround *Fencer.*

Whitetree said, "Can you cruise at Warp Factor Four, Captain?"

"Quite comfortably, Admiral," Krenn said, thinking, *Of course you knew that, just as my computers are filled with data on your ships. But we will play the game as if it were Blind, instead of only Clouded.*

Thermal sinks on the *Mann*-class cruisers glowed dull red, and the convoy moved toward the space the Federation claimed as its own.

Chapter 5
Players

Fencer held station ten thousand meters off Federation Starbase 6. The Klingons had an excellent view of the Starbase, a dished circular hull some five hundred meters across, mounting an antenna-and-sensor cluster at its center. The web forms of work docks floated beyond the hull, marker lights flashing. The docks all seemed to be empty. Kelly had reported no subspace traffic in or out, even encrypted.

There was a squadron of small, hunter-type ships, all built for speed and firepower; Krenn supposed they could be frontier patrol on normal station leave. But there were those empty docks: ships could not need so little maintenance, else why build so many docks? And there were the five cruisers still englobing *Fencer*.

"You say, Captain Krenn, that your total ship's complement is less than three hundred?" Admiral

Whitetree said. The disbelief in his voice was not open, but it was there.

"Your recognition data are correct, Admiral. Our normal complement is larger. But this ship is carrying only a few Marines as honor guards for the officers. It did not seem necessary to bring more. . . . I believe your sensor systems can verify the number of living organisms aboard?"

The Admiral said, "In that case, permission granted to deboard your crew. We'll give you approach routes for your shuttlecraft."

"From which we will not deviate. Until we meet face to face, Admiral. Krenn out."

Kelly broke the link.

Maktai said, "Shuttlecraft?"

"The Admiral's suggestion," Krenn said, thinking hard.

"It'll take eight trips with all shuttles running, if we don't have a *kherx* on the staging floor. Are they afraid we'll use the troop transporters and overrun them?" He pointed at the Starbase. "There must be thousands of troops on that thing. If the whole hold was full of *frozen* Marines, we—"

Akhil said, "They may just not want to drop shields, even a crack. Or there's another possibility." He looked at Krenn. "Are you thinking what I am, Captain?"

Maktai caught on in a moment. "They don't *have* particle transporters."

Akhil said, "We haven't had them for so very long."

Maktai said, "If that's true—"

Krenn said, "If it's true, they still have shields. And there's another possibility: they have transporters, but they don't know that *we* do. . . . I think we ought to avoid mentioning transporter systems while we're on this leave. Mak, you'll let the crew know—and tell them that they might, without attracting any notice, be

120

looking for anything that might be a Federation transporter?"

The Security Commander grunted agreement.

Krenn's shuttle entered a landing deck that could have held thirty such craft; tractors pulled it to a lighted square on the dark surface, and an elevator carried it down to a pressurized staging room larger than *Fencer*'s entire shuttle deck.

The ship's doors opened. Two honor guards preceded Krenn out.

A small, slim Human and a Vulcan were waiting. Behind them were six beings of assorted races, all carrying sidearms. All wore dress uniforms of glossy fabric, with bright gold trim; the Human and Vulcan showed a large number of award pins on their tunics.

"Welcome aboard Starbase 6, Captain," the slender Human said, in rather good *klingonaase,* not machine-translation. "I am Takashi Onoda, senior Diplomatic representative to this station. May I introduce Captain Sinon, the Starfleet attaché." The Vulcan bowed slightly.

Onoda said, "The rest of your officers are coming? We're of course pleased to accommodate your crew; if Admiral Whitetree expressed himself badly—"

"My officers are coming. My Executive, the Security Commander, and I do not ride in the same shuttlecraft."

"Of course. A sensible precaution. And this is your . . . " Onoda paused. ". . . Consort?"

"This is Lieutenant Kelly, my Communications Officer," Krenn said. He stepped aside, so that Kelly's uniform and sash were clearly visible, and thought This is one of their *diplomats?*

Onoda paled slightly. "A moment, please, Captain." He turned to the attaché, said something in the Vulcan language. Krenn wondered if Sinon were *tharavul.*

Onoda said, "If you and your company will follow

121

me, please? We have a reception planned. I hope it's to your liking."

"Diplomat Onoda," Krenn said, "are you the Ambassador we are to take to Klinzhai?"

"Oh, no," Onoda said, "oh, no." He gestured, and the group started out of the room. As they funneled toward the door, Onoda turned to Sinon and said, in Federation, "Whitetree's going to *explode.*"

Then they have not contacted him, Krenn thought. Which means he is coming by shuttle as well.

Perhaps we should not have used their language so soon.

One of the Federation guards was speaking, to one of his companions. He was discussing Kelly, and clearly he did not know she could understand him.

Krenn said to her, in Battle Language, "Subspace silence. Hold fire."

"It doesn't bother me to tell you," Admiral Whitetree said to Captain Krenn, "I wanted you quarantined here. Give you the Ambassador and send you home again. But the Diplomatic Corps overruled Starfleet."

Krenn said, "I have no disagreement with your caution."

They were sitting in a private lounge on the rim of the Starbase; the lights within were dim, and a panoramic window showed a solid wall of naked stars.

The Admiral got up from his chair. "Another?" he said, pointing at Krenn's glass.

"Please," Krenn said. He had had a hard time getting used to the word. But after a day on the Starbase, Krenn had realized that the Humans used it continually, across all levels of authority, for requests of any or no importance: the word simply had no meaning.

"Apple or orange?" Whitetree said. "We've got pineapple and grape, too . . . and prune, but the Medical Corps would have my ass for antimatter if I gave you that."

"Apple juice is fine."

Whitetree came back from the wall unit with two glasses. "I understand the climate here's a little out of range for you."

"It is acceptable."

"Onoda wanted to reset temp and humidity for the whole damned base. We just couldn't do it; you know the size of this place, you can imagine the inertia in the enviro system. It'd take a week and a half to even try, with a good chance of making it uncomfortable for everyone."

"This is understood." And, Krenn thought, Starfleet was not always overruled by the Diplomatic Corps.

"I'm glad. I've stayed in enough alien cabins to know what it's like. . . . I suppose your homeworld's star is a spectral class . . . F-something? Or is the orbit very tight?"

"I am not an astronomer. My Science officer would know. But I am not certain that he could tell you."

After a pause, the Admiral said, "Yup. I can think of a dozen different things I'd usually talk about, with a Captain just off a cruise like yours, but most of them would violate military security. And I'm not sure I want to go near the others."

"I have killed a few who insulted me," Krenn said, "but I do not think you mean any insults. Please speak."

Whitetree said, "Well, there's your Communications person . . . I never knew your Empire used female officers."

"Your Empire does. Why would we waste an intelligent one with talent?"

"You have women . . . females in command, then?"

"Lieutenant Kelly's orders are obeyed."

"I mean, in command of ships. Independent command." There was a set to Whitetree's creased, dark face, a light in his eyes.

Krenn said, "No."

Whitetree said, "My daughter commands a survey ship. The *Avebury*."

Krenn said nothing.

Whitetree said, as if pressing the same point, "How does a Klingon Captain get chosen for duty like this? Was it a reward? Or punishment? Or did you just draw the short straw?"

Krenn's taped learning did not include the last idiom, but he supposed it meant bad luck. "The Empire ordered me here; I came. The mission is not dishonorable."

"So you were just following orders?"

"Do officers of the Federation not follow orders?"

Whitetree leaned forward, about to say something; then he sat back slowly. His expression had changed wholly, though the shifts of flesh were small. "I'm . . . sorry, Captain."

Krenn had heard that word too: it seemed to have more of its meaning left than *please* did. And, watching the Human, Krenn thought he intended that it should have meaning now.

"I am not insulted, Admiral."

"Maybe you should be. I was—" Whitetree shook his head. "My son was killed by Klingons."

"Did the one fight well?" Krenn said.

"He was on a ship called the *Flying Fortress*," the Admiral said. "You may have heard of the incident. The ship was one of our *Rickenbacker*-class, what we used to call Maximum Security Transports. Only one of them was ever hijacked . . . *pirates* broadcast a fake distress message from a fake Federation scout. When *Flying Fort* answered, the *pirates* put a shot straight into her crew compartment.

"There was an automatic subspace alarm aboard, though, that the *pirates* didn't know about. A patrol was scrambled, and when it showed up, the *pirates* dropped the loot and ran."

"I have indeed heard of this incident," Krenn said. "Those who fled were executed, for cowardice."

Whitetree said, "I didn't know that. I suppose . . . it ought to please me, or at least satisfy me, but . . ."

In a low voice, the Admiral said, "You see, Captain, Starfleet sent me out here because they thought I'd really show you the hot end of the lasers. And I really thought I would.

"So what happens? I show up with a task force that could level half a planet, to meet one cruiser with a light crew and sealed guns. You don't drip spittle from your bloodied fangs, you don't keep your women in chains—Spirit, you speak the language better than some of my crew, and you're a damn sight politer."

He stood up, went to look out the window. No ships were visible. Krenn wondered if Humans believed in the power of the naked stars. Whitetree said, "So everyone involved with the hijack is dead?"

"The one who planned it was named Kethas. He also is dead."

Whitetree turned. "Kethas? We've heard of him. The Klingon Yamamoto. Dead too . . . damnation."

"My family," Krenn said, "was killed by Romulans. It was also an ambush of a ship not at war."

"Don't misunderstand me, Captain," Whitetree said, his voice hardened again. "I still hate you, and all Klingons. I don't think I'd stop hating you if I found out Jesus Christ was a Klingon. But you've . . . made me think. It's as if . . . dead things were alive again."

The only truth about death, Krenn thought but did not consider to say, *is that it is death, and the end.*

The wall communicator chimed, and the Admiral went to it. "Whitetree . . . Yes, I see. The Captain's with me; we'll be there shortly."

Whitetree turned to Krenn. "Some of your crew are in a brawl with some of mine. We'd better go and untangle them."

Krenn said, "Was the combat started by Klingons?"

"They didn't say." Whitetree swallowed the last of

his juice. "And I really don't think it's going to matter a damn. Do you?"

Krenn, Akhil, and Maktai had Lieutenant Kalim in a three-way fire: Krenn was aware it was probably harder on the young officer than time in the cube, but they could not afford even the usual leave tolerances just now. The Klingons had left the Starbase under the tubes of guns and eyes hardly less threatening, and *Fencer*'s authorization to proceed to Earth had come none too soon.

"We were just talking," Kalim said, "with some of those fringe-patrol Feds. Some of them had fought Roms, you see, Captain, and they knew good Rom stories, like 'How many Roms does it take to change a transtator?' "

"Don't digress," Maktai said. His usual easy manner made his growl all the more effective.

"Yes, Lieutenant," Krenn said calmly, "you were talking with the Starfleet beings. Did the fight start over old Rom stories?"

"No, Captain, it wasn't that. One of the Feds mentioned Lieutenant Kelly—"

Not *that* again, Krenn thought, surprised at the strength of his feeling.

"—he didn't know her name, not then, but he talked about her, and that translator-pipe of theirs isn't very subtle, if you know what I mean, Captain, and it was clear who he was talking about. And I said, 'That's our Lieutenant Kelly, and you be careful how you talk.' "

"You said that?" Akhil said.

"Well, Commander, it may have been Konli, but I was about to say it."

According to the taped testimonies, every one of the twenty-six Klingons involved in the brawl had been first to defend the Communications officer. Krenn said "Proceed."

Kalim said, "So one of the Feds said 'Personal deity,

they have an Eirizhman in the crew.' That's what the translator-pipe said."

Krenn said, "'Irish' is a place of origin on Earth."

"I thought it ,,25was an insult, Captain."

"A reasonable assumption. Proceed."

"So then a Human said 'That makes nothing. I heard there is a Skots'man also, a . . . Maktai.' And then the Feds started arguing with each other."

"That was when the fight started?"

"No, Captain. We didn't even know what the argument was about, not then. But then Ensign Kintata said—"

If the speaker was a Lieutenant, it was an ensign who had said the key phrase; if an ensign, a Lieutenant had. It was that, or admit one had been drinking with non-officers. Krenn supposed they were fortunate to have no cadets aboard.

Akhil read from the computer screen in his lap, "Asked a Starfleet Human his name. Was told it was 'Marks.' Announced that he knew many Klingons named Marks, and all were Marines."

"Yes, Commander," Kalim said, nodding vigorously.

"And *that* was when the fight started."

"Affirm."

Krenn said, "A small surprise."

The Lieutenant started to nod, but instead came to laser-locked attention.

"This is not a raid," Krenn said. "We are not to provoke combat, though we have the right to defend ourselves." He paused. *"Did* we defend ourselves?"

"Oh, yes, Captain," Kalim said. "Humans can take a lot of hitting, but they're slow. And those stunners of theirs, the beam ones, they don't work well at all. I was hit, oh, eight or nine times and I still took down—"

"That's sufficient, Lieutenant." Krenn stood up. "The Exec has a punishment detail in mind for you."

To his credit, Lieutenant Kalim did not react at all as Krenn went into his inner office, followed by Maktai.

The door closed; Krenn touched on a monitor with a view of the outer office.

". . . confined to quarters during non-duty or meal hours until the ship reaches Earth," Akhil was saying. "Confined to the ship during the duration of the Earth stay . . . "

"It'll be a Security directive when it comes," Krenn said, "but no one's going downside on Earth but the landing party . . . me, 'Khil, you if you want, but I'd rather have you in command here." And away from the Feds, Krenn thought.

"How about Communications?"

"I'll have a communicator. I'll want Kelly listening for me." And away from the Humans, doubled.

Beside which, Krenn thought, if she is from II, the two of you are best kept in the same place . . . in fact, if either of you are, or both.

Maktai said, "How many guards?"

"None. Akhil and I will carry dress weapons. If they want to kill us, they have a whole planet to do it with."

"It isn't the bite, it's the showing of teeth."

"They expect us to show teeth—*khest,* they expect us to bite. It doesn't scare them. But they feel wrong when they send out a great force, and are met by a small one. They feel . . . " Krenn found the Human word. ". . . *silly.* This has enormous power over them. I want them to feel as *silly* as possible while we're there."

Maktai said, "Oh, that Vulcan attaché—the one you thought might be *tharavul* to the diplomat?"

"He wasn't, was he."

"No. One of my people saw him mind-touch one of the Starfleeters, after the fight. A Human. She seemed to consent to it."

"Humans seem to consent to a lot of things," Krenn said. "But then, the Vulcans consent to having a piece of their brains cut out, just so they can live among us, watch how we live."

"What do Vulcans care?" Maktai said. "And, no one reported seeing or hearing anything about particle transporters. Not that they gave us much freedom to look."

"I wonder what they'll let us see on Earth," Krenn said.

Akhil came in. "That's the last of the disciplines. At least there weren't any deaths . . . I think we're lucky the crews didn't know much of each other's anatomy. The Surgeon had to set six dislocated jaws, did you know? Humans like to punch at the jaw. . . . " He shook his head. "In Keth's years, I've never heard such a story."

"Speaking of stories, 'Khil," Krenn said.

"Yes?"

"How many Roms *does* it take to change a transtator?"

Akhil stared. So did Maktai. Almost together, they said, "You don't *know?*"

"I never much liked Romulan jokes."

Maktai said, "One to change the 'stator . . . "

Akhil said, ". . . and 150 to blow up the ship out of shame."

And Krenn, who had not laughed at a Rom joke in many years, found himself full to bursting.

Seen from parking orbit, most of Earth had been ocean, and clouds covered it in vast white ruffs and whorls.

So how, Krenn wondered, could such a planet have a place so incredibly dry, with so much bald white sky arching over?

"Don't breathe deeply," Akhil warned, as they stepped from the shuttle onto the hard soil. "There's no moisture at *all;* it'll burn your lungs out."

And it was hot, like a fusion torch is hot. Krenn's head was aching in a moment. He looked around, feeling his eyeballs beginning to cook: there was a ring of Humans and vehicles all around the shuttlecraft, all waiting for something. Krenn saw that all the Humans had weapons; so did all the vehicles, except for one, a blocky thing the size of the shuttle, all white metal below and black glass above. NORTH AMERICAN PRIME STARPORT, said letters on the metal side, WHITE SANDS, CIBOLA, USA.

"Bloody Ishtar," a Human voice said, "if they have heatstroke it's our tails," and four of the soldiers ran to help Krenn and Akhil toward the half-glass vehicle. "I thought they *liked* it hot," one muttered.

Within the vehicle it was dark, and moist, and cold: but as Krenn recovered, he realized it was only the effect of sudden change. The interior of the vehicle was actually very close to Klingon ship's environment.

"Sit down," another Human voice said. "It isn't that they were afraid of you; they just didn't know what they might have to be afraid *of*."

Krenn sat. Then he realized that the Human voice had spoken in quite casual *klingonaase*.

Krenn looked up. There were leather swivel seats along both sides of the vehicle, which was moving now: an operator was visible through thick glass in the front. There was no door to his compartment. With him was one of the Human soldiers, rifle at ready arms, head encased in some kind of breathing helmet.

Krenn turned again. In a seat opposite him sat the smallest, frailest Human Krenn had yet seen, including some who had spent days in the agonizer cube.

This Human was dark-skinned, almost as dark as a Klingon—Kelly's color, Krenn thought. His hair was thin, gray-silver, almost white. His face was bony and lined, but his eyes were brilliant behind discs of glass in a wire frame. He wore a long belted tunic of smooth white fabric; there were single traceries of gold wire on collar and cuffs, and a supernova of award triangles on the breast. If they were the medals they represented, Krenn thought, they would outweigh the wearer.

"There is no more absolute zero of land," the Human said, looking through the heavily tinted windows, "not since we have begun to live on the icecap. Only white sun, white air, and a pan of industrial

130

abrasive the size of Chesapeake Bay, with no good line dividing them."

The Human looked at Krenn again, and his face made Krenn uneasy: the bright eyes in the old face made him think too much, far too much, of Kethas.

"Things are done here," the Human said, *"you* are here, because this place is nothing, and nothing can ever happen here. When we were inventing reaction-drive spacecraft, the fueled rockets were allowed to crash here. Nuclear weapons were set off here, just to satisfy curiosity as to what would happen, because *it would not matter,* you see. There is no mind in this land, and no memory. And that is why you were caused to land here.

"I am Dr. Emanuel Tagore," said the Human, "Ph.D. several times, University of New Bombay, Universities of Chicago, Edinburgh, Akademgorodok and the Ocean of Storms, late of the Makropyrios College of Political Science, and probable candidate for the Museum of Antiquities on Memory Alpha. I will have the honor of accompanying you on your return home, Captain . . . if we reach the lands of memory."

Krenn watched a monitor, showing Humans fighting one another in the streets of a city. The city's location was not given, and its name was meaningless to him. He, and Akhil, and *Fencer,* were the subjects of the riot; Krenn wondered how far away the Humans were rioting.

He also wondered what their purpose was in letting him see this.

The Klingons and the Ambassador Dr. Tagore had been transferred, at a place called Juarez–El Paso Station, to a gravity-suspended train of cars riding elevated tracks. Akhil had asked one of the train crew their speed: the Human seemed startled to hear the Klingon speaking his language, but then rather proudly gave the speed as three hundred kilometers an Earth hour. Akhil gave a suitably impressed thanks.

131

The sun had set; Dr. Tagore assured Krenn it was safe to watch, and the colors were indeed dramatic. Now Krenn was alone in the last car of the train. Akhil was one car forward, dozing in a small bedroom. Dr. Tagore was further ahead, in conference with the other Federation officials aboard. There was a soldier visible through the door to that car, not threatening, merely armed and ready.

The door to Krenn's car opened, and two Humans came in. The first was a Starfleet Admiral, Marcus van Diemen; the second was a Colonel of the Earth Surface Forces named Rabinowich.

Van Diemen was a large, impressive male with yellow hair and light skin; he wore a Starfleet dress uniform with plenty of gold braid, more by far than Admiral Whitetree had worn. Jael Rabinowich wore a uniform like those her soldiers wore, with rank badges of dark fabric that would not show to an enemy's scouts or snipers, and a sidearm of dull black metal that was clearly not for show. She was darker than van Diemen, much smaller, though not slight. Krenn thought about Whitetree's comments on female commanders. He looked at Rabinowich's face, and wondered what tools she would use to lead.

Admiral van Diemen said, "We have a change of plans." His voice was large as well. "A gentleman of some importance has asked to speak with you, and the diversion and meeting have just been approved. It will delay us perhaps half a day . . . will your crew become alarmed, if you are stopped for a few hours before reaching Federa-Terra?"

Van Diemen looked at Krenn's communicator. Krenn had supposed the Federation would be screening them from search; but then, no one could ever quite know what the enemy's sensors could sense past. And if they did not in fact have the transporter . . . "I will inform them. To where is the diversion?"

"The city of Atlanta, State of Georgia, United States of America."

Wherever that was, Krenn thought. "And whom are we to meet?"

"His name is Maxwell Grandisson, the Third. He is a private citizen, but, as I say, influential. In fact, it was partly through Mr. Grandisson's efforts that the embassy to Klingon is being established."

"Klinzhai," Krenn said.

"Excuse me?"

"The Homeworld's name is Klinzhai."

"Ahh. I see." Van Diemen acted as if he had just discovered a major military secret. Krenn wondered if the Admiral understood any *klingonaase*.

Krenn said, trying not to sound too curious, "Will the stop in this city complicate your security arrangements?"

Van Diemen looked past Krenn, at the monitor screen, and took on a vaguely distracted expression. Colonel Rabinowich said, "Complicate them, yes. This citizen insists on meeting you at the place of his choosing. And the Atlanta Metroplex is very large. But we can control our people." Her voice was surprisingly soft, though not smooth. She nodded toward the rioters on the screen. "To protest, to demonstrate, these we may not interfere with. But we will not let them cause lasting damage."

Admiral van Diemen said, "You must understand, Captain . . . many of our people have lost relatives and friends to Klingon action. I myself had a brother killed on the frontier. This is why we must have peace."

Both the Humans had used the phrase "our people"; the same possessive, yet Krenn felt they did not mean the same thing by it.

"I assure you, Admiral, I shall do my best," said a voice from the car ahead. Colonel Rabinowich instantly moved to let Dr. Tagore pass. She would be a good Swift, perhaps, Krenn thought. But her bearing seemed more that of a Fencer.

"Yes," van Diemen said, uncertain for only an

133

instant. "Well. We'll be returning to our car now; there's still a lot to do and not much time to do it in. Good night, Captain . . . Mr. Ambassador."

"Good night," Dr. Tagore said. Krenn bowed slightly. The Admiral went out. "Peace," the Colonel said, and followed.

When the door had closed, Krenn said in *klingonaase,* "Peace? Was that sarcasm? At you?"

"Not at all. It's a common greeting, or exit line. I see your companion has retired; do you need to rest?"

"Not for some time."

"Your day is longer than ours?"

"Somewhat."

Dr. Tagore smiled. "I ask only as one who expects to live there soon. Shall we sit and talk, then? You said you drank coffee, so I brought some."

Krenn turned the monitor off as Dr. Tagore filled cups. When they were settled, Dr. Tagore said, "You are vestai-Rustazh. Is the line a large one?"

"No. . . . Only I am this line."

"Then you are a founder."

"You have authentic knowledge," Krenn said, surprised that the Human had so quickly drawn the conclusion.

"There are reports, mostly from Vulcan. And there are books and tapes . . . they filter from your space into ours, in Orion loot and Rigellian trading hulls. I suppose I shouldn't say this, but a spy was captured on Argelius III, and the one had dozens of books and tapes, a closetful of them. Starfleet Intelligence was convinced the one was using them in an elaborate code scheme, and as the nearest available reader of *klingonaase* I was called in to read the lot."

Krenn sipped the *kafei*—he found he was actually coming to like the stuff—and wondered that the Ambassador should so casually reveal his connection with the Intelligence service. "Were they a code?"

"Not at all. They were solely for his pleasure. As he said, as soon as the matter was found: but Intelligence did not believe this. I told them, once he was discovered, and no longer a spy, the one would say nothing, or tell the truth. But I was not believed, either."

Perhaps that was the point of the story: indirectly, the Human was discounting his tie to Intelligence.

Dr. Tagore said, "I'm pleased to find my knowledge is valid. There are some famous fictions about our history that I should not like an alien ambassador to take learning from. . . . Though I confess I have become quite fond of *Battlecruiser Vengeance*. Is it still in production?"

"Yes," Krenn said, trying not to choke.

"I was correct that you are founder of a line, Captain; do you have a sole consort, or many?"

At least this one asked in private, as one with a concern. "I have no consort at this time."

Dr. Tagore paused, said, "I see. My own wife—" he used the Human word—"is dead."

Krenn waited: every Human seemed to have a close relative killed by marauding Klingons.

"A disease of the nerve sheaths," Dr. Tagore said, looking away from Krenn. "Gualter's neuromyelitis. There is a chemical therapy, but one patient in twenty cannot tolerate it; that one dies in a few years." The Human looked at Krenn, said in a very mild, almost apologetic tone, "I am told the symptoms are similar to the effects of your agonizer device. . . . " In Human he added, "I'm sorry; I meant nothing by that."

That made still another inflection of the word *sorry*.

Dr. Tagore said, still in Federation Standard, "I know your race has no tradition of ghosts or revenants, no rites for the dead. Ours has too many of them. I say this to explain certain of our actions, that might otherwise seem strange. I have a theory . . . but this isn't the time for it. Please, let's find another subject."

Krenn waited a moment. The Human's eyes seemed even brighter than before, yet the face was older, more crumpled. At once Krenn also wished to change the subject. He pointed at the darkened monitor. "Those

135

people . . . who hate us . . . how many of them are there?"

"Enough," Dr. Tagore said. "Always enough. The Klingon Empire has been a very convenient devil, these twenty-odd years. Whenever a ship vanishes in that general direction of space, someone claims, with or without evidence, that it's 'fallen prey to the savage Klingon.' All too often the claim is made on the floor of the Solar Senate, or even the whole Federation." He sighed. "From the Galactic Bermuda Triangle to the Klingon Twilight Zone."

Krenn said, "Twenty odd years?"

"An idiom, pardon. In *klingonaase,* twenty-plus—which is also an idiom of ours; I must be sure to use that one from now on. First contact with the *komerex klingon* was, if I can unwind it from the Stardate system, twenty-two Standard years ago. That would be twenty years Klingon standard, if I have the ratios right."

"Yes, that is the difference as I understand it." Krenn was not really thinking about year lengths, but the fact that the first Federation ships had been taken by the Empire fully thirty years ago: thirty Klingon years. Obviously no prize had reported its fate for a long time.

"There was a novel, written long before we had starflight and even longer before warp drive," Dr. Tagore was saying, "in which the accidental loss of some starships coincided with first contact with nonhumans—who had also lost ships. Both sides resorted to the communication that needs no translation. The war, in the story, lasted a thousand years."

"A war of a thousand years. . . ?" Krenn said. It was an astonishing idea, still more so from a Human. Yet Krenn could, thinking on it, see how it might be conducted: dynastic lines ruling over lines of battle, fifty generations born and dying in the pursuit of a single glory. A war like that would mark worlds deeply, so that if, a million years after, when all the warriors

136

were dust, a new race should come upon the space, they would know what had happened there.

Dr. Tagore said, "Perhaps we will not take so long to communicate. I do not have a thousand years left in this life, and I fear I have about used my karma up."

"I do not know the word."

"Neither do I." The Human was smiling whitely; his teeth, Krenn saw, were square-cornered, without points. "At least, not so I could explain it properly, and that's the same thing. My enlightenment is all of the immanent sort."

Krenn wondered at this little Human, who seemed to think he could dismiss an idea as potent as a war of a thousand years in a single moment . . . who would stand between two Empires, like waves of the sea, or colliding stars, and hold them apart. It was absurd; it was *silly;* perhaps it was insane.

Krenn thought then of the Willall, and the Tellarites, all hollow great words . . . but no, he did not think this Dr. Tagore was *kuve.* He drank more *kafei;* it had gone cold. It was not good cold. Dr. Tagore saw Krenn's grimace, tasted his own drink, said, "I see what you mean. I'll get another pot."

When the Human had gone, Krenn turned on the monitor again, set it to the channel that gave continuous news reports. There was a report of an industrial accident, a display of new clothing by "famous designers" that was little short of bewildering, and then more tape of the rioters. They were breaking windows of buildings, which seemed strange, since Krenn and Akhil were the only Klingons on Earth—at least, the only Klingons known to be on Earth. A group burned a wooden model of a D4 cruiser. Krenn laughed; no one had told him Humans believed in primitive magic.

Then the picture changed again, to two streaks of light in darkness, and Krenn leaped to the train window; slowly, he opened a curtain.

The train's guideway was elevated on castrock piers, twenty to twenty-five meters above the ground: below,

137

as the train flashed by, were long dashes of light. With difficulty Krenn resolved them into Humans with torches, electric and flaming and cold chemical. He tried to calculate their number: Akhil said the train covered five thousand meters every local minute. Krenn looked at his communicator's time display.

Krenn turned as the door opened. It was Akhil. He did not look rested at all. He pointed at the glass. "I saw them from the window. They've been with us for at least an hour."

"How many, do you figure?"

"A hundred thousand, probably more. I suppose they could be relaying a smaller group, behind us to ahead; a flier could just outrun this train. But what I'm really thinking is what a couple of good shots into one of those support towers would do."

"That is also Colonel Rabinowich's thought," Dr. Tagore said from the doorway. "She does tell me that the construction is very strong, and hand weapons would not serve, and they have sensor vehicles searching for any larger weapons." In a smaller voice he said "She also says that a certain number of the demonstrators are actually her troops, disguised."

"Kai Rabinowich," Krenn said, impressed.

"Yes," Dr. Tagore said, speaking *klingonaase* again. "Her family have been soldiers for more than ten generations, and I think your praise would please her, if it were properly explained." He looked down at the torches streaming by. "It is the explanations which are hard . . . especially in a culture which knows no difference between a machine translation and an understanding of language."

He paused, filled two cups with *kafei,* then a third for Akhil, who seemed genuinely glad to have it. Dr. Tagore said, "You have noticed, perhaps, that in Fed-Standard *klingonaase* is pronounced a little strangely?"

"*'Klingoneeze,'*" Akhil said.

Dr. Tagore nodded. "That suffix is common in several of Standard's root languages, including, dear me, Rigellian Trade Dialect, to turn a nation-name into the nation-language—which itself is a less than wholly useful notion. And so we have Japanese, Terchionese, F'tallgatri'itese, and, when the circuits got the word in their clutches, 'Klingonese.' The whole significance of the *aase* suffix, that the language is the tool for manipulating the embodiment of the *klin* principle . . . all that is lost, in the leap of an electron across an Abramson junction."

Krenn said, "What do the lights out there mean? The flames? Can you translate those? Or is it your language that needs no translation?"

"They need to say something," Dr. Tagore said calmly, "but they do not know just what. Not yet." He went to the monitor, which was showing close views of the chains of Humans, showing their faces, lit by torchlight and searchlight and the flash of the train's passing. Krenn could see the strong emotions there, and knew that he must be seeing fear, and hate, and pain, because those were the only things he knew that could bend the face so, but he was not at all sure which was which, or what else might be there as well.

"You understand, now," Dr. Tagore said in *klingonaase*. "You do not know yet, either, what to say. There must be a little time."

Krenn said, "And if, in time, they still hate us?" He was aware, even as he spoke, that he said it only to get a little time to think.

Dr. Tagore put his thin-fingered hand across his eyes, as if to hide them from the faces on the screen; but at once he took it away, and looked at Krenn and Akhil. "I said that Colonel Rabinowich's was a line of warriors. That line is rooted in a hate that ran deeper than blood runs in the liver, that many people of the best intention though could only end in the separations of walls and wire, or in the mass grave. And there were those things. But the walls are down, and the graveyards . . . they are remembered, and kept, which is a thing our race does.

"And Admiral van Diemen's people had their war, too, for hate instead of territory. And the walls, and the graves. But finally the peace. The city of Atlanta, to which we are making a side excursion, was burned to nothing a hundred years before nuclear explosives made it so much less laborious a task. . . . And my own ancestors were the second nation of Earth to use a nuclear explosive against an enemy, though not the last, not the last.

"We know what hate is, Captain, and we practice it with great finesse. But sometimes we achieve things in spite of it."

Akhil said, without force, "But if they want the war?"

"If they do, Commander, I will oppose them. I am a public servant; I am not a servitor."

Krenn saw Akhil's eyes flick. He realized that he had failed to take this Human's measure. And the advantage he had found was—at least with this one—gone: this one could have no concern with being made absurd. He might die—they all might, Krenn thought, as another hundred Human fires flashed by—but silly he would not be.

Wondering if he had now been twice maneuvered into changing the subject, Krenn said, "This diversion . . . do you know this person we're to see? This *important* person?"

"Maxwell Grandisson III," Dr. Tagore said, stretching out the syllables. "I know *of* him, who doesn't—sorry, Captain—but we've never met. I have only once been to Atlanta, and he never leaves the city. Which indirectly answers your indirect question: he is powerful enough that he does not have to leave. If he wishes to see a mountain, the mountain comes to him." The Human smiled. "Figuratively speaking, of course.

Though I do not doubt he has the resources to move mountains. Small ones, at any rate."

Akhil said, "How much wealth is concentrated with this Human?"

"Enough . . . always enough, somehow. But faith is the power that moves mountains, and of that he has access to a great deal more than enough."

Krenn said, "What does he want from us, then? Trade? Or just the satisfaction of his curiosity?"

"Certainly not the first, and not just the second." Dr. Tagore hesitated. "Mr. Grandisson is a leader of a large—still growing, I regret to say—movement, spread throughout Human space. This . . . movement is not known so much for what it wants, as what it does not want."

"War?" Krenn said, and then remembered that Dr. Tagore had *regretted*.

"The stars," Dr. Tagore said.

The sun was rising behind the city called Atlanta. The entire city seemed to be built of glass and crystal and bright metal, cylindrical columns and truncated pyramids endlessly reflecting one another, all tied together with flying bridges at every level. Morning light colored all the glass a pale red: Krenn thought of Dr. Tagore's comment, of the city burning. A century before nuclears, the Human said, however long ago that was. It was a Vulcan calculation that a culture's lifespan was either some fifty years after basic fission was discovered, or else indefinite.

There were still Humans at the base of the guideway as the train hurtled into the city, now holding colored flags instead of torches. Colonel Rabinowich said, "We'll be going underground a few klicks before the terminal. And an identical train will come out of the southbound pipe. We'd have done it at the Baton Rouge shunt, but there wasn't time."

"And the change of course?" Dr. Tagore said.

"Let 'em think we tried to fool 'em, and failed."

"An excellent strategy," Krenn said, careful to draw no comparisons with Klingon methods, though any Imperial officer would have hailed the trick. "You honor your craft and your line." He understood well now which of the leader's paths she had mastered: the way of greater cunning.

Rabinowich cast a side look at Dr. Tagore, who sat across the dining car, placidly drinking coffee. He had had no sleep, Krenn knew. Admiral van Diemen was in the sleeping car now.

The Colonel said, "Thank you, Captain," in her customary soft-coarse voice. "That's more than Star-fleet usually gives us dirtballers."

The terrain rose past the train. Interior lights came on, and then the windows went black, except for flashes of light that were gone before the eye could catch what was illuminated.

"Sit down, please, Captain, Commander," the Colonel said, going to a seat herself; Dr. Tagore gulped the last of his coffee, held tight to the ceramic cup. "Gravitic braking," Rabinowich said.

It was not a bad deceleration—certainly nothing like a combat maneuver when the deckplates were already straining—but Krenn was glad of the chair as invisible drag pulled him toward the front of the train.

In less than two local minutes they were at a full stop. Cool blue lights showed a platform beyond the windows, and more soldiers.

"All out," Dr. Tagore said lightly, "change here for the *Southern Crescent.*"

Colonel Rabinowich looked at the Ambassador for a moment, then said, "Your escort to the hotel's on the platform. We'll be meeting you at a different platform: right now we've got to get the numbers scraped off this train and a different set on. Enjoy your breakfast."

"You aren't coming with us?" Krenn said. "Or the Admiral?"

"Or the Ambassador," Dr. Tagore said.

142

Rabinowich paused. "You must—no, of course you don't know. The invitation wasn't to us. Grandisson doesn't like Starfleet people."

"You are not with Starfleet."

"Never been off Earth, in fact. Max Grandisson doesn't like me for a reason I thought was extinct until I was twenty-eight years old." She gave a flat smile. "It goes a long way back. Unto the tenth generation, and then some. *Shalom aleichem,* Captain Krenn, Commander Akhil."

"Aleichem shalom," Krenn said, and as the Colonel's mouth opened in surprise, and then a grin, Krenn caught Dr. Tagore's nod in the corner of his eye.

The building was ancient, dull stone among all the bright glass, with new entry steps that led down where it had settled into the earth. The Klingons' escorts—Humans in plain clothing, driving a vehicle that was like a dozen others on the street—surrounded Krenn and Akhil as all walked briskly inside.

Within, the hotel was a hollow box, balconies lining its interior; the roof, many floors above, was of an age-darkened glass that let only a few shafts of light through. Spindle-shaped lift cars rode up a central black pylon. The lobby was quite empty, and quiet. Bright green plants stood next to dying ones.

All this Krenn saw on the move. Within seconds they were at the glass-walled lifts, which more Humans in plain suits were holding ready; Akhil and half the guards went into one glass capsule, Krenn and the rest into another.

A young Human male in a red and white uniform walked past Krenn's lift just then, carrying a tray. He looked up. Krenn looked back. The tray fell with a crash Krenn could not hear, as the car moved upward.

They emerged into a curved room: windows ran around the outer wall, giving what must have been a panorama of the city when the building was new, but which now showed only a curtain of glass.

143

A tall, slender Human came around the curve. The cut of his clothing was almost as restrained as the security guards' suits, but the tailoring was much sharper, the fabrics more exotic by far. His shirt had a high collar and a lace front. His face was rectangular, with a large jaw, a high forehead from which brown hair fell back straight to the collar. His nose was a blade, his eyes sharp enough to draw blood. There was a wireless phone in his ear, and a black device, the size of a communicator, clipped to his breast pocket.

"Good morning, gentlemen," he said, and the device in his pocket repeated it in *klingonaase*. Not only was the black device much smaller than the usual Federation translator, its sound quality was better. "I'm Max Grandisson. Glad you could join us."

Krenn thought a moment about his answer, not only what to say but which language to say it in. Finally he decided that, while speaking Federation might cost them some interesting side comments, a deception might backfire. "Thank you for the invitation, Mr. Grandisson. We're here to make peaceful contacts. I am Krenn, Captain of the *Fencer;* this is Commander Akhil, my Science officer, and also my Executive."

Grandisson held quite still, his sharp eyes narrowing slightly; he touched his earphone, then extracted it, smiled. "Pardon my surprise, gentlemen. No one told me you spoke our language." From his tone, Krenn was certain that someone would regret the lapse.

Grandisson said to the guards, "Why don't you fellows go on down. Have breakfast if you like; I don't suppose you're allowed to drink on the job, but anything you like, just charge it to me." He waved a hand before an objection could properly be raised. "I don't think you need worry about our guests; I'll vouch for the gentlemen with me, and no one comes up here without my approval. Go on down, now, and relax."

It was one of the most gently delivered absolute commands Krenn had ever heard. And, though they looked doubtful, the Security people got into the lifts and descended.

"Now, Captain, Commander, if you'll come with me, we can get started. Pardon me a moment." Grandisson took another black device from inside his coat, pressed buttons on it. "Sally? This is Max. There's some boys coming down right now, you won't be able to miss 'em, they've got Government written all over 'em in big red letters. You see they get what they want, but give 'em a seat with a good view of the kitchen."

There was a sound from the speaker. Grandisson said, "That's right. Don't annoy them. But keep them out of mischief.

"And, Sally, if anyone from the *Constitution* comes by, there's nothing happening here, and there certainly aren't any Government hound dogs around. . . . I know you will, Sal. That's what I pay you for." He put away the communicator.

Akhil said, *"Constitution* is what class of starship?"

"What? Ah. Not at all, Commander. The Atlanta *Constitution* is a news service. Honest men, but not always prudent ones. Now, if you'll all come this way." As they went around the curve, past partitions, desks, and bookshelves, Grandisson said, "This was originally a restaurant, built to revolve, you see. But after two hundred years the mechanism became rather delicate . . . not that there was anything left to see by that time. I wish I could show you gentlemen the old city."

"Before the fire?" Krenn said.

Grandisson stroked his smooth brown hair. "I dare say, Captain, you have me at a loss." Krenn thoroughly doubted that. "No, Captain, I wasn't thinking that far back. That's a sight I'd like to see myself. Do you know of—ah, here we are."

Three Human males were seated at a table set for six. Two of them rose as Grandisson and the Klingons approached; the third, Krenn saw, sat in an antigrav chair, because he had no legs. One of the standing men

145

was young, with eyeglasses and a thin mustache; the other had a neat gray beard, and a gold chain across the front of his coat. All were well-dressed, though not so expensively as Grandisson.

Grandisson said, "May I present Commodore Amos Blakeslee of the Starfleet Exploration Command, now retired." The legless Human nodded. Krenn wondered about Colonel Rabinowich's comment: how *did* Grandisson feel about Starfleet personnel?

"Doctor Samuel Landers, of the Inner Space Corporation." That was the young Human. "And T.J. McCoy, M.D., Chief of Medicine at the Emory University Medical Center."

Introductions completed, all sat down. The chairs were carved wood with leather padding; not really comfortable for Klingon anatomy, but tolerable. The table was of highly polished wood, the service of heavy ceramics, apparently solid silver, and cut crystal that broke the indirect light into rainbows.

"I understand that you gentlemen can eat our cooking," Grandisson said, as platters were unloaded onto the table. Krenn wondered, if Grandisson should be told the words, if he would consider the Human servers *kuve* or *straave*.

"We've done so without harm," Akhil said.

"That's fine. Of course, just in case, I called T.J. up here to join us. Best doctor in the state."

Dr. McCoy turned, slowly. His accent was much stronger than Grandisson's. "Actually, Captain, I'm just a G.P. from Union County, not a xenophysician at all. And I doubt there's anyone inside of twenty parsecs with any experience of Klingon medicine. I would, however, give you the medical advice not to eat those."

"What is that?" Akhil said.

"Those, sir, are called grits."

Krenn had already tried a forkful. They were, he decided, no worse than Romulan emergency rations. But it was a near thing.

The soft-cooked eggs in silver cups required mechanical mastery, but tasted good, if bland. The peach nectar was blood-thick and incredible. The coffee was void-black and incredibly strong.

The places were cleared; the Humans, except for Commodore Blakeslee, sat back in their chairs.

"I've asked you here, Captain," Grandisson said crisply, "because you're about to be hustled down to that Florida land swindle they call a Federation City, and double-shuffled past some diplomats and Starfleet officers, and sent home again heavily weighted with one point of view. I'd like to expose you to another, one that a great many Human beings subscribe to."

He turned, settling into a comfortable three-quarter pose. "For a long time, our leaders have been telling us that we had to progress in certain directions: greater speed, greater height, greater sheer mass and volume. There was a time when this city was filled with architectural masterworks, like the building we're in now; but progress tore them down, *blasted* them down, and gave us *that* in their place." Grandisson pointed out the window, at the sheer glass cliffs. "We have seen the future, gentlemen, and it is vastly more expensive.

"The other direction we were told we must go was out. A *long way* out. First to the Moon, then Mars, and some gravitational holes just as far away as the Moon but no more hospitable; and now, the stars. On every one, we were told, we'd find the answers to all our problems. But when we got there, somehow the answers had moved on."

Dr. McCoy burped lightly, excused himself, and said, "It seems to me, Max, that it started with Columbus, or maybe Lucky Leif, before the Moon got into it. Or maybe it was when some little thing that lived in a pond decided that it had better try the dry land, before the pond took it to dry up."

"If it was Space he'd had to cross," Commodore Blakeslee said in a rasping voice, "cold, hard Space,

Columbus would have been a shoemaker and glad to have the work."

Grandisson was watching both the other Humans, with a faintly calculating smile. Krenn wondered if he were delivering them cues. Finally Grandisson said, "When I spoke of expense, I also meant the personal kind. Amos was . . . hurt, looking for one of those worlds full of answers that always seem just out of reach. As it was, he was caught out of reach . . . with an injury that, if he'd only been nearer home, would have been fixed—"

"People die on the front steps of hospitals," Dr. McCoy said. Krenn saw the physician's hands were folded very tightly in his lap.

Grandisson said pleasantly, "Tom's always being modest when he doesn't have to. That's why I keep him around; I need a conscience." McCoy tapped a finger on his gold vest chain. Grandisson went on: "I'm not a mathematician, but I know the ratio between a sphere's diameter and its volume. And I know how much of my money the Federation taxes away every year, trying to fill that bottomless bucket."

Krenn wondered, if this Human were so powerful, how the Federation managed to take his wealth.

Grandisson was looking directly at Krenn. His eyes were very blue, and very cold. "Captain," he said, "in Federa-Terra they're going to tell you that we've got to grow in your direction, that if we *don't* grow we'll die, and so on; and I'm telling you it's a bill of goods. We don't need your space. We don't need the space we've got now. All we need is the Earth. And I speak for almost one billion Human beings when I say that the Earth is all we want."

"Well, you don't speak for me, Max," Dr. McCoy said, and stood up. "You want your goddamn neutral witness, invite those *Constitution* reporters up here." He turned to Krenn and Akhil. "You officers will kindly excuse my bad manners, but I've had my intelli-

148

gence insulted enough for one day. Good day to you; I hope the rest of your stay here is pleasanter and more productive than this morning has been for me . . . and if your ship's doctor should feel like visiting, I'd admire to buy him a bottle of whatever he's drinking.

"And good day to you, too, Max. I'm gonna go change my grandson Leonard's diapers now, but I'll be thinkin' of you the whole time." He turned, and walked toward the lifts.

"Oh, come on back, T.J.," Grandisson said, smiling. McCoy did not break stride. Grandisson's smile wavered. *"Tom,* come back here."

McCoy did stop then, and turn. "I'll see you at the Clinic on Thursday, won't I, Max?" he said, rather quietly. And then he walked away again.

"McCoy!" Grandisson shouted, but the Doctor was already out of sight. Grandisson pulled out his communicator. Commodore Blakeslee looked violent and Dr. Landers looked baffled.

"Sal? *Well, get her.* . . . Sal, Tom McCoy's coming down, and he's in another of his moods. You just—no, *listen.* You just make sure he doesn't talk to any reporters. No, *don't* have Billy follow him, if he doesn't do it right off, it'll blow over. Yes, honey, your job and then some."

Grandisson looked up; Krenn was looking at him. To have looked at anything else would have been an absurd gesture.

"I have," Grandisson said, recovering with amazing speed, "a somewhat dramatic conscience.

"But I assure you, Captain, that I, and the Homeworld Movement on whose behalf I speak, are entirely serious and committed. Dr. Landers heads a multi-megacredit corporation that is, right now, developing the technology to make the Earth not only habitable for the many millions who will return, but a self-sufficient paradise for them."

Akhil said, *"Komerex tel khesterex?"*

149

Grandisson turned, reached to his ear. He took the phone from his pocket and inserted it. "I'm afraid I didn't—"

Krenn said, "What of the Humans who do not wish to return?"

"Naturally we can't explain everyone's motives. But we also cannot take responsibility for those who choose irresponsible paths. A Human not on Earth will be . . . homeless. As, in a way, they always have been.

"Now, all I ask is that you take this message back to your leaders, along with the 'official' one. Will you do that?"

Krenn said, "Which message do you mean, Mr. Grandisson?"

The Human stared, then laughed shortly. "I suppose I have gone on a bit. Tell your people that not all Humans want their territory, and endless rounds of gunboat diplomacy and saber-rattling."

Krenn had no trouble understanding the idioms. He rather liked them. But he was tired of this meeting.

Grandisson's *dramatic* was an interesting choice of words, Krenn thought. The stage was effective, the lead performance good, the three Human props adequate . . . though Krenn wondered about the character of the physician McCoy.

It did not matter. What mattered was whether Krenn and Akhil were supposed to take the presentation at its face value, or find some secret meaning.

It was simpler in the Empire, Krenn thought. One had the *komerex zha:* one was always safe in assuming the other player was enemy, the next move a trap.

Well. He would show the Human a Klingon face. But perhaps not the face he was expecting.

Krenn said, "If you wish, I will take that message. But there is something I ought to tell you. We have a word, *komerex:* your translator has probably told you it means 'Empire,' but what it means truly is 'the structure that grows.' It has an opposite, *khesterex:* 'the structure that dies.' We are taught—by those you wish

150

to receive your story—that there are no other cultures than these. And in my years as a Captain, I have seen nothing to indicate that my teaching was wrong. There are only Empires . . . and *kuve.*" Krenn saw Grandisson's long jaw go slack; he knew how the Human's machine had translated the last word. "And this is the change you say you wish to make in yourselves. . . .

"So, yes, Mr. Grandisson, if you wish I will take your message. But I tell you now: there are none Klingon who will believe it."

Chapter 6
Games

Krenn had some vague ideas about what a diplomatic conference might be. None of them prepared him for the reality. He shortly began to doubt that he could have been prepared: there were ideas so new and strange, as the epetai-Khemara had taught him, that they must be shown by example.

There were two days of "opening ceremonies," during which the delegates showed short dull tapes of their planets and held long dull parties at which everyone pretended to be drunker than they actually were, presumably hoping to catch carelessly dropped information. Krenn did discover that Earth made some excellent black ales, and whenever an "important secret" was tossed in his direction he dutifully caught it, as he was meant to.

After the opening came meetings with political representatives and military ones—Krenn was startled to discover how different the two sorts were, even when they represented the same population. Akhil reported that the scientists were just as isolated from their "colleagues" in the other branches.

Each meeting took half an Earthly hour to begin, with recitations of each present delegate's credentials for being present, invocations to three Federation religions chosen randomly, and a song. Krenn was certain that he was misunderstanding the anthem's lyrics. At least, he hoped he was.

The shape of the meeting table was different for every session: now round, now polyhedral, now scalloped, now long and narrow . . . "Part of the system," Dr. Tagore said. "Used to be, you could hold up a conference for weeks over the shape of the table."

No one shot anyone else, at least while Krenn was present.

For all the protocols, the meetings did not seem to be *about* much of anything. Trade was mentioned, but not what might be traded. Peace was a constant topic (". . . but there is no peace," Emanuel Tagore said once, and silenced the room, and departed it with a small strange smile). It was suggested that a true Neutral Zone in space be established; they could not, Krenn thought with distasteful irony, have known just how empty a thought that was.

There seemed to be a huge game going on, with dozens of pieces on an indeterminable number of sides, and most of the board obscured. Krenn did not deny the *komerex zha*, that was not his strategy, but the *komerex zha* was *for* something. Each night, after the long ritual of ending the day's discussion and an aimless social function, Krenn returned to his hotel room and sank into a warm bath . . . the Humans *did* know how to build a bath . . . and wondered what any of it was for.

And if perhaps Maxwell Grandisson III was not such a fool after all.

During the sixth day, or perhaps it was the seventh—

Krenn was losing track—a diplomat offered an elaborate plan of exchanging prisoners across the boundary —he kept saying Neutral Zone, of course; Krenn had forgotten whether that plan was a precondition of *this* plan—anyhow, at the recitation of the twenty-sixth Point Governing the Treatment of Federation Prisoners, Krenn stood up from the table, excused himself in Fed-Standard, said in *klingonaase* that he must have time to think, and used all he knew of the Kinshaya language to curse the Humans and their riding animals.

Krenn sat down in a small lounge, expelling the Human servitors and xenophysician sent after him.

Dr. Tagore came in. "The one is well?" he said, then tucked his hands inside his gown and sat a polite distance away. He said, "The one asks the wrong question."

"Does the one know what will happen," Krenn said, feeling rage tearing at him, "if this proposal is set before the Imperial Council? *Orion pirates* take hostages for ransom. *Kuve* in desperation take hostages for their lives. And now the Federation shows us more rules than a Vulcan would make, about selling hostages! I will tell you what the Klingon law of hostages is: A dead thing is without value."

Dr. Tagore said, "Klingons do take prizes. For the Year Games, and the Thought Masters of medicine."

"Of course," Krenn said. "How else to supply them?"

"And prizes have a value."

"This need not be said." Krenn was puzzled.

"Then might not the sale of prizes be arranged? I do not speak of a universal rule, but only a case for discussion. Either side might refuse the trade, but that is the nature of trade. And the one taken as prize might refuse to be part of a sale . . . or might refuse to be taken."

Krenn had an unsettling thought. "Are . . . many Klingons taken?" He thought about the Human fondness for stunning weapons. And he knew that the

Federation kept its criminals in cages, for years, or their lives. The idea made him slightly sick.

"There are not many," Dr. Tagore said. "But it is a common belief that the Klingons take no living prizes at all."

"But you know this is not true—you just said—"

"*I* know," Dr. Tagore said. "A very few know. If more than a very few were to know, then it would not be this one going to Klinzhai, but a thousand warships. And if you were to see the pain of those we take, and keep in the places without memory . . . "

Dr. Tagore paused, hands to his eyes. Krenn could not react: the little Human seemed huge before him. The Ambassador uncovered his face, and began to speak again, and while his voice was like no commander's Krenn had ever heard, still it held him tight.

"It is not the one with his thousand rules who must speak to the Imperial Council, but I, and I must have the right thing to tell them, for while too many are dying for fear's sake right now, it is nothing compared to those who will die if those fears take their true shape, and if the naked stars see what we have done to one another."

A clear fluid was running from Dr. Tagore's eyes. Tears, Krenn thought; he vaguely recalled that pain brought them. The Human wiped the fluid away with his sleeve; his gaze did not leave Krenn.

Krenn said, "It is that you do not want the war. You do not want it, even if your people should be certain of the victory. You do not want the war *as a thing*."

"Yes," the Human said, and his voice was thick with the fluid but still very strong. "I do not want it, as a thing. And if it comes, I will have no part of it, except to save what peace I may."

Krenn stared. The other diplomats, and they had been many, made clear that the war stood behind their plans, as a cruiser squadron escorts a convoy of freighters. But this one denied that, and this was the one who went to Klinzhai.

155

Why would the Federation send one who cared not enough to fight for it?

Unless, Krenn thought, this was the trapped move in the game. Krenn remembered Admiral Kezhke's strange advice: *You must bring him alive . . . no matter what you are told.*

This was such a little Human, to start a war of a thousand years: but only a little antimatter started a great reaction.

"I don't . . . understand," Krenn said finally.

Dr. Tagore sat down, his eyes no longer running, but red-colored. "That's all right," he said. "There's still a little time."

The only good thing about the Embassy reception, Krenn thought, was that it was not also a dinner. Those present were frcc to wander around a large building, starting or avoiding conversations as desired.

It was now common knowledge that the two Klingons understood the Federation language without translators, and discussions tended to sputter and shift as Krenn approached. This made little sense to him. Not only did half the beings present carry translating machines (or have servitors to carry them) but Krenn could not even hear very well. Akhil said it was the thinness of the air.

The air seemed thick enough to Krenn, but not pleasantly so. The Federation beings preferred talking around him than to him, but when he was asked questions, they were the same. Yes, he had been a privateer. No, he had never taken Federation prizes. Yes, he had killed with his hands. *And* his teeth. Krenn thought he should have a tape recorded.

In one of the larger rooms, the Vulcan Ambassador to Earth stood near a fireplace, speaking to a moderately large circle of guests of a dozen miscellaneous races. A Human female, even-featured and light-haired, stood near the Ambassador: Krenn recalled from the first day's shock wave of introductions that she was the Vulcan's sole consort. Interested, Krenn went that way, not quite joining the group; no one turned to notice him as the tall Vulcan talked on.

Krenn could not understand any complete sentence of the lecture. The Ambassador's Federation Standard was Vulcan-flawless, of course, but there was no machine program that could make a Vulcan's technical conversation intelligible. Krenn supposed the other listeners must all be Thought Masters, or one of the equivalent Federation degrees. Or perhaps they had other reasons for standing in the barrage of words.

Krenn watched the Human female. There seemed to be a tightness in her expression; if it was humor, it was not any sort he had seen. It looked more like distress, but at what? Krenn? No, she was not looking at him. She was not, Krenn saw, looking at anything.

A few of the Vulcan's words registered on Krenn: something about *chromosomes* and *intersplicing*.

Krenn withdrew, and wandered from room to room until he found Akhil, who was amusing himself with an electronic pattern-matching toy.

"Where did you get that?" Krenn said.

"There's a games room upstairs. Want to try this? It helps if you drink something strong."

"How does that help?"

"You don't mind losing. Here."

"Not now. Come with me. I need a Specialist to listen to something."

They went back to watch the Vulcan Ambassador, and listened until the two Klingons together began to attract the attention Krenn alone had avoided.

"What was he talking about?" Krenn asked Akhil.

"I'm an astronomer, not a geneticist." There was a hesitation in his voice.

"That still tells me more than I knew. What was he talking about, even generally?"

"Oh, I know more than generally. He's discussing genetic fusion. Don't you remember, when we were meeting half the Federation, that son of theirs—seven

157

or eight years old? He's a fusion, and the Ambassador was describing the process.''

"With his consort present?'' Krenn said, astonished and disgusted.

"What? Was she there?'' Akhil said, distracted. "He said something really interesting, in with all the technical detail.''

Krenn said, carefully, "Interesting?'' He had heard Akhil call off incoming fire as if it concerned him not at all; he had heard the Exec tear a slacking junior officer into raw protein with his voice. But only very rarely had he heard Akhil angry. It was not a loud effect. The sharpest knives are the quietest. And 'Khil was angry now.

"He was saying that the fusion techniques were 'only recently perfected by Vulcan scientists.' *Recently perfected?* If that gets back to the Imperial Institutes of Research, there are going to be some *tharavul* headed back to Vulcan, Warp 4. Without a ship around them.''

"How can he say that? If he lies—'' Krenn thought that, if it should be found that a Vulcan could lie, the *tharavul* would soon be more than just deaf telepathically.

"Lies?'' Akhil said, and stopped short; the anger slipped out of his voice. "No. He doesn't lie. He reports scientific results.'' Akhil laughed. "Scientists know some tricks Imperial Intelligence will never master.''

Krenn asked Akhil the way to the Embassy game room, and they separated again. Krenn climbed a curving white staircase, carpeted in black velvet with tiny crystal stars, and turned down the corridor Akhil had indicated. He passed a door, and despite that it was closed and his hearing diminished, he could clearly hear a Human voice within, saying, ". . . not whether Tagore's a competent negotiator, we're not even that far along in the argument. First I want to know if the bastard's *sane.*''

There was an unintelligible reply.

"I'll *grant* you that . . . volunteering for this should be grounds for confinement. But you know his record . . . all right, sure, but would you send Gandhi to argue Hitler out of . . . How do we *know* he won't?"

The rest was lost in a sound of plumbing. Krenn moved on to the room he wanted.

It was dim within, pleasantly so after the Earth-level lighting of the main rooms. Spotlights shone on tables set for several different games; Krenn examined the unfamiliar ones, and sat down at a chessboard with pieces lathe-turned from bright and dark metal.

"Would you wish an opponent, sir?" said a voice behind Krenn. He turned, hand dropping to his weapon. There was a small being a few meters from him, in a spotlit alcove of the room; it had been reading a book. It came forward.

It was only a child, Krenn saw at once. The hair was cut in the Vulcan style, and the ears were unmistakable.

"My parents are downstairs," the young Vulcan said. "I did not wish to be an annoyance. I will leave."

This must be the Ambassador's son, Krenn thought, the fusion. "You do not annoy me," he said, as the boy moved toward the door. "And I would welcome a chance to play this game."

Krenn won the chess game, but he did not win it easily. "A pleasant game," he said. "My compliments to a worthy opponent."

The child nodded.

Krenn said, "That is a phrase we use at the conclusion of our game, *klin zha*. In my language it is *'Zha riest'n, teskas tal'tai-kleon.'*"

"Zha riest'n," the boy said, carefully copying Krenn's pronunciation, *"teskas tal . . . la . . . "*

"Tal'tai-kleon."

"Tal'tai-kleon."

"Kai," Krenn said, and laughed.

"Are you the Klingon Captain, sir, or the Science officer?"

"I am the Captain . . . of the cruiser *Fencer*," Krenn said. He had been about to give his full name and honorific, but it had suddenly seemed unnecessary. *Rather silly*. And he was tired of introductions. "Have you ever thought of being a starship Captain?"

The boy's lips compressed. Then he said "I plan to be a scientist. But perhaps I will join the Starfleet."

"The sciences are a good path. I'm sorry my Specialist isn't here to talk to you."

"No insult was meant, sir—"

"None was assumed."

"There will be a logical choice."

"Sometimes there is," Krenn said. "Another game?"

They talked as they played. It did not affect the boy's play, but Krenn let a bishop get away from him, and lost. The boy gave him the whole *klingonaase* phrase, perfectly accented.

"*Sa tel'ren?*" Krenn said.

"What does that mean, Captain sir?"

"Two out of three."

Krenn wondered what Vulcan children said to a fusion in their midst. The two races were similar to start with, and this one's physical characteristics leaned to the Vulcan. The ears especially. Krenn tried to think what would have happened, in his House Gensa, to one with Vulcan ears. He seemed to feel the blood on his fingers. Would it be green, he wondered.

The boy moved a knight, taking one of Krenn's rooks. He waited.

Krenn slid a pawn forward.

"Given the established balance of our skills, Captain, and other factors being equal, you cannot defeat me with the odds of a rook. It would be logical for you to resign."

"Klingons do not resign," Krenn said. Seven or eight years old, Akhil had said. Krenn had killed his first intelligent being when he was this one's age. A Human starship crewman, a prize, in the Year Games.

"The sequence of moves is predictable, and barring suboptimal strategies, inevitable. The time consumed—"

"If I go to the Black Fleet, what matter that I go a little slowly?" Krenn thought of the Human, who had shouted challenge into Krenn's face even as he died. It was an honorable death, and a glorious kill.

"What is the Black Fleet?" the Vulcan asked.

Krenn was pulled back from his memory. "One who serves his ship well, in the life we see, will serve on a ship of the Fleet when this life ends." Krenn's Federation vocabulary was not right for this; the words would not fit together as Dr. Tagore could make them to fit. "In the Fleet there is the death that is not death, because not the end; there is the enemy to be killed a thousand times, and each time return; and there is the laughter."

"Laughter?" the boy said. "And enemies?" His eyes were calm, and yet almost painfully intense to Krenn, who struggled to make the languages meet, and wondered why he so badly needed to.

"Fed, Rom . . . others," Krenn said. "Without *kleoni,* what would be the purpose?"

"My mother says that the spirit is eternal," the boy said. "My father says this is true in a purely figurative sense, as the wisdom of Surak is not forgotten, though Surak is become unstructured."

"We have one who is not forgotten," Krenn said. "His name was Kahless. When his ship was dying, he had his hand bound to his Chair, that no one could say he left it, or that another had been in the Chair at the ship's death. Then all his crew could escape without suspicion, because Kahless had taken on all the ship's destiny.

"Kahlesste kaase, we say. Kahless's Hand."

"This would seem a supremely logical act."

"Logical?" Krenn said, and then he understood. The boy was raised in his father's culture. It was the highest

161

praise he knew. "I think you are right," Krenn said. "I had not perceived the logic of the situation."

"My father says that this is his task: to communicate logic by example."

Is that why you were caused to exist? Krenn was thinking. As an example? He could see that the boy was proud of what he had just done—communicated to a Klingon! Was that not the victory? And yet he could not shout it. Vulcans did not shout.

"My mother is a teacher," the boy said. "She also communicates. My parents are—" He looked away.

"My mother," Krenn said, "was not of my father's race."

The boy turned his eyes on Krenn once more. It could not be called a stare, it was absolutely polite, but it did pierce, and the arched eyebrows cut.

"It is a custom on Earth," the Vulcan said, "on concluding a chess game, to shake hands."

Krenn's liver pinched. That was not a Vulcan custom, he knew well enough. Touching a Vulcan's hand opened the path for the touch of their minds. And *that* touch could pull out thoughts that the agonizer or the Examiner's tools could never reach. It was said by some that it could burn the brain; Krenn did not believe this, but . . .

The touch, Krenn thought, *the touch.* And he raised his right hand, slowly held it out over the chessboard, palm up.

The boy extended his own hand, above Krenn's, palm down. A drop of water fell into Krenn's palm.

A Vulcan sweating. And I am drenched already.

There was a choked cry from the doorway, a scream stopped at the last instant. Krenn and the boy turned together, and saw the Ambassador's consort standing there, her whole body rigid, her knuckles bone-white against the sides of her face.

"What is this?" the Human said.

The boy said, "We were playing a game—"

162

"Game!" It was half a gasp. The female looked at Krenn, and the hatred in her look was like a blow against his body.

Then she said, very calmly, without looking away from Krenn, "Your father's looking for you. Go to him now."

"Yes, mother." At the door, the boy stopped, turned, held up his hand with fingers at an angle. "Live long and prosper, Captain."

Krenn nodded. He could still feel the hate and fear radiating from the Human. He raised his hand and saluted the boy, who bowed and went out.

"I don't . . . " said the Ambassador's consort, still angry and frightened, but now with the tension of confusion as well.

"You would fight for your line," Krenn said. "That is a good thing. I think that is the best honor I know. That one is . . . " He tried to think of a praise the Human could not misinterpret. ". . . worthy of the stars." He was, now, a little relieved that events had ended when they had.

The woman's face had softened, though her stance was still rigid. "Perhaps I misunderstood," she said. "I am sorry. It can be hard to . . . protect a child, on Vulcan."

"You fear the Klingon," Krenn said. "In this is no need for apology."

The meetings dragged on for three more days. Krenn had a sort of waking nightmare that the Federation had lost or forgotten the procedures necessary to end their conferences, and the sessions would continue until all those present crumbled into dust around rotting tables.

Then, rather suddenly, a hammer came down on a wooden block and it was all over, and even more suddenly diplomats and attachés were headed for their homeworlds, each packing a shuttle-load of luggage . . . each but one.

163

"These are all the goods you require?" Krenn asked Dr. Tagore. "We do not have such a mass constraint."

"There's more there than I can carry, and that's already too much. But I've become used to having certain things around . . . softer than I used to be." Krenn looked at the Human, who seemed made of dry brown sticks, and wondered at that.

The Ambassador bent over one of his cases, examined the label. "They're going to seal my apartment, I hear, and fill it with nitrogen. If I don't return, I suppose they can just bolt a plaque on the door." He pointed at one of the smaller cases. "This is a data encryptor. I'll have to warn your Security people that it'll destroy itself if the case is opened. Starfleet wanted me to take a complete subspace radio rig, three hundred kilos plus spares, not that I'd know what to do if it needed spares. The ComInt man said a Klingon set would be bugged." He looked up, smiled. "Monitored, that is. Of course it will, I said. What would I be saying that I would not want heard?"

He sat down on a suitcase. "I've brought quite a few clothes. *Zan* Akhil tells me your ship's laundry doesn't synthesize from basic fiber, as ours do. And I'm not built much like the Imperial Race." He looked at the time display on his wrist. "That 'demonstration' of Marcus van Diemen's, whatever it is, is in twenty minutes. Shall we go, Captain?"

"It would please me, Thought Master, to be called Krenn."

"Honored, Krenn. And you must call me Emanuel." He laughed. "Hoping that isn't blasphemy."

They went to a small auditorium, half full of Starfleet Naval and Technical personnel. Akhil was already there, in a front-row seat; Krenn sat next to him. As Dr. Tagore prepared to sit, a junior officer whispered in his ear. "A moment, Krenn. I seem to be wanted." The officer led him away. Krenn looked after them until they were lost in the crowd; he was remembering that the people along the train route, the ones with torches, had been called *demonstrators*.

The Humans all found seats. Admiral van Diemen stepped onto the dais, looking the very image of heroism in his full-dress uniform and weapon with gilded hilt. "Good afternoon, fellow officers . . . and our honored guests. It is a Human custom to provide something special at a guest's departure, so they may carry with them an enduring memory.

"Now, through the latest breakthrough in Federation scientific research, we wish to present to you something very special indeed. *Lights.*"

The room darkened. "Another *gagny* hologram show?" Akhil muttered.

There was an electronic squeal, a rising, oscillating hum. On the dais, three columns of light appeared, took shapes.

Three armed soldiers were transporting onto the stage.

Krenn went for his pistol. It was, he thought, a crude trap, but deadly enough; but there were many targets behind him, and he would die spitting challenge at them, and not all of them would live to hear his last words.

His arm would not move. He turned his head. Akhil had three fingers tight on Krenn's arm, pinching the nerves, blocking the muscle. "No," he said, not loud but urgently. "Not yet."

"What are you doing?"

"If I'm wrong," Akhil said coolly, "kill me first."

The armed Humans solidified; the mechanical noise died away. The soldiers did not move, nor did their weapons come to bear on the Klingons; Krenn saw they were frozen in a sort of heroic tableau.

The lights came up. Krenn winced. No one was moving yet.

"The most important development in transtator applications in fifty years," Admiral van Diemen was

165

saying. "Thirty years in development, and now certified safe for intelligent life."

The Humans were applauding. Krenn looked at Akhil. Akhil released Krenn's arm, said very quietly, "Now we know."

As the clapping subsided, Admiral van Dicmen said, in a completely friendly tone, "I hope, Captain, that you and your Science officer will take word of this breakthrough to your own physicists."

"Of course I will, Admiral," Krenn said. He took out his communicator, glanced at Akhil; the Specialist nodded.

"Captain to *Fencer*."

Kelly responded. Krenn snapped a line of Battle Language.

"Captain, are you—"

"The situation is stable, Kelly. Action."

"Acting."

Akhil stood, muttering, "Don't want to land on my butt," and flickered golden, and evaporated without a sound.

Around Krenn, there was a silence like the silence of vacuum. Then there was a single sound of applause: Krenn turned to see Dr. Tagore clapping furiously, the fluid called tears rolling down his cheeks as he laughed.

"Our physicists will indeed be interested," Krenn said to Admiral van Diemen, who stood gripping the podium with both hands. "They will want very much to know why your system makes that terrible noise."

"All right, *why?*" Krenn said.

"Specialist Antaan worked it out," Akhil said. He seemed extremely pleased, and Krenn could hardly argue: they were bringing back a major piece of scientific intelligence, and they could hardly be accused of having pirated it.

"Antaan got a sensor lock on the corona leakage from the Feds' 'demonstration'." Akhil pushed a key,

166

and a multicolored trace appeared on the display of Akhil's Bridge station. "Do you see this line?"

"You're pointing to it, I see it," Krenn said patiently. He was thinking that since they had this data, *Fencer* had indeed had sensors trained on them the whole time. Just like home.

"Antaan calls it a super-carrier wave, polarized in three dimensions plus warp-time. They're overlaying it on the ordinary transporter signal. At reassembly, it superheterodynes with the main signal; the heterodyning produces a set of parasitic sound frequencies. Like the fact that a disruptor beam is blue, even though the disrupting wave itself is invisible."

"So it's noisy," Krenn said, wondering if 'Khil might secretly be a Vulcan fusion. "Is it better?"

"I can't see how," Akhil said flatly. "The super-carrier repeats the main signal information, but the reduction in assembly error is trivial, maybe one percent. And the power cost is twenty percent higher, not to mention the cost of extra equipment. *Plus* being able to hear a boarding party a boom's-length away."

Krenn leaned against one of the main ceiling struts. He looked at the main display, just past his empty Chair, at the stars passing at Warp 4 and the Federation ships surrounding *Fencer.* They had only three escorts for the voyage from Earth, all of them the new-model cruisers with the saucer hulls and outriggered warp engines. There was *Glasgow,* that had led them in, and *Savannah,* and *Hokkaido.* Admiral van Diemen had said with quickly recovered pride that they were of the *Baton Rouge* class, and they also were on Starfleet's leading edge of technology. And all of them did have transporters, Krenn was told.

"One percent, you say?"

"One percent of the error rate, Captain, not the number of transports."

"Yes . . . I'd thought that was what you meant." Krenn looked at Kelly. She had been watching him;

167

quickly she turned away. "Still," Krenn said, "they seem to have a powerful desire for personal safety."

"Humans?" Akhil said, disbelieving. "Most of them weren't even armed."

"Maybe their idea of danger isn't the same as ours."

Amused, Akhil said, "How many things are there to fear?"

"I don't know," Krenn said. "That's what scares me."

Akhil took it as a joke, as Krenn had intended.

"The room is comfortable?" Maktai said.

"Very much so," Dr. Tagore said, looking around, at the clearprints on the walls, the newly installed furniture, and his still-sealed baggage. "Much larger than I had expected. This isn't normally a stateroom?"

"It's my office," Krenn said. "I'll be using the Exec's office down the corridor."

"I hadn't meant such an inconvenience."

Krenn said, "An advantage of this cruise is that there isn't much office work. Anyway, we had to put you somewhere; this has its own washroom, and an individual lock code. There aren't any regular passenger facilities, and you can't have expected us to give you Marine quarters." Krenn noticed Maktai watching him; as casual as Mak was, he had not expected the informality between his superior officers and the alien.

Dr. Tagore said, "Starfleet has done just that, on occasion." He turned to Maktai. "And I have had my bags examined by a number of Federation member worlds, including Earth. I'll gladly assist your crew in a search, Commander Maktai."

The Security chief scratched his forehead. Krenn was amused, and interested: if Mak's style aboard were really only a mask, this cruise might put some wrinkles in it.

Maktai said, "We do not search others' property without cause."

"I hadn't meant to suggest you would. Many cultures

168

consider my profession itself not only sufficient cause, but necessary."

"We . . . do not," Maktai said. "You're aware that you will be the only resident of this deck . . . besides this office, and the Executive's, there are only the forward transporter rooms at the corridor ends. And the ship's computers . . . but I must advise you not to enter those compartments."

"The doors to the computer room are secured, I assume?"

"This . . . need not be said."

"Then it need not be said that I shall not enter. The same for the transporter rooms; I find it a fascinating invention, much pleasanter than shuttlecraft rides, but I should not like to accidentally disassemble myself."

"It is good that you understand."

"Commander, that is the reason I am here."

Krenn said, "Mak and Akhil and I are three decks below. You're not alone in the pod." He gestured at the wall. "We've disabled the priority call on your communicator, but it'll call any open location. And we'll have a computer screen in here in a day."

Dr. Tagore said gently, "What you may have heard is true: my kind die if we are isolated. But you need not worry." He pressed the seal on one of his cases, and it folded itself open. Within were books, more than a hundred of them, and a case of crystal slides with a reader. In the bottom of the case was a flat black plane, like a computer terminal, but with very different controls that Krenn recognized at once: he had played a thousand games of *klin zha* on just such an electronic game grid.

"You see," Dr. Tagore said, selecting a book, "I am not isolated."

Maktai said, "There is one security matter . . ."

"Of course, Commander."

"Your weapon."

"Weapon?" Dr. Tagore said, sounding slightly distressed.

169

"Of course you may keep your personal arms. But I must know their type, for the record. So that if an incident occurs, yours may be . . . eliminated from consideration."

"Commander . . . Captain . . . I have not carried a weapon in forty-four years. Since I would not use one, I would not tell the lie of wearing one."

"On Earth," Krenn said, startled, "I saw your people with dress arms—" He had assumed the Ambassador carried his weapon well concealed.

"It is permitted," the Human said, "though many of us hope it ceases to be the fashion."

"I may," Maktai said slowly, "be forced to search your bags, to confirm this . . . "

"My offer to assist you still stands."

"I think that's all for now," Krenn said. "I would be pleased if you would join me for dinner, Dr. Tagore."

"Honored of course, Captain."

In the lift, Krenn said to Maktai, "As strange as it sounds, Mak . . . I don't think he has a weapon."

Maktai shook his head, plucked at his hair. "I *know* he doesn't. We scanned his equipment for weapons, routine, you know the drill. *Nothing. G'dayt,* I'd been thinking he had something that our scanners couldn't pick up."

Krenn could see how Mak felt: he felt *silly.*

"So tell me, Captain, *why* doesn't he have a weapon?" Maktai spread his hands. "He's not *kuve* . . . Kagga's crown, he's not *kuve.* So what *is* he, Captain?"

It was the late watch, and *Fencer* was quiet; quieter now than in a long time. The ship was ten days across the Zone, in Klingon space again.

Krenn moved a pawn upward one space. "Do all Humans play chess?"

"No," Dr. Tagore said. "Actually very few play, though everyone knows the pieces, and most have an idea of the moves. There is a common belief that truly exceptional chessplayers, grandmasters, must also

be . . . " He touched a rook, moved it downward.
". . . insane."

Krenn took a bite from a gel pastry, washed it back
with *kafei*. "Is this belief true?"

"I don't know. At least partially, I suppose. Certainly some grandmasters were mad, or went mad. But so
have any number of people who never touched a
pawn. . . . The other factor is that computers play
chess. In solitaire mode, this unit—" he tapped the
game grid—"plays so well I cannot beat it. And one of
the new duotronic computers cannot be beaten at all,
not even by a Vulcan."

"What difference does that make?" Krenn said.
"What honor is there in playing a machine whose only
function is to win?" Krenn shifted a sub-board, the
projected pieces descending through his fingers.

Dr. Tagore looked up, pleased. Krenn stared at the
position again.

"Oh, don't worry, I'm mated in two or so," the
Human said. "I'm just delighted to hear you say that.
Not even Vulcans seem to be able to see that it is not
the game, but the player."

The checkmate actually took five moves. At least the
Ambassador never tried to resign, Krenn thought.

Dr. Tagore blanked the board. "Another? Or would
you like to give me another lesson in *klin zha?*"

"I would like to have another lesson in *pokher.*"

"Gladly." Dr. Tagore went to his library, returned
with two decks of cards and a rack of tokens. "You
realize that I've still got nothing of value to play for,
and I doubt that Strip would be of more than academic
interest."

"It is important that the stakes be real," Krenn said.
He had been waiting for this, trying to perfect his
strategy for the moment when it came.

"As I've said, Chess and Poker between them sum up
the Human psyche. And Chess is the supreme game for
itself, just as Poker is the supreme game for stakes."

Krenn stood up, went to the library shelves, pulled

out one of the thin, plastic-covered books. "There are these," he said.

Dr. Tagore laughed. "Krenn, if I've ever grudged the loan of a book, may the spirit of Ben Franklin choke me with a kitestring. You're welcome to any of those."

"No," Krenn said, and walked to the services wall. He tapped the book against the spring doors of the disposal slot.

Dr. Tagore said, "One of the hardest parts of xenoculture is understanding humor. . . . Are you joking, Krenn?"

Krenn started to put the book through the slot. It would have taken only a snap of the wrist, but he looked down, and read the title on the cover, and his hand did not move. After a moment he said, "No, Emanuel. I am not joking."

Dr. Tagore nodded. He said, "And what will be your stake, Krenn?"

"The books are my stake," Krenn said. "I already hold them; you may win them back."

"Despite that they have no value to you?" The Human's calm was like an unexpected cold wind.

"It was you, was it not, who told me one might trade for hostages, that also have no value."

"Very well. Cut for first deal, Krenn."

Krenn said, "If you were armed, you could fight me for this."

Dr. Tagore paused in his shuffling; then he resumed. "But I am not." He split the deck. "Jack of spades. Your cut."

"Perhaps I have selected one that means nothing to you. I shall destroy it and select another." The book seemed to twist in Krenn's hand, and would not enter the slot. Krenn resisted looking at the title again.

"That one is as precious as the rest, as I imagine you know. Take your cut, so we may begin."

Krenn went to the table. He put the book face down, picked up a block of cards, turned them.

"Nine of diamonds," Dr. Tagore said. "Dealer chooses five-card draw, nothing wild."

"Is *that* what you will say to the Imperial Council?" Krenn said. "When they ask you why you go unarmed like a *kuve,* when they ask you what the Federation can be worth to you, since you will not fight for it—" He had not meant to shout, but he was shouting. "When they ask why they should deal with you, will you tell them it is because you have drawn a higher card?"

"If that is the game we are playing."

Perhaps this one was insane, Krenn thought. Perhaps he went into the Empire like a Romulan, to find his death close to the enemy's heart. "The game they play is the *komerex zha,*" Krenn said, "and if you lose, it will not be your books that burn, but yourself."

Dr. Tagore reached for the book.

(Kethas reached for the dead green hand.)

The Human said "There is no difference." He picked up the book, held it out to Krenn. "Here. It's yours. Read it or destroy it; but if you destroy it, you will never know what it had to say to you."

Krenn took it. He did not even look at the disposal slot. He knew he had been beaten, by one unarmed. He read the book's title: *Space Cadet,* it said. The book could say nothing to him; how could it? He was no longer a cadet.

And still he knew he would have to read it.

Dr. Tagore was casing the decks of cards. "Pleasant rest, Krenn," he said.

Now Krenn was being ordered out of his office. "It was . . . a good game, Emanuel."

"An excellent game, Krenn. *Teskas tal'tai-kleon.*"

Krenn took the lift down to his cabin. He put the book on the bedside table, unfastened his vest and was about to slip out of his tunic when there was a tap at the door. Krenn looked at the communicator panel; the idle lights were on. He went to the door.

Akhil was in the corridor, his portable terminal

under his arm. Krenn was about to ask if whatever it was could wait, but the expression on the Exec's face said it would not. Then Krenn saw that Akhil was wearing, not his usual duty arms, but a heavy disruptor pistol.

"What is it, 'Khil?"

"Not here. Get something to shoot with and come with me."

"Where's Mak?" Krenn said, but the suspicion was already rising.

"Mak's asleep. At least, I hope he is. Now *come.*"

They took the lift aft, down the boom to the cargo hold. The deck was lit only by small directional lights; indicators flickered in the darkness.

Akhil said, "Wait." He paused by a communicator panel, put a key into the access lock. Krenn held the terminal as Akhil swung the wall panel open, exposing a maze of components. Akhil took a rectangle of green circuit board from his sash, slipped it between two junction blocks. He said, "Now if one of Maktai's crew takes a look down here, they'll get noise. It'll look like normal circuit transients for a little while, but not long. Over here."

They stopped again at one of the cargo modules, an insulated food box. Akhil took his terminal, opened the black case, and uncoiled the cord of a coding wand. He ran it over the cargo module's invoice plate. "This is the one." He stood, gave the terminal to Krenn. "Better read it for yourself."

Krenn wiped the wand over the code lines, and read the terminal screen.

"*Cold-sleep capsules?*" he said, and looked automatically toward the invisible ceiling, the invisible monitors.

"Should be fifty Marines, if this is the only one," Akhil said. "Instant mutiny. Just thaw and serve."

"How did you find this?"

"Checking the cargo manifest." Akhil gave a toneless laugh. "The Feds consider zentaars an intelligent species. I thought it might bother our passenger if a

174

zentaar haunch showed up on his dinner tray. . . . I suppose it's an honorable debt we owe him, for this."

"If it's on the label and manifest, then the Cargomaster has to know," Krenn said. "Who else?" He counted through his officers.

"Someone's got to command this instant army."

"Maktai . . ."

"Would they trust a lower rank?"

"I haven't decided who 'they' are yet." He thought of Meth of Imperial Intelligence, with his plastic face.

He thought of Kelly. "But I don't suppose it matters. Let's go."

"Who. . . ?" said the voice from the other side of the door.

"It's Krenn, Mak." He pushed the heavy disruptor inside his sash, out of sight.

Maktai opened the door. *"Parkhest . . ."*

"Just the way I feel, Mak. We've got trouble aboard."

"The passenger?" Maktai looked at his wall monitor. "There's no alert."

"Not yet. Get some clothes on, and come with me. Rapid action."

"Acting, Captain."

"And, Mak—light weapons."

"Khest diplomacy."

Krenn stepped into the cabin, letting the door close, and watched Maktai dress, noting carefully where the Security chief put the small projectile pistol he favored for light work. If Mak were not Klingon, this would be easier, Krenn thought. But he could not show Maktai the gun. And he could not order Mak to come unarmed; the one would have known he went to arrest, if not execution, and that must not happen until Krenn knew who else was part of the mutiny.

And it was possible still that they would not have to execute more than a few crewmen, as strong example. It was not necessarily a crime to *consider* mutiny.

Krenn and Maktai met Akhil and Kelly in the lift. Kelly looked, confused and sleepy, at Krenn; then she looked at Maktai. Mak gave a faint shake of his head.

Krenn felt his lips pull back, his liver turn to lead.

They arrived in the hold. Akhil went to the cargo module, plugged in a keypad and pressed buttons. Seals cracked, and the thick insulated door swung open; a cloud of white vapor flooded out.

"What in the name of the Nameless Emperor *is* this?" Maktai said, shivering in the wave of cold air.

"See for yourself," Krenn said, and motioned Maktai and Kelly forward. Akhil brought the deck lights up as they reached the door, and the glowing white fog was blinding. Krenn thought briefly about what Admiral Whitetree would have said, if he were told fifty Klingons had entered his space without even rippling his sensors.

Krenn's vision cleared, and he looked into the module.

Whitefang and zentaar carcasses stood ranked along the inner walls, impaled on frost-covered rods.

Akhil's fingers thrust into the base of Krenn's skull; a shock ran down Krenn's spine, and he fell forward, carrying Mak and Kelly with him into the freezer. He felt ice burn his face, saw the arc of light from outside sweep down to nothing as the door swung shut.

Maktai crawled from beneath Krenn, reached for the opening, got two fingers on the frame. The door closed regardless. There was a hiss as the gaskets resealed, and then total darkness.

Krenn rolled over. His legs were still paralyzed: they struck a carcass. Maktai said, *"G'dayt, v'kaase,"* in an almost disinterested tone. *Shock,* Krenn thought.

"Freeze it, Mak," Krenn said. "Freeze the stumps before you bleed out."

"Right . . ."

"Kelly, can you reach Mak?"

"He's got it," she said.

Krenn felt muscle control returning to his lower

body. He realized the floor was sucking heat from him; knew he would freeze to it in a moment. He levered himself up, burning his hands.

"Kelly to Bridge," she was saying. "Kelly to Security. Kelly to any station, priority call." A flash of light came from nearby; Kelly had done something to her communicator so the blue-white call light shone bright and steady. "That won't last long," she said, "but it might as well be good for something. I can't call out through this thing."

Even in the darkness, it was still not much light, and it was cold and pale. Kelly reached inside her tunic, produced a palm-sized object. "I've got a light sonic. Will that do any good on the door?"

"We'll try it," Krenn said. "Mak, you've . . . " But of course he knew.

"Slug-thrower. You said small weapons."

"I did." Krenn drew out the heavy disruptor. Its grip froze to his fingers; he pulled it free, wrapped it in the end of his sash.

"Small?" Maktai said, as Krenn's pistol caught the light.

Krenn held the gun close to the doorframe, thumbed fire. The blue flash was dazzling, and fragments of plastic erupted; Krenn felt them shower his arms. He examined the target spot. It was disappointing: the insulation had absorbed much of the blast energy. But Krenn had heard metal tear. The sonic would be worthless, but the disruptor would work, if there was enough charge.

And enough heat, and enough air.

"Could you explain," Maktai said, his voice very tight, "what we're doing here?"

Krenn tried to do so, shouting to be heard as he cut the door.

Maktai said, "All right," and there was no condemnation in it; no Klingon would require excuses of a Captain threatened with mutiny. "What does Akhil want, then? It can't be the ship, not this way."

"It has to be the ship, or else the passenger," Krenn said. "And I don't think it's the ship, either."

"Captain, permission to speak?"

"For the duration of the crisis, Kelly."

"Did the Captain suspect this one from the first?"

"Yes," Krenn said, and bore down on the disruptor. The cold was in his lungs like death's own hand now, and only the flash of the disruptor gave any warmth at all.

Maktai's head rolled to the side. Kelly moved toward him, shook him. Maktai grunted, stirred, then slumped again.

"In his sash, near his pistol," Krenn said. "He's got . . ."

Kelly knew. She had the metal cylinder out, and was tugging Maktai's tunic open at the collar. She held the agonizer to the communicator's light, checking the setting, and applied it. Maktai's limbs twitched.

Krenn said, "I'll tell you when I need a touch of that."

As Kelly had warned, the communicator's battery died shortly. A knife-thin light came in around the doorframe, where Krenn had made his cuts. Kelly began firing her sonic into the frozen meat; the noise was worse than the disruptor on the door, but it seemed to generate a little bit of heat.

After years of darkness Krenn reached the last corner. He struggled to stand; his skin hurt as he moved. He wondered if the blood was frozen in his small surface vessels. He had seen that happen. The flesh went greenish-black, and sloughed away like bark from a dead tree.

Krenn slammed his shoulder against the door. Pain exploded inside him. Frost crashed. The panel did not move.

Maktai got up, wavering, Kelly helping him. The three of them leaned together.

"Action," Krenn said.

With a tearing crash the door fell out. The Klingons

staggered onto the cargo deck. Krenn felt his lungs open up to receive the hot air, tried to control his breathing so his heart would not burst.

The wall communicator had been shot apart. At the lift doors, Maktai hit the call button. The indicator did not light. "He's locked them off," he said, hammered the panel with his maimed hand, then looked at the stumps of his fingers and said, "I didn't even feel that." He took a step, then leaned against the wall. Ice crystals fell from his shoulders. "The stairway's around the corner . . . we'll have to take the boom corridor forward."

Krenn said, "That's two decks up, then the length of the ship, *then* up three more decks to Emanuel's room." Ignoring Maktai's look, Krenn looked back the way they had come. "But there's a stage right back there."

"I'll set the controls," Kelly said.

"Krenn," Mak said, "there are only cargo transporters on this level. . . . Oh, *khest* it, I'm coming." He took one step, two, then slumped against the wall again. Krenn knew it wasn't muscle keeping him up, but pure *klin*.

"You're no use to me as you are," Krenn said, "and less use dead."

Mak slid down to the deck. He wrapped the fingers of his good hand around the other wrist; it might have been to slow the bleeding once his blood thawed, but Krenn saw Maktai's look. *Kahlesste kaase*, it said. Kahless's Hand.

Krenn and Kelly made for the transporter stage. He had not seen her run since she had come aboard Fencer: it pleased him to know that she still could run.

"Your arm," he said then, because it hung like a dead thing nailed to her body.

"My shoulder froze," she said, and Krenn knew it was literal truth; she was metal there, within. He remembered the feel of the pistol butt in his hand, for only an instant.

179

There was not enough pain in Akhil's body to pay for all of this.

They reached the transporter, a flat plane of rhomboidal segments. Krenn could not remember the scramble rate for living things sent by the less finely tuned cargo units, and was glad of the lapse. "Starboard stage, Pod Deck 4," he said.

"Acting." She worked the controls one-handed with an ease that was more than manual dexterity: Krenn suddenly realized that he had not known she even knew the transport routines. He supposed those in the Unassigned pool must master as many skills as possible, to more often get out of the pool and on a ship.

She would not be going back to the pool after this cruise, Krenn thought.

"Energizing," she said, and pushed the levers. Krenn held dead still; it couldn't hurt.

He turned golden and vanished.

Krenn flickered in on the disc of the passenger transporter: Deck 4 Starboard, the room sign said. He still hurt in all the same places, and now he had a headache, but a scramble error never left the victim able to notice his problem.

The corridor was empty, its far end, with the portside transporter, just out of sight around the curve. One door along the forward wall was open, and Earth-bright light spilled out. Krenn moved to the open door. No sound came from within.

He might, he knew, be a long time too late. But *Fencer* was still his. He went through the door.

The outer room was empty. Dr. Tagore's game grid was in pieces on the table, shattered by a disruptor bolt. A book lay on the floor, by an overturned chair; *The Innocents Abroad,* its cover said. The door to the inner room had been burned open.

Krenn heard the sound of a fresh charge slide going into a weapon. He moved, quickly, to the inner door.

Akhil stood by the bathroom door, which was closed;

he spun as Krenn entered, disruptor level. He fired. The doorframe exploded next to Krenn; metal struck him, and the shock wave knocked him down, took the gun from his hand.

Akhil said, "I knew you'd get out of the freezer," he said, "but how . . . oh. The cargo stage. *Kai* the Captain."

Krenn groped for his disruptor. Akhil fired again, high. Molecules of wall tore themselves apart. "Don't, Krenn. Don't force me to kill you. It isn't *necessary*. Is Maktai dead?"

"Not . . . quite."

"It can be an execution, then. Too bad for Mak, but someone has to die for killing the Human, and it's not going to be me, and why should it be you? The Navy won't mind—it's the Security chief, after all. But it has to be one of us; anyone any lower, and they'd fry us for incompetence."

"Why?" Krenn said.

"You *can't* see, can you?" Akhil said, sounding very tired and sad. He gestured at the bathroom door. "How that thing in there has you . . . *enslaved?*"

"What did you call me?" Krenn said, and almost succeeded in sitting up; but he fell back again.

"Not willingly," Akhil said, shaking his head violently. "Maybe it's psionic, I don't know. The rest of the race we saw on Earth—we'll have no trouble with them. But we're taking *this* one to the Imperial Council. That just mustn't happen, Thought Ensign." Akhil turned back to the door, pressed the cone of his disruptor against the panel, thumbed fire.

There was an explosion that blew the door out of its frame, throwing Akhil backward in a cloud of steam; he clutched at his face with scalded hands, fell nearly on top of Krenn as a wave of water drenched them both. Krenn grabbed for the Specialist and missed; Akhil crawled away, staggered to his feet, went for the corridor door.

Krenn found his pistol, pulsed the trigger. The shot shattered a clearprint on the wall. Krenn pulled himself up; his midsection felt like a bowl of lumpy pudding.

Akhil disappeared through the door. Krenn stumbled after. When he reached the corridor, Akhil was working at one of the Computer Room's security doors. They dared not use weapons in the machine room, Krenn knew; if Akhil got inside he would have to be pried out with bare hands. And long before that could happen, he could kill *Fencer* and all of them, by killing *Fencer*'s brain.

Krenn braced against the office door, fired. The pistol buzzed dry of charge. Akhil did not even look up from the lock.

The heavy shielded door moved inward, then slid aside. Krenn tensed to leap; it hurt enough to make him dizzy.

Kelly stepped around the curve from the portside transporter, pointed Maktai's pistol and fired. Akhil was slammed against the edge of the door, but stayed on his feet. Kelly shot him again. He took a step, and she ran to where he stood and kicked, Swift-like, to the back of his knee.

Akhil fell down and did not move.

Kelly turned to face Krenn; her arm still dangled. Krenn felt hands touching him: Dr. Tagore, his clothing wrinkled and wet but otherwise undamaged, was guiding Krenn to a chair.

"You weren't . . . in the bathroom."

"I closed the drains and opened all the taps, then went out again, closing the door. I'd merely hoped the water would distract him, but Commander Akhil did not even check that the door was not locked."

"Klingons always lock doors," Krenn said. "Where were you?"

"A custom of my race, in the presence of danger. . . . I was underneath the bed."

"You almost convinced me," Krenn said. "I thought you would not fight. It was . . . a good trick."

"I did not fight," Dr. Tagore said calmly. "I simply did not allow myself to be too easily killed."

And Krenn laughed, not because it was absurd but because he saw the reason of it. "Emanuel . . . *are* you psionic?"

"No, Krenn. I have been tested, on Vulcan. I am not."

"Then Akhil was right," Krenn said, feeling his senses fading, as in a warm bath. "The Imperial Council must beware. Now that their Imperial Intelligence has failed to protect them. . . . "

"Akhil did not act for II," Krenn heard, and though he could no longer see, the voice could not be anyone's but Kelly's.

"I do."

Krenn and Dr. Tagore were playing *klin zha,* with Krenn's set, when the call came to announce that Akhil's body had been transported into space at maximum beam divergence. Krenn acknowledged and made his next move.

Dr. Tagore said, "I believe I once told you I had a theory, about the Klingon observance of death."

"You did not say what it was."

"Well, it isn't popular among my colleagues. . . . At any rate, when one of our race dies, we hold a ceremony, sometimes simple, sometimes very elaborate."

"You *celebrate* a death?"

"Commemorate, rather."

"And the one dead appreciates this."

Dr. Tagore smiled thinly, said, "That depends on the culture. But the practical function is to allow the survivors a vent for their grief, a time when emotion may be released, shared."

"Sharing diminishes the . . . grief?"

"Such is our experience."

Krenn said, "We do not do this."

"I know. And I wonder what happens to the energy,

the stress. . . . I think it helps to drive your culture. To expand . . . to conquer, if you like."

"Nal komerex, khesterex," Krenn said, distracted from the game, annoyed to have even such a small reminder of Maxwell Grandisson III.

"I know that, too. And your environment is hostile, and your life-cycle is short and rapid. As I say, my hypothesis is not popular."

Krenn massaged his jaw.

"Klingons do not weep, as many races do," Dr. Tagore said idly. "A different set of facial nerves is stimulated by stress. The Klingon in deep emotion bares his teeth, as if to say 'stay away, until this feeling is past.'

"The isolation that results is . . . not unknown among Humans."

Krenn won the game, congratulated Dr. Tagore on his growing skill at *klin zha*, and went out.

He found Kelly in the Officer's Mess; she was alone, her plate empty, watching the naked stars flow past.

She did not turn as he approached, and he knew she was being politely deaf; twenty days after the incident there was still a plastic splint on his hip, and he made a good deal of noise in motion.

He understood, now, why her movements had become deliberate, un-Swift-like: she had been imprisoned in her body for far longer than he would be.

Now there was a sheathing of surgical plastic on her shoulder, where *Fencer*'s Surgeon had again replaced the joint with a new metal one. This time it was minor, though. Only the changing-out of a part.

Krenn sat down. She greeted him.

Neither of them spoke for a while.

"I wonder," Krenn said finally, "what Meth of Imperial Intelligence will say about this whole affair?"

"Operations Master Meth is never concerned with methods," Kelly said. "Only results."

Krenn nodded, watching her: the curve of her throat,

the slant of her white eyes. He reached over and touched her arm, carefully avoiding the nerves.

She stood, looked at him. Her face was quite empty, though never so dead as Meth's. "You are the founder of a line," she said. "I can be no part of that; I am a fusion, and I do not even know what manner of fusion, so that children might be created."

Krenn said, "Does Meth have that information?"

She said, "You know that Meth only uses those he controls. I have been part of injury and death to your crew. And . . . you are injured; I would cause you . . . pain."

"I know that," Krenn said.

She began to walk away. He caught her hand, held it; she shook at the movement of her shoulder. She said, "I cannot be trusted, and I am not Klingon."

"Akhil was Klingon."

"What do you want?"

"I want you to tell me," Krenn said, "something that I do not already know."

He released her hand. She looked at the stars racing by, and nodded, and went out, walking again slowly, each movement carefully chosen.

But if one knew how to look, Krenn thought, she was dancing.

He followed in her steps.

PART THREE
The Falling Tower

Only a fool fights in a burning house.
                                    —Klingon proverb

Chapter 7
Mirrors

Twenty-six select members of the Imperial Council sat and reclined facing Krenn. There was a large Navy faction, some Marine officers, several political Specialists, and two Imperial Planetary Governors.

The Audience Chamber was an enormous, multi-sided room. Random panels of colored and reflective glass dissected the space near the ceiling, bouncing and diffusing soft light. The air was pleasant, though not so warm and damp as to induce sleep. Woven into the carpeting was an Imperial trefoil some ten meters long: Krenn stood behind a narrow glass podium at the figure's center.

"Supply of arms to the worlds Tcholin III and Wilda's Planet has caused the dominant factions to favor the Empire as a partner in development," Krenn said. He had no notes to read from: he was allowed none. He watched the audience. Admiral Kezhke was there, aging and still overindulgent. And there was Admiral Kodon, the hero of the Romulan Frontier. Krenn did not look directly into Kodon's face.

"These arms are of course all inexpensive sonics. No transtator technology has been supplied. The sale is aided by the fact that Federation machines translate all *vird'dakaasei* as *disruptor*, regardless of their actual operating mode. . . . "

There were half a dozen *tharavul* standing like sculpture behind the Klingons they served-observed. A few servitors carried trays with food, drink, and incenses: they were *tharkuve*, deaf in a more literal sense than the Vulcans.

"Four more worlds along the Alshanai Rift have made advances of peace. They will not commit to abandoning the Federation, but they have been made to understand that the Federation cannot protect them from Orion pirates.

"If this technique is to be expanded, it will be necessary to simulate Orion attacks, as the cost of purchasing actual pirate raids will become unacceptable."

There was a throne in the Chamber, but it was empty. A crown rested on it, in token of the Emperor's presence. Kadrya had chosen iron as the substance for his crown. It was generally a free choice by each Emperor, though none since Keth the Centenarian had presumed to wear imperishable gold. And none had imitated General Kagga, who despite that he was under sentence of death for rebellion had been granted the accession, allowed to reign for the twentieth part of one day, and executed upon the throne: a grand end move of the *komerex zha*. Kagga's crown had been branded, on the flesh around his skull.

"The Federation authorities propose to convene one of the meetings of all members they call *Babels*, to discuss their terms of union. Such meetings require roughly one year to assemble all delegates, because of travel time.

"That concludes this report of the Imperial Contacts Branch, Captain Krenn sutai-Rustazh reporting."

There were polite nods. Krenn saluted and went out of the Chamber. There was a transporter link to his hotel; he nodded to the operator and stepped onto a disc.

Krenn found himself standing on the smallest transporter stage he had ever seen: there was only a single disc, which was enormously wasteful of control equipment; even home stations had three. The only other things in the room were an unattended control console for the transporter, and a blank metal door.

The door receded a few centimeters, then slid aside. It was a good fifth of a meter thick. Supposing his presence was either invited or commanded, Krenn went through.

He entered a small, dim room. The only furnishing was a desk, with a computer and a flask of pale liquid on its top. The far wall was all glass, tilted slightly outward. A tall, broad-shouldered Klingon, dressed entirely in black, stood looking out the window, his back to Krenn.

Without turning around, Operations Master Meth said, "Do join me, Captain Krenn."

Krenn took a step; the door closed behind him, and he heard it seal. He went to the window.

He was looking down on the Audience Chamber he had just left. The Council members had changed slightly; more Administrators were present, fewer Navy. Approaching the podium was Dr. Emanuel Tagore, dressed in a straight-lined white gown with a dark red sash.

They were hidden among the glass panels of the ceiling, Krenn understood; *how* they could be here, he did not know.

Dr. Tagore bowed, began to speak. His words were inaudible.

Meth held out a wireless earphone to Krenn. He took and inserted it, noticing that Meth did not wear

191

one. Krenn wondered if he had a direct implant. Klingons rarely had such things, wary of taps, of mind control, of feedback signals to set the mechanism burning. But Meth . . .

"The exchange of athletes between the Year Games and the Pan-Federation Olympics," Dr. Tagore was saying, "would reduce the need for prizes to fight in the Games, and allow trials other than deadly combat. There are already many such events in the Year Games, and they are honorable.

"As for the passage of damaging medical data, the required screenings could be conducted entirely by medical tricorder, the machines' recording function being disabled: even if a contestant were to be disqualified, none would know the exact reason. Dr. T'Riri, *tharavul* to Thought Master Ankhisek, tells me this is easily possible for Vulcan technicians . . . "

Meth said, "It is remarkable to watch him. Given only a little more time, the Council would approve this proposal. . . . After four years, most of them believe he has taken their part. When in fact they have taken his." Meth's lips curled in his plastic smile.

Krenn said, "Does he know he's been called back to Earth?"

"Oh, yes. Since you were so readily available, there was no need to delay the message. . . . " Meth looked down again. "He knows, and still he delivers the speech, as if there were still a Federation united behind him. One could almost believe the one believes in his proposals for their own sake."

"Perhaps the one does."

"Ah, I had forgotten you were close," Meth said. Krenn knew he had done no such thing. "No, I don't think so. That technique is useful, on the lower levels. The assassin's gun may believe it is a surgeon's laser. But the assassin must know the task." Meth gestured toward Dr. Tagore with a disguised hand. "I have become very respectful of this Human, Captain, and I

192

think he is a craftsman, not a tool. . . . His reaction, when he received his message of recall, was interesting to watch. If you would care to see it, a tape may be arranged."

"No," Krenn said. "Is the ship ready?"

"Quite ready. Kezhke was most helpful, again. . . . He has strong beliefs about you, sutai-Rustazh." There had been no change in Meth's tone. Krenn realized, for the first time, that he had never heard the Intelligence chief's linename.

Before he could say something dangerous to himself, Krenn said, "And the ones requested?"

"Commander Maktai and Lieutenant Commander Kelly are of course yours, and excellent choices."

"Commander Kelly?"

"As of tonight, yes. Ranks are not difficult to obtain. Authority is rather more so . . . but that, of course, is your problem. As for the other, it has been arranged. You understand the limitations?"

"Thought Master Ankhisek himself explained them."

"And you understood him? *Kai* the thought, Captain." It was almost a joke: Thought Captain. Krenn wondered if it were meant as one.

Meth said, "I'm certain that you understand the mission, so I suppose you are ready for cruise. The Red File will be transferred aboard just before you depart."

"I will be ready whenever the Ambassador is."

"He is already. He is leaving all his effects, except for some clothing and his library. He explained that he is only traveling to a conference; the Embassy remains in existence." Meth looked down at Dr. Tagore, as did Krenn. Krenn found that even from the high angle, the Human did not seem diminished. Krenn turned, a very slight movement, to watch Meth, but Meth's face gave away nothing, his eyes might as well have been glass behind holes in the plastic, even his powerful body—or was that another concealment?—was neutrally posed.

Meth was a black hole of information: he drew it in from everywhere, with a reach as infinite as gravity, but nothing ever escaped the event horizon around him.

There was, in theory at least, one way to get information out of a black hole. It involved high energies just at the event horizon, and for every particle that escaped one of equal value must be lost.

Akhil had told Krenn that.

Meth said, "I shall regret the departure of the epetai-Tagore." There did not seem to be any irony in the honorific. "Like myself, he is absolutely loyal to his Empire, and will do anything at all to protect it."

"Perhaps not anything," Krenn said.

"A natural error, sutai-Rustazh. You do not understand, because you are not absolutely loyal."

"*I am*—"

"It is not an accusation, Captain. Only the truth. You *serve* the Empire, and very well. But some of your loyalty is always reserved for yourself. . . . This is true of all Klingons but I. It is true of the Emperor." He pointed downward. "I suspect that it is also true of all Humans. Except this one."

Krenn recalled what Meth had said about the Council, wondered if the Intelligence Master had also come to see himself reflected in the Ambassador. He said, "Still, I have come to believe that the one would use no weapon."

Meth smiled, and Krenn thought there was somehow amusement in it. "Have you ever seen my weapon, Captain?"

Krenn was too startled to answer.

"You think there is a *komerex zha*," Meth said calmly, "but there is only the *komerex*." He indicated the throne, the iron crown upon it. "Kadrya is nearly sixty now, and Kadrya is no Keth. Though it may be criminal now to speak of rust on iron, in time he will die, and the Council will fight for the crown, and I will fight for the Empire.

"And if the Federation should choose to war with

itself, then it must occur while there is an Emperor, and we may take advantages."

Meth filled two glasses from the bottle of pale liquid. There was a strong scent of herbs. "Speaking of loyalty . . . I noticed that the Contacts Branch did not tell the Council their next speaker had been recalled? . . .

"And you know your mission, and it is not my habit to repeat myself. Pleasant voyage, Captain."

Kelly moved the levers, and Dr. Tagore silently flickered in. Krenn thought perhaps the Human's hair had become whiter, but there was no great outward change.

The Ambassador stepped off the disc, nodded to them all. "Honored again, Captain Krenn. I was pleased to hear it would be you taking me home. And Kelly . . . full Commander, now? *Kai*. And Maktai. Good to see you all. I'm in need of good signs, this cruise."

Then Krenn saw the tiredness—but it was a small thing, where Krenn had expected a greater.

"This is a new ship, isn't it?" Dr. Tagore said, and while he spoke the small tiredness was not visible. *"Mirror,* they said. Is *Fencer,* then . . . "

"Fencer still exists, still mine," Krenn said. "She is in the docks. *Mirror* is new, a Class D5, though the changes are mostly not visible. The interior is the same, with only small exceptions . . . one being that we have a stateroom for a passenger, on the officers' deck."

"With a private bath," Maktai said. There was a moment's cool silence, and then Dr. Tagore began to laugh, and then they were all laughing.

"You see," the Human said, "I have learned to know when you are joking."

"The reason I was recalled?" Dr. Tagore said. "To . . . now what was the exact phrase . . . 'reevaluate the mission, and expose the Ambassador to the mood, as well as the decisions, of the Babel Conference.' How many cards?"

Krenn took three cards. He adjusted his hand: a four, a King, and three nines. Maktai tapped his three-fingered hand on the table and took one card. Mak caught his tongue between his teeth and let his cards fall, face down. Krenn looked at him; it had taken a long time to teach Mak that folding was not the same as resignation: that the courage of the game was not in throwing resources into a pot already lost. Still, they were losing to the Human.

Dr. Tagore said, "The gentleman drops. And dealer takes two. Bet?"

"Check," Krenn said.

"You've stayed in practice."

Maktai said, "I paid for it."

Dr. Tagore said, "All right. Dealer bets three." He separated three fruit drops from a pile near his elbow, pushed them into the pile at the center of the table. "Of course, the actual reason for the recall is that many UFP members do not want a single negotiator to represent them to the Empire. They want to make their own deals."

"Call, raise two," Krenn said. "As I understand it, you have won the Federation a number of points."

"Thank you, Krenn. I'll see that, raise you five. But of course the Federation is a coalition, not a super-government, though sometimes it forgets that . . . if the members do not wish the Federation to act for them, then it must not do so."

Krenn looked at his three of a kind, at Dr. Tagore's face. He was wondering what the Operations Master of Imperial Intelligence would have said to that.

He let his cards fall. Maktai looked sidewise.

Dr. Tagore put his hand face down. Maktai reached out; Dr. Tagore's finger came down on top of the cards. "You didn't pay to see those," he said.

Maktai withdrew. "I forgot the rule," he said quietly.

196

Dr. Tagore nodded. "No insult was assumed. But not every game is as friendly as this one."

One ship was waiting for them, at the far side of the Zone: a single saucer-fronted cruiser, the *Savannah II*. The first of that name, Krenn recalled, had taken them outbound from Earth, years ago. He wondered who had destroyed it.

The Human in command was younger-looking than the other Human Admirals Krenn had seen. He had reddish hair, moderately pale skin by Human standards, and a remarkable, bushy growth of hair down the sides of his face and over his upper lip.

"Captain Krenn," he said, in reasonably good *klingonaase* without translating machine, "a pleasure to meet you. I'm Douglas Tancred Shepherd, commanding this Task Force, such as it is. Starfleet is spread somewhat thin just now, ferrying delegates."

Krenn wondered about that: would the Human so casually admit to a Klingon that the frontier patrols were stretched thin? Yet there were still the hunter-killer squadrons. So perhaps it was a challenge, however er slight.

Shepherd said, "Chief of Staff van Diemen sends his respects, Captain, and regrets that he could not meet you. And please give my regards to Dr. Tagore; I was once a student of his."

Krenn said, "And my respects to Admiral Luther Whitetree."

Admiral Shepherd said slowly, "Lou Whitetree . . . died two years ago, Captain."

Krenn wanted to ask if he had died well, but Shepherd already showed discomfort, and Humans had too many ideas about death to be all comprehended. Someday, he thought, I will meet you, Whitetree, in the Black Fleet, and kill you a thousand times laughing. And perhaps you will even kill me, for the glory of your son.

What Krenn said was, "I regret to hear that. My

Executive also is dead . . . I would have liked for the Admiral to meet his replacement." He looked at the Communications station, but Ensign Kreg was in the seat.

"My . . . sympathies," Shepherd said, sounding very puzzled. "Your authorizations are fully in order, so if you're ready, Captain Krenn . . . Warp 4?"

"Warp 4, Admiral."

When the ships were under way, the Bridge-to-Bridge link broken, Krenn said, "Lieutenant Klimor, you have the conn," and nodded to Maktai. They took the lift down eight decks within the pod, to the Intelligence Operations level.

All doors here were heavily shielded. To Krenn's left was the Interrogation Room, empty now. Krenn and Mak went right; Maktai inserted a key in the lock. Only Maktai's personal key could open this door; those within could not even leave at will. The door opened. Within were three rows of consoles, each with an elaborate cluster of displays.

In every other cruiser of the Navy, this was the Internal Surveillance Room, from which Security could monitor any part of the ship at will. Here the room was called Special Communications. *Mirror* did not in fact have continuous Internal Surveillance. Most of the crew did not know this, and would not have believed it if told. It was the least of the ship's secrets.

Kelly came around the consoles. "They're sensing us, Captain. I'm maintaining the level of screens they expect; they've found the guns off and the hold empty . . . power level's taking care of itself, and mechanical shielding covers the rest."

"Perfect, Kelly. What are you reading from them?"

"Normal subspace traffic. Admiral Shepherd is pleased to report you courteous as described to him."

Krenn laughed. "Soon they'll lose their fear of the Empire, and then what shall happen? . . . Nothing further to the Red File?"

"Not since the Section Two confirming message several days ago."

Krenn nodded. "You should put in an appearance on the Bridge. I'll be in quarters. Emanuel expects me for *klin zha.*"

Dr. Tagore moved the Lancer on the Reflective board.

Krenn examined the position, sat back, letting out a long breath. "You have also stayed in practice, Emanuel."

"Zha riest'n," Dr. Tagore said. "And compliments indeed; in four years I do not think I found a finer opponent. Certainly not for the Reflective Game."

"I was well instructed."

"The name of Kethas was mentioned. A Thought Admiral, the epetai-Khemara."

Krenn said, "In what connection?"

"Reflective *klin zha,*" Dr. Tagore said, as if the question were unexpected. "I would mention the game to a potential opponent, and more than half the time the one would say 'that was Kethas's game.' Did you know the one?"

"I of course know of him. He died when I was young."

Dr. Tagore sighed. "I still have not lived among Klingons long enough. I still think of you as aging as we do . . . you must be, what, twenty-five?"

"Nearly so."

"And I will be seventy-nine on my next birthday. And still we aren't so far apart . . . we both have twenty or thirty years left, if we avoid violence." Krenn was not insulted by that. "Maybe even longer. Coffee?"

"Yes."

"We work slowly on improving our genes, except for what we've borrowed from the Vulcans. Ever since the Eugenics Wars . . . " He shook his head. "Anyway, to

199

return to the original point, Kethas had a reputation with Starfleet, I recall. They called him the Klingon Yamamoto, after a strategist of our history . . . the one was an extraordinary poker player. And he had three fingers on one hand."

"I'll tell Mak." Krenn was wondering if this discussion was about games.

"He seems in an ill mood lately," Dr. Tagore said. "Is the one well?"

"He's lost dreams. We both thought he should learn Federation."

"Ah. My sympathies."

Krenn said, "The commander of our escort is an Admiral Douglas Tancred Shepherd. He mentioned your name."

"Doug Shepherd's an Admiral now? Now that does make me feel old. Reminds me of when . . . " He paused. "Did you read the book about Arthur and Camelot? The long one?"

"With the changing into animals."

"Yes. Well, when I was teaching boys like Doug Shepherd, I tended to think of myself as Lancelot . . . the terrible sinner, looking for a miracle, just one miracle of his own." He touched one of the Reflective pieces. "I have spent a large part of the last four years with the Imperial Council. It became apparent long ago that I was not the only ambassador to the Council from Federation worlds, though I was the only one with portfolio."

Quietly Dr. Tagore said, "Although I hope I will be returning to Klinzhai when the conference ends, still you could have saved a long voyage by transferring me to Admiral Shepherd's ship at the Zone. Are you proceeding to Earth . . . " He paused. "Are you being allowed to proceed to Babel because I am aboard, or because you were yourselves invited?"

"The Empire was asked by several to send an observer."

"Yes . . . I'd supposed that was it. You see, I gave up believing in miracles.

"Shall we play again? I don't know anyone on Earth who plays *klin zha.*"

This arrival at Earth, there was no game with shuttlecraft. Krenn, Maktai, and Dr. Tagore beamed down directly to Federa-Terra. They were met at the stage by a heavily armed Security force, and an official wearing Babel Conference insignia who seemed in an extreme hurry.

"Admiral van Diemen sends his regrets," the functionary said. "He's been delayed in San Francisco, but he'll be sending a visual message tonight. We have rooms ready for you, Captain, and you, Commander . . . and, Doctor, you'll be in the delegates' quarters."

They were almost instantly separated. Krenn and Maktai were loaded, with several armed and uniformed Starfleet Military guards, into a small vehicle with curtained windows, and moved off at speed.

The car stopped a few minutes later, and the guards practically leaped out; Admiral Shepherd entered, the door closed, and the car started moving again, at a somewhat lesser speed.

Krenn understood now, as he had not six years ago, the term *double-shuffle.*

"Welcome to Earth, truly this time, Captain Krenn," Shepherd said. "I find I've been appointed as Marcus van Diemen's deputy until he arrives, so I won't be able to spend as much time with you as I'd hoped. I suppose you're aware that you're the most in demand of all the non-Federation observers?"

He produced several sheets of computer printing. "These are the delegates who have asked for interviews."

Krenn flipped through the listing. "How many names are here?"

"One hundred thirty-one."

Maktai said, "And how many members has the Federation?"

"Five hundred forty," Shepherd said, with just the right *klingonaase* inflection for irony.

Krenn said, "This is an impossible number."

Shepherd said, "In several senses I agree. It's entirely your decision whom you wish actually to see, if anyone. The delegates' worlds are listed there; if you need more data, there'll be a computer terminal in your hotel suite."

"Where may we meet . . . such of these persons as we decide on?"

"Your suite is electronically scrambled. If that's not sufficient, we can arrange a secured conference room at Starfleet Headquarters." He paused, said delicately, "The hotel will be shielded against transport, of course. . . ."

"This need not be said." Krenn read through the names of planets. Contacts Branch knew most of them. Some they knew very well indeed. Krenn mentally crossed those off at once. He said, "You are being very cooperative with us, Admiral."

Shepherd put his hands together on his lap. "I'm against dissolution, Captain Krenn. And I know perfectly well that the beings on that list are for it, a little or a long way. But I can't think of a better way to guarantee their votes than to put pressure on them, or even give the appearance of pressure." He reached out, tapped the paper. "If Starfleet tried to tamper with the vote . . . the Federation wouldn't deserve to exist."

Acutely reminded that Dr. Tagore had taught this Human, Krenn looked up; Shepherd's look was quite intent, but there was nothing of a threat in it.

Krenn and Maktai walked into the hotel suite. A uniformed Human shifted their traveling bags from an antigrav carrier to the deep carpeting, went silently around the room indicating closets, lights, and environmental controls, opening the heavy drape across the windows: the fiftieth-floor view of the city and the sea was dramatic. The porter stood by the door for a moment, as if expecting something, then gave a small quick bow and went out.

"Humanai kuvest'?" Maktai said.

"A paid worker," Krenn said, though he had been thinking of Odise, in his father's house so long ago. *"Tokhest*—I don't know."

Maktai grunted. "They have anything that passes for a bath here?" He disappeared into the next room.

"I saw some good ones, last time . . . they call them 'Roman,' after an Empire from their history."

Mak stuck his head back around the corner. "A what?"

"Komerex Romaan."

Mak made a hands-up gesture and turned around again. Krenn followed him, into a room with two enormous beds.

"I've been on ships smaller than these quarters," Maktai was saying. "This must be the—Maskan's *liver,* Captain. . . ."

The Security officer stood in a doorway that opened on a circular room, the size of a small ship's Bridge; it was decorated with columns of veined white stone, mirrors around the walls and on the ceiling. Green vines trailed down from a wooden lattice that diffused the overhead light. In the center of the floor was a sunken bath wider than the span of Maktai's arms, with golden taps and sprays in bizarre shapes.

"We've got to meet those delegates, Mak. . . ." Krenn heard his mouth saying, and wondered why his mouth was saying such a stupid thing.

Maktai had a wildly dreamy grin. "But you really ought to relax before then, Captain. And I've got to check this thing out first. Security rules."

"Captains put up with a lot," Krenn said. "All right, make sure it isn't a Romulan trap. I'll find the computer

. . . we'll see who wants us badly enough to wait a little while for the privilege.''

"When the Federation was incorporated, ninety standard years ago," the Rigellian delegate said, "we requested the sum of eight billion credits to cover the administrative and other costs of in-federation. This sum was, however, never paid; instead, crude threats of Andorian reprisal were used to coerce our signature to the Articles of Federation."

The Rigellian brushed the fur on its nose, and curled its silver-ornamented tail across its shoulders. "The original amount, invested at four percent annual interest compounded annually—a modest rate of appreciation, you must agree—would now equal . . . " The delegate consulted a wrist computer. ". . . two hundred and seventy-three billion credits. Unfortunately, the membership as a whole still shows no understanding of our position, and in fact has reverted to its original approach—except that now we are threatened with Klingon devils instead of Andorian ones."

"Klingons do not believe in devils," Krenn said.

"A very pragmatic approach."

"Klingons also do not believe in bribery."

"That's a *terrible* word to use for—administrative expenses."

"In our experience it is the most accurate one."

"Perhaps . . . the interest could be discounted for risk."

Krenn showed the points of his side teeth.

"Or even waived," the Rigellian said. It tugged at its tail, which had somehow become wrapped around its throat. "Or perhaps a certain positive consideration—"

"I have only a single diplomatic cruiser," Krenn said. "I doubt there is room in its holds for two hundred seventy-three billion credits." He stood up, bowed slightly. "This concludes the interview."

"Of course," the Rigellian whispered, and left with its tail around its neck.

Krenn went into the suite's bedroom. Maktai was watching a monitor; the pictures were of delegates arriving at Babel, with extra tape allotted to those of particularly non-humanoid forms. Mak said, "I'm glad now I learned the language. They showed a tape of the *g'dayt* ugliest Klingon I'd ever seen, all fangs and scars, and were talking about him as if he was just run of the Imperial Race. Then I saw it was me."

"Have you tried the entertainment channels?"

"What's this?"

"News."

"I thought it *was* the entertainment channel. The others all look like children's indoctrination tapes."

The picture changed again. A crowd of Humans was seated on a hillside. There were long banners stretched above them, reading ONLY ONE SPACESHIP: EARTH and LOOK HOMEWARD HUMAN. Balloons, painted to resemble the Earth, floated on strings.

"In major cities on all points of the globe," a disembodied voice said, "members of the Back-to-Earth Movement met peacefully to protest . . . "

"Points?" Maktai said.

"They don't like to go into space."

Maktai had his tongue between his teeth, watching the crowd of Humans. "There must be thousands of them, all there together."

"They turned out a quarter million for just two Klingons."

"I remember 'Khil . . . you saying that . . . but . . . " he shook his head. "I don't think I've ever seen ten thousand of anything in one place before. Not even *kuve*." He pointed at the blue sky above the crowd. "A few fliers with weapon pods, and a cordon force around them . . . not fifty would get away. But they don't . . . and that mob doesn't even look like they've thought of it." Maktai looked up at Krenn. "Is that what you meant, when you said we weren't afraid of the same things?"

"Partly."

205

The picture changed again, to an old building against a sky of glass, with a blue-domed disc on its roof. "In Atlanta," the announcer said, "Maxwell Grandisson III, leader of the well-supported Homeworld faction of Back-to-Earth, was unavailable for comment. But a tapetext release to the press, signed by Grandisson, included the phrases 'a major development is near' and 'years of faith are about to be vindicated in action.'" The words appeared on the screen. "Speculation on—"

Krenn struck the monitor's off switch. Maktai was silent for a few moments, then said, "How did it play, with the Rigellian?"

"Well enough. We wouldn't buy and we wouldn't sell, so they don't know what to do about us; they're off balance, and it won't take much to push them over." He looked at the curtained window; it was fully dark outside. The clock beside the bed read 22:36. "I think it's time."

Maktai nodded, began unfastening his tunic.

Krenn said, "There are two more interviews set for tonight, and three tomorrow morning. Think you're ready?"

"I think I'll enjoy it." Mak gestured toward the monitor. "If any of them saw those tapes, the real me ought to scare them to death."

Krenn laughed. "Don't do that, or they won't be able to vote."

Mak reached inside his loosened clothing, drew out a flat black display panel, then a small keyboard, and finally a metal box that unfolded itself in four stages to become a meter-wide antenna array. Cables linked all the devices together: indicators came to life, and the display screen showed first noise, then a data line.

Maktai worked at the keyboard, then said, "Shepherd gave me the key to shut off the spy screens."

"How convenient," Krenn said. "I'm sure someone's waiting for us to use it. Besides, Kelly'd be insulted."

"She's the proudest female I . . . um."

Krenn laughed.

"They're answering," Maktai said. "Decrypting the shields now. . . . *Mirror* has lock-on. At least, as locked as we can expect."

"Have them energize," Krenn said.

"Captain . . . " Mak said, "I think one gets only so much luck with transporters, this side of the Black Fleet. You understand?"

"I understand, Mak. Action."

"Acting."

The golden flicker was very slow, and pulsed much brighter than normal, as the warp-accelerated transport signal found the dead oscillations of the standing shield wave, and cycled through them.

Science Officer Antaan had devised the technique, though Kelly's hands were on the console. Antaan claimed the Federation could not have guessed at the technique, because their transporter's super-carrier (or, as Antaan called it, the Noise Wave) could not get through the null spots. That was his thought, anyway.

Krenn felt his head throb with the transport pulse, wondered if they should not just have announced some unnamed emergency, and beamed up openly: the Federation surely would not have dared to forbid it. That was Mak and Kelly's thought.

But it was necessary that no attention at all be called to *Mirror,* not while it was within reach of Earth, and Earth's Specialists, and whatever equipment they might have. There were secrets aboard that must be kept.

Including, Krenn thought as he finally faded, from Kelly and Mak.

Chapter 8
Images

Krenn stepped off the disc, felt himself sway, put his head against the wall. A hand tried to touch an agonizer to his ear, and he snarled and swept it away: then he realized it was the Surgeon, and the tool was a neural scanner. It wasn't so much of an error after all, Krenn thought; they were the same device, only wired differently.

Kelly said, "You were almost nine minutes in transit."

"It would have been . . . a long swim."

"Artifact errors build up geometrically while you're in the system."

Krenn nodded, almost caring. "Have I missed van Diemen's message?"

"No. It's being open-channel broadcast; I routed it to the forward Theatre. Unless you'd rather lie down and watch it in your cabin."

"I'm all right. Auloh."

"Captain?" the Surgeon said.

"I think you'd better go down to the hold and get started. There's a data tape in the container."

"I've thawed out more Marines than a squadron can carry," Auloh said diffidently.

"Not like this, you haven't. Run the tape. We'll record van Diemen for you."

Marcus van Diemen, Chief of Staff for Starfleet and Chairman of the Babel Conference, stood before a panoramic view of the city called San Francisco: lighted buildings stretched away for kilometers, and the moon shone on water beneath a long bridge that was strung with lights in a double arc. Van Diemen wore a uniform that stated his rank in unrestrained terms: Krenn supposed there were enough Federation members who needed to see the metal.

"Though unforeseen events will keep me from the Conference until tomorrow, I am with you in spirit, through this message."

The Chief of Staff himself was no less dramatic a figure than he had been at Krenn's first visit: a wind seemed to lift his yellow hair as he spoke, and his hands gestured like fists striking blows.

"Perhaps, all unintended, this may be a symbolic opening for this Babel; for what we are to discuss is keeping contact between peoples who are sometimes held apart. This Babel is, more than any before it, about sending messages to ourselves.

"There are those who say that Starfleet cannot protect the Federation members. I cannot deny that we have been spread thin, that there have been losses on the frontiers; and we must find a better answer to this problem. But is that answer to disband the Fleet, each world defending itself in isolation? I think the frontier would find itself imperiled indeed without the ships of the line provided by the inner worlds, and the trained crews produced by Starfleet Academy.

"Conversely, the claim that the frontier defense bleeds the inner worlds simply misses the fact: the frontier defense *is* the defense of the inner worlds. Has Earth ever been raided by Romulan or Klingon? Has Centauri, or Rigel, or Vulcan?"

Above the skyline behind van Diemen, a small ship was rising on gravs, marker lights strobing. Krenn reached for his communicator. "Special Communications, Commander Kelly," he said.

"And finally there are those," van Diemen said, "who claim the Federation is unresponsive to the needs of its members. I could give several answers to this; casually say 'the Federation *is* its members,' callously say 'the members get the Federation they deserve.'

"Instead, I will mention some events of Federation history. The halting of Rigellian Fever. The evacuation of entire planets doomed by supernovae. Peace with the Romulans—peace forged with blood and iron, certainly, but a real peace nonetheless. Concessions won from the Klingon Empire, which not ten years ago was thought to be beyond the reach of reason—"

In the Inspirational Theatre aboard *Mirror,* there were several comments from the officers listening on translator. Krenn only smiled.

Van Diemen said, "The truth is that we do not, from one day to the next, know what our needs will be. Medical aid, disaster relief, united defense against an unimagined new enemy or a resurgent old one—these have been our needs, and who can say what will follow them?

"As a great Human said centuries ago, at the joining of another great Union, 'We must all hang together, or we shall assuredly all hang separately.'"

Krenn heard more comments from the Theatre audience, and wondered how the translator had converted the hanging line.

"Delegates to Babel . . . until we meet . . . good night."

Krenn kept his seat as the others filed out of the

Theatre. Shortly Kelly came in, holding two clear-prints. Krenn took one; the film was still warm from the printer. The image showed the spacecraft he had seen behind Admiral van Diemen, enlarged so that its markings were clearly visible. "Cargo tug?" Krenn said. "About a kilometer altitude."

Kelly nodded, handed Krenn the second print. It showed San Francisco from *Mirror*'s orbit; the city was easily identifiable by the bay and bridge. Krenn held the print to the light of the Theatre screen, flexed it for maximum depth effect. A ship a thousand meters up should have stood out clearly, floating above the land-scape. But there was nothing but a few wisps of cloud.

Krenn checked the reference strips along the prints' edges; they were simultaneous exposures.

"So it was a recorded message," Krenn said. "Was the window real, or a display?"

"It seems to have been real. The resolution matches that of van Diemen's image. But the analysts are still working. We may be able to find out when the tape was made, from light cues in the city and the angle of the moon."

"*Kai* Special Communications."

Krenn's communicator chimed. "Captain. . . . Yes, Auloh. I'll be there." He switched off, said to Kelly, "He's almost ready. Shall we go?"

"I'd . . . rather not, Captain." She held very still: Krenn realized it was to keep herself from trembling. Involuntarily, Krenn looked at the ceiling, though he knew very well there were no watchers on this voyage. Sometimes death is better, he thought, death is the end. But the thought did not improve his feeling.

Krenn said, "No reason why you have to. Finish assembling the Red File, and put these into it." He handed back the clearprints.

"Section One or Two?"

"Section One. Then do a full sort, and download a copy of One."

"Affirm." Kelly went out, walking cautiously, holding her arm to herself. After allowing her time to get a lift car, Krenn left the Theatre and rode up three decks to Sickbay.

A male Klingon lay naked on the surgical bed, strapped down securely, still half-surrounded by thermowave projectors and scanning gear. An empty coldsleep capsule stood against the wall.

Surgeon Specialist Auloh pulled a contact away from the body, cleaned off the conductive paste. "You were right about the tape," he said to Krenn. "If I'd gotten these neural readings on anyone else, I'd have figured he was a candidate to go back in the freezer, not on duty. And some of these 'recommended procedures' aren't recommended by any authority I know of." He picked up a pressure injector. "This is one."

Krenn said, "What is it?"

"Masiform-D, Tri-Ox, *and* four times the therapeutic dose of Cordrazine."

"Lethal?" Krenn said, looking at the body on the bed. The sleeping Klingon appeared to be about Krenn's age; in a way, that was right, but it was also very, very wrong.

Auloh said, "This wouldn't just kill you; you'd *explode.*" He gave the injection. "I'll be in my office. I need a jolt of something strong, too. Call if he goes over the lines."

After a few minutes, the body began to stir. The bed displays ticked higher, many of them into the yellow critical ranges; Krenn saw that Auloh had marked new lines onto the display with a wax stylus, and the indicator bars hovered near the marks.

The Klingon on the bed twitched. A wrist tore through the heavy plastic of the restraint as if it were wet paper. Then the arm stopped moving, lowered again. The eyes opened; Krenn imagined he heard a click.

212

"Welcome aboard, Zharn," Krenn said. "I am Krenn, Captain of the *Mirror*. Are you well?"

"I am indeed so," Zharn said. "You have a mission for me, Captain?"

"I do," Krenn said, and began unfastening the bed restraints.

"You are Captain . . . "

"Krenn."

"Captain Krenn. Have I acted for you before?"

"Not I. But I know your record."

"Is it a good record?" The question was almost absurdly eager.

"It is full of glory." Krenn released the last strap. Zharn began to sit up; Krenn started to assist him.

"Do not touch me, Captain. I have a reflex to attack anyone in physical contact, and I might become distracted and fail to suppress the reflex. You would die."

"I . . . understand. This was in the background tape."

"It is a thing I always remember," Zharn said. "Do you have my target briefing?"

"Yes. But we have a little time. Would you like anything—food? Something else?"

"I will need to eat. . . . " Zharn stood up. He moved like oiled machinery; naked, he seemed not at all vulnerable. "And of course I appreciate your hospitality." He smiled vaguely. "But after the mission, I will be more . . . able. And I will . . . remember it longer. The sleep damages memory."

"As you wish, *zan* Zharn."

"You are gracious, Captain . . . Krenn. Are you . . . certain I have never acted for you?"

"It is not impossible that we have met. Perhaps long ago. In the Year Games?"

"I was in the Year Games. Perhaps then. Was it long ago, that you were in the Games? For me it was not."

Krenn looked casually at his chronometer. In Federa-Terra, on the Earth below, it was 03:14. "I have your equipment ready," Krenn said. "And your target briefing."

"How did you get such precise coordinates?" Krenn asked Kelly, as they rode the lift to the transporter room.

"We tapped into their public communications grid at an open microwave link. It's a very easy system to use, there are any number of directories. I called the University of Emory, and they connected me directly to his office: we locked on the call impulse."

"You *spoke* to him?"

"He wasn't there. But a secretary told me when he would be."

They stepped out of the lift. They were wearing long hooded cloaks over their dress uniforms: Krenn's was black velvet, Kelly's a metallic gold.

In the transporter room, she handed Krenn a computer cassette. "These are the settings for Antaan's transmission technique. We've held lock on Maktai's focal referent since you beamed up . . . don't let Antaan try to set the transporter manually."

"Why?"

"Because the Captain's transport is my responsibility," she said, and began working at the console. "Energizing," she said, and stepped onto a disc next to Krenn's.

They flickered into an office with wood-paneled walls, and wooden furniture with the dark tone of age. Along the walls were glass cases, holding peculiar devices of glass and wood and metal; Krenn saw a few that were similar to Auloh's instruments, and supposed they were a collection of medical tools. A pendulum clock's hands pointed to 10:25.

On the wall above the office desk was a large framed document, with script so ornate Krenn could not read most of it: he made out DOCTOR OF MEDICINE and THOMAS JACKSON MCCOY.

Beneath his credentials, Dr. McCoy was seated, staring, hand frozen in midair on its way to a stylus plate. After a moment he said, "That's quite a trick, gentlemen . . . excuse me, sir, madam."

"Doctor McCoy, I am Captain Krenn . . . we met some years ago, at Maxwell Grandisson III's table. This is Commander Kelly, my Communications and Executive officer."

"Well, I'll be damned," McCoy said.

"Do you remember, Doctor . . . "

"I'm not likely to forget that breakfast," the Human said, and stood up. "Won't you all please sit down?"

The door to the office opened, and a woman came in, carrying a stack of note plates. She was wearing eyeglasses on a cord around her neck; she stopped short, and the glasses fell off.

"Not just now, Lucy," Dr. McCoy said. "I think I'm in consultation."

The woman put back her glasses, took a very long look at the two Klingons, and another at Dr. McCoy. Then she smiled. "Of course, Doctor. Hold your calls?"

"Sounds like a good idea."

The woman nodded to Krenn and Kelly, still smiling. "Since I've already barged in on you folks, can I get you something? Coffee?"

"Coffee would be most pleasant, thank you," Krenn said.

Dr. McCoy said, "Bring the pot, Lucy. And I hope to Lucius Beebe there's something strong for it."

Krenn thought of Auloh, and smiled to himself.

When they were supplied and seated, Dr. McCoy said, "Now what can I do for you?"

Krenn explained briefly.

Dr. McCoy was sitting back in his chair, stroking his square gray beard. He said, "I assume this isn't a professional referral?"

"I don't understand," Krenn said.

"The legally constituted authorities don't know you're here. And if they find out you *are,* it's gonna make the Last Trump sound like a tin whistle."

The phrase was bewildering, but its tone was clear enough. "The Federation will not be pleased," Krenn said.

Dr. McCoy said, "And if even some of what I hear about your culture is true, *they* won't be any too happy either."

Kelly said, "This is true." She began to stand up.

"Good!" McCoy said. Kelly dropped back into her chair. McCoy said "I won't play anybody's politics. But for the lady, that's just fine." He picked up the communicator handset on his desk. "Lucy? Get me Dr. Nesheim in the path lab."

Krenn had never seen any being but Dr. Tagore smile so warmly.

Krenn took out his own communicator. "I have to meet other appointments," he said. "The Commander will call for transport when you are finished."

"You understand, this'll take a few days," Dr. McCoy said. "We'll have to use some of our research gear, and do a little midnight requisitioning."

Cargomaster Keppa had used exactly that phrase in *klingonaase.* "I understand, Doctor."

"Then don't worry, Captain. We'll take the best care of her."

Kelly said, in *klingonaase,* "Use the control cassette."

"All *right,* Kelly."

"And use caution."

"Affirm." Krenn pushed the call key. *"Zan* Kreg, this is the Captain . . . ready to beam up."

Krenn materialized in the hotel room, took a few steps, and sat down hard on the bed. He put down the pouch containing the Red File, Section One.

"You look terrible," Maktai said.

"It is a good thing to be so cared for," Krenn said.

216

"The interviews?" Maktai's laugh was enough answer. "Good," Krenn said, and looked at the bedside clock. 11:18. He had been nonexistent for eight minutes since leaving *Mirror*. "Turn on the monitor . . . news channel."

The screen showed the dedication of a housing unit in a place called Antarctica: Krenn remembered Dr. Tagore saying that was the planet's south polar cap. He felt cold just looking at the pictures. Maktai was rubbing his three-fingered hand, and had a rigid expression.

The screen changed abruptly to a sign reading UR-GENT BULLETIN. The next image was of a crowd of Humans, some of them armed soldiers in the Earth Forces and Starfleet Military uniforms. The picture shook, evidently taken by a hand-held camera; the camera seemed trying to go forward, and the troops were holding it back. In the background, a concrete pillar was just visible. Then the soldiers pressed in again, and the picture retreated.

A Human wearing a headset dodged into view. "This is Judith Rozmital, in . . . where? . . . Byron, Georgia, USA. We have word that Admiral Marcus van Diemen's train has been attacked. . . . " An insert appeared in the corner of the screen, with a still picture of van Diemen. The cordon of soldiers continued pushing outward.

"We're trying to get some pictures . . . there's no official statement yet.

"Admiral van Diemen was on his way to Federa-Terra, where he is to be Chairman of the Babel Conference. He left San Francisco this morning . . . " The reporter turned her head sharply, said in a low voice, "Jack? This line doesn't go to Frisco . . . " Rozmital turned back to the camera. "I'm told we're about to get an official statement."

The URGENT BULLETIN sign appeared for a moment. Then the unsteady camera showed a group of civilians, all wired in some way, around an Earth Forces officer in

217

field uniform. Lines of superimposed type read COL. WALLACE DUQUESNE and EGF SECURITY. Krenn was glad it was not Colonel Rabinowich.

"I regret to announce," the Colonel said, "that Admiral Marcus van Diemen . . . is dead."

The reporters crowded in. Someone screamed in the distance.

"The cause of death . . . is unknown at this time.

"Attack? No . . . no, the train was *not* attacked . . . *heart attack,* someone may possibly have said, and if so it was totally without authorization, or responsibility.

"No, other than that I don't . . . We're looking into the route. . . .

"No, there is *no* evidence of an attack. Not by aliens, not by Humans, not by killer bees. There is . . . Oh, that *concludes* the goddamn statement." Colonel Duquesne turned, drew a finger across his throat.

The screen went white.

"Him I understand," Maktai said.

Marcus van Diemen appeared on the screen, frozen-framed, standing in front of San Francisco by night. A voice said, "For the benefit of our viewers who did not see the original broadcast, we present again Admiral van Diemen's last message . . . once again, Starfleet Chief of Staff Marcus van Diemen is dead at 67. More details as they become available."

Krenn turned off the sound, but not the monitor. He picked up the hotel communicator, watching the screen. On the bed, Maktai was dismantling the transporter referent.

"Good afternoon," Krenn said. "I would like to arrange a meeting with the Deputy Conference Chairman, Admiral Douglas Shepherd. . . . Yes, I am certain he is very busy. Tell him this is Captain Krenn sutai-Rustazh of the Klingon Empire.

"Thank you. Tell him also that one other Human must be present at this meeting. His name is . . . " Krenn reached into his tunic, produced a small plastic card. ". . . Carter Winston, delegate to Babel from the planet Deneva.

"Yes, I shall be pleased to have the Ambassador there, but it is not required. Mr. Winston's presence is *required*.

"It is indeed related to that. I suggest a place more secure than my suite. I suggest the most secure place Admiral Shepherd can arrange.

"Thank you."

Krenn broke the link. He flexed the card with Winston's name between his fingers, cracked it across, and dropped the pieces into a metal wastebasket. They glowed orange as they fell, and were burning whitely before they touched the bottom.

On one wall of the conference chamber, a display panel showed colored wave patterns, continuous proof that the room's electronic defenses were functional. Overhead, a circular ventilator moved cold, damp air with a continuous rush.

Krenn supposed all security meeting rooms looked alike: all blank and bare, as if any hint of warmth or comfort were an entrance for the enemy. This room even had access by transporter only, like Meth's window on the Council: but there were three discs on the stage, and of course it was the screeching Federation device. Krenn listened to the irritating sound of the ventilator and wondered if, should the power fail, they would all suffocate, sealed inside the Starfleet Tower. He had no disruptor to burn an exit.

Krenn sat at one long side of the long black table. The Red File rested near his left elbow. At the narrow end to Krenn's right was Douglas Tancred Shepherd, for the last forty minutes the Acting Chief of Staff for Starfleet. At the other end Dr. Tagore sat, a little back from the table, fingers interlaced in his lap.

The door hissed open, and another Human came in: he wore a narrow-waisted suit of purple velvet, with a white silk scarf at his throat. There was a silver ring on his left hand, of simple and elegant design, mounting a red-gold stone. His hair was a medium brown, long, caught at the back of his neck with a plain silver band. His face would have been smooth, except for the lines of worry in it.

"I understand that the situation is difficult, Admiral Shepherd," he said, firmly, not angrily. "But I don't appreciate being rousted from a business lunch in a public place by rude men in cheap suits. We don't do that on Deneva, and I certainly didn't expect it on Earth. I'm going to—" He turned, saw Krenn. "—Oh, my stars."

"We apologize for any embarrassment that may have been caused, Mr. Winston," Admiral Shepherd said, "but I doubt that troops in uniform would have been any less so, and the matter is very important.

"This is Captain Krenn, of the Klingon cruiser *Mirror*. And Dr. Emanuel Tagore, our Ambassador to the Klingon Empire."

"Carter Winston," the young Human said. "Resources Corporation of Deneva . . . " He looked at Shepherd, then Dr. Tagore. "I don't, ah, have a translator with me . . . "

Krenn said, "I understand you, Mr. Winston."

Shepherd said, "Please sit down, sir."

Winston sat.

Krenn said, "Admiral, what is the latest word on the death of Admiral van Diemen?"

Shepherd said, "We're still investigating—"

Dr. Tagore said gently, "I think, Doug, that if Starfleet knows anything, it had best be said."

Shepherd tensed. Measuring the words, he said "At 1552 hours Universal Time today . . . 1052 locally . . . an electrical fault in the guideway control system stopped Admiral van Diemen's train, just south of Macon, Georgia. Colonel Duquesne, the Security officer in charge, sealed the cars at once.

"Six minutes twenty seconds after the stop, Colonel

220

Duquesne checked on Admiral van Diemen, who was in a sleeping compartment. When the Admiral did not respond, the Colonel had the compartment door forced.

"The Admiral was on the bed inside, wearing his dress uniform, with a holstered, fully charged pistol. He appeared to be asleep, and the first assumption was of a stroke or heart attack.

"However . . . the military physician who examined the body a few minutes later discovered that cause of death was a clean cervical fracture."

"What?" Winston said.

Dr. Tagore said, "The Admiral died in bed of a broken neck."

Shepherd said, "In the physician's opinion, death had occurred within the last twenty minutes, which is to say, no more than ten minutes before the train was stopped, or immediately afterward."

Winston said, "Couldn't they have frozen him—or something?"

"The spinal cord was entirely severed. As by a knife, the doctor's report says, though the skin was unbroken. Even if the Admiral had not suffered irreversible brain damage from loss of oxygen, there would be little hope of restoring function to his body below the neck." Shepherd paused. "Marc van Diemen wouldn't want that."

"So he was murdered," Winston said.

Admiral Shepherd said, "I've seen men die of broken necks, and they . . . twitch when they die. Not for long, but . . . Marc's body was as composed as if he was sleeping. Which means someone composed it."

"And your suspects?" Dr. Tagore said.

"There were eight soldiers, including Colonel Duquesne, three train crew, and two members of the Chief's personal staff. The blow was very precise, but superhuman strength wasn't necessary, only knowing how, and anyone could know how. All of Duquesne's troops admit they do know. The compartment was latched, but a screwdriver could open it, and all the train crew knew how to do *that*. As for alibis, a train is a very small place, distances are short. It would have taken perhaps a minute, perhaps thirty seconds or less. And in the confusion of the sudden stop . . . well.

"We have thirteen suspects, and unless one of them confesses, we are not likely to have a prosecution. And a confession is unlikely." Shepherd looked at Krenn. "As the means we may use to extract confessions are strictly limited."

"Our facilities are at your disposal, of course," Krenn said, in *klingonaase*.

Winston looked at Krenn, said to Shepherd, "You haven't mentioned a motive. But I don't suppose I need to ask that, do I? He was on his way to Babel."

"Via the eye of the needle, it would seem," Dr. Tagore said very quietly.

Winston said, his voice rising, "Why are you *sitting* on this? Don't you realize what'll happen when the truth comes out? The Dissolution forces will be discredited completely—anyone who voted to dissolve would be linked to the murderers."

Dr. Tagore said, "I think you underestimate the flexibility of the members. The greater the excess of an act, the more easily it is disassociated from oneself."

Winston looked rueful. "Yes . . . I suppose you're right." He gave a short, unhappy laugh. "What am I saying? I've dealt with the Pentalians, not to mention Rent-a-Rigellian. I *know* you're right."

"Please do not congratulate me," Dr. Tagore said.

Krenn said, "Are you then in favor of Federation unity, Mr. Winston?"

Winston looked up. He seemed to have forgotten Krenn's presence until now. "Of course I am. I wouldn't be in business if it weren't for my Federation contracts. If it weren't for Starfleet, I wouldn't *be* here; my parents were nearly killed by . . . well, pirates."

222

"And peace concerns you."

"No businessman in his right mind wants a war. Trade patterns go to perdition, goods get seized, currencies devalue . . ." Winston laughed again, somewhat less bitterly. "Even my friends in the arms trade prefer a wide-open market."

"Yet Dissolution seems quite popular."

"I didn't say we were all in our right minds."

Krenn reached into the Red File pouch, brought out a tape cassette. "Is there a means to play this?"

Shepherd took the tape, went to the light panel on the wall. He touched a button, and a panel slid open to expose a playback unit. He put in the cartridge.

A section of the gray wall brightened, showed visual noise. The swirling dots resolved into small squares, then into a picture: here and there, squares still dropped out black, but the Human on the screen was clearly Marcus van Diemen.

"What's wrong with the picture?" Winston said.

Shepherd said, "It's a descramble . . . an unauthorized descramble." He looked at Krenn, who looked back with a slight smile.

"Standard procedure, as before," van Diemen was saying to the unseen recipient of the message, "no names, numbers, coordinates. Burn any recordings or notes." He touched keys on the desk before him, and a transparent starmap appeared in front of him. Stretching from one corner to the other was a wide amber band.

Krenn said, "That is the zone of space which the Federation calls the Klingon Neutral Zone."

Shepherd said, "That could be tested."

"A hunter squadron and two scouts to these points," van Diemen said, indicating them with a fingertip. "Engage, exchange fire, and break off. If you're pursued, signal code TRIPWIRE for support in strength."

Krenn said, "Is there such a code, Admiral?"

"That would be . . . classified," Shepherd said, staring at the screen.

223

Van Diemen said, "Your desirable losses are one-third of the hunters and moderate damage to one scout. Loss of one scout is acceptable. However, if a TRIPWIRE directive appears certain to result, any loss may be—"

Shepherd snatched the cartridge from the machine. "This is a fake," he said. A burr had come into his voice. "Sweet Mary O'Meara, it's got to be a phony."

Krenn took a document from the file pouch. "This is a voiceprint and image-source analysis. I do not understand all the technical aspects, but my Communications officer tells me that your signal-intelligence staff will be able to reach the same conclusions." He touched the File. "There are more intercepts, all of the same general meaning."

"If these are real," Shepherd said, *"if . . . "*

Krenn said, "Speaking as a Naval officer, I would think the best way to test their validity would be to examine the pattern of skirmishes across the . . . Neutral Zone."

Shepherd's voice was thick with confusion and anger. "You're sayin' he was tryin' to draw you . . . *the Klingons* . . . into a war. Sendin' crews out deliberately t'be killed. You tell me why the Chief would do that, Captain. An' it better be a damned good reason."

Winston said quietly, "Every delegate to Babel knows *why,* Admiral. We'd never dare dissolve the Federation if we thought some alien menace was waiting to gobble us up piecemeal. I admit, and I'm not proud of it, one of the reasons I was for unity was that I was . . . afraid of the Klingons."

"In this," Krenn said, "there is no need for apology."

Shepherd said, tightly controlling himself, "Are you telling us, Captain, that the Klingon Empire has no desire for war? That every shoot-out on the frontier has been provoked by Starfleet? For that matter, are you telling us that the Klingons even *minded* having an excuse to attack across the Zone?"

Krenn smiled, showing teeth. Winston paled slightly;

Shepherd stood impassive; Dr. Tagore's face was calm. Krenn wished that Emanuel were not here; the Ambassador was the only one here who might see through Krenn's performance.

Krenn said, "I am telling you one thing only. I intend to release this file to the Babel conference. Being no diplomat, I cannot calculate its effects. But I would expect them to be strong. And the killing of the Conference Chairman may seem then to be no more terrible a crime than . . . " Krenn paused, as if searching for the phrase. ". . . the shooting of a mad dog."

Shepherd flushed red, and he was shaking. The plastic cassette creaked in his grip. "I don't care what you've found out wi' your dirty window-peeping, *Captain*. You say another such thing about Admiral van Diemen an' we'll have it out, right here between us."

Krenn said nothing. But he saw the tilt of Dr. Tagore's head, and thought, Emanuel knows, of course. He understands that the Klingon who comes as a friend will always be thought a liar.

Carter Winston pulled gently at his hair, said, "All right, Captain Krenn . . . what's the asking price for these documents?"

Shepherd said, "You've no authorization—"

"Of course, trade with the Klingon Empire is illegal," Winston said coolly, "even though it happens on a regular basis. But under the Uniform Law of Space Salvage, any item recovered by a ship Captain from a wreck abandoned by its owner becomes ship's property. This is certainly a wreck we're looking at: does Starfleet want to claim it?

"And Federation law is quite clear that the right of individuals to hold, transfer, sell, use, destroy, or otherwise manipulate nonliving personal property may not be infringed. I told you, Admiral, I've been to Rigel and come back with most of my shirt." He looked at Krenn. "Besides which, there must be a reason I was . . . invited here. Tell me, Captain, do you know our word, 'blackmail'?"

"I know it."

"Good. That saves all the threats and counter-threats. What do you want for the original file, and destruction of all copies?"

Krenn said, "Dilithium."

There was a silence. Winston pulled off his ring, set it on the table in front of Krenn, with the red-gold stone showing. "There's a piece," he said. "Five carats, worth about eighty thousand credits. Or how much did you have in mind? I warn you, it's a horror to cut; tougher than diamond. You need high-output lasers."

"Or antimatter," Krenn said.

Winston said, "That sounds *very* dangerous."

Krenn said, "Over two years ago, a geophysicist at the Lalande 8 mining complex discovered that dilithium crystals could focus and channel the energy from antimatter annihilation reactions. The difference in output, his preliminary report said, was similar to the difference between white light and a laser."

"I think I read about that," Winston said. "In some mining journal or another. Pretty dull stuff."

"Yet the Federation immediately began an engineering development project, which was highly classified. A few months ago, this project issued a report, also very secret.

"Mr. Winston, Resources Corporation of Deneva owns Lalande 8. You were the contractor for the dilithium development project, and you have access to the report. I want a copy."

Winston put his ring on again, examined the stone. "Yes, I guess that explains my invitation well enough. My compliments on your research, Captain."

Dr. Tagore said, "Not being an engineer, would someone explain this invention in political terms?"

Admiral Shepherd said, "It means a new generation of warp drives. Warp 6, at least . . . maybe Warp 8 or 9." He looked very black. "And the same sort of advance in weapons systems. Is that political enough, Professor?"

"Yes, Admiral. Those terms I understand."

Shepherd said, "Then you understand why we can't possibly do it."

Winston said, "It'll take the rest of today to get hold of one, Captain. Is that acceptable?"

The Admiral said, *"What in God's name are you saying?"*

"I'm closing a deal, Admiral. That's what I'm here for."

"The Dilithium Report is still under Starfleet classification—and if you think you can space-lawyer your way around *that,* you're wrong. As a Federation citizen—"

"Admiral," Winston said calmly, "There are over five hundred Babel delegates out there, and every one of them is scared of the Klingons, even the ones that weren't scared a couple of days ago. I don't suppose the Vulcans are, but they've only got one vote.

"I assure you, if those tapes are released, in forty-eight hours there won't *be* any Federation citizens, or any Federation, or any Starfleet: just five hundred tiny little Empires. And the Klingons, and the Romulans. And if you think *this* deal is rotten, just wait and see what happens *then.*"

Shepherd sat down. "I know now," he said, exhausted. "I know why Marc wanted the war."

Dr. Tagore said, "But you don't want it, Doug."

Shepherd looked down the length of the table. "Not you too, Emanuel . . . you of all people haven't started believing in the balance of terror."

"You know what I believe in, Douglas."

Shepherd nodded. "You're right. I don't want a war." He stood again. "Gentlemen . . . let's all go back to our hotels and betray our trusts."

Krenn almost laughed. But the Humans would not understand. Not even Dr. Tagore, this time.

Admiral Shepherd's hand paused on the way to the door control. "I suppose I understand, now, where the

227

Chief's train detoured to . . . who he was meeting. Who else would demand a meeting at the last minute, and get it?"

"The File contains evidence," Krenn said, "not all of it recent."

"If you were watching . . . are you selling us that, too? Will that file tell us who killed him?"

Krenn smiled. "Sorry. You didn't pay to see those cards."

Chapter 9
Reflections

It was morning over Federa-Terra and Atlanta when Kelly beamed up. Krenn pointed at a cloth bag she was carrying: it had a pattern of flowers embroidered on the side. "What's that?"

"They called it my 'discharge kit,' " she said. "One of the nurses gave it to me, to carry all the records. . . . "

"They found it?"

She nodded slowly. "They gave me some . . . 'pattern slides,' they called them. Auloh can . . . match a shoulder joint to me now." She looked at him. "Or anything." She took a step toward the door, a little crookedly. "Too much time in bed . . . it's been three days; I'd better check the station. Both of them."

"Kreg's done all right on the Bridge, and we haven't needed Special Communications," Krenn said. "But it will be good to have you back."

"Pleased, Captain." There seemed to be a light in her, as if the glow of transport had not entirely faded.

On her way to the door she stopped, said, "Is Zharn still . . ."

"For the rest of the day."

She nodded. "I'll find him."

"Kelly—he doesn't know us. He's only still called Zharn because he had to have some name."

"I understand," she said. "But I'd like to see him anyway." She reached into her bag. "Dr. McCoy sent this to you . . . and a message with it." Kelly pulled out a roll of densely printed paper.

"What's the message?"

"'I guess I oughta be happy,'" she said, in a fair imitation of McCoy's accent. "'But I'm not.'"

Krenn felt a coldness as he took the paper; he nodded as Kelly went out, then unfolded the sheets. But there was nothing there about the Communications Officer.

THE ATLANTA CONSTITUTION, read heavy type at the top of the front page. There were several columns of text, each with its own heading shouting for attention. KLINGONS LEAVE BABEL, one said, DELEGATES EXPRESS RELIEF. But Krenn had no difficulty deciding which story he was meant to read.

ATLANTA INDUSTRIALIST DIES

Maxwell Grandisson III, billionaire local businessman and key figure in the "Back-to-Earth Movement," died early yesterday afternoon in a freak accident at the Atlanta Regency, where he had resided for several years.

Grandisson plunged through the glass wall of one of the hotel's scenic elevators, falling more than twenty stories to his death. It was suggested that fatigue stresses in the glass and frame, parts of which are more than two hundred years old, caused a sudden fracture when Grandisson leaned against the elevator wall. Ms. Sally Parker, a spokesperson for the hotel, said that as a historic building the Regency is exempt from certain types of safety certification.

The Fulton County Coroner officially declared cause of death as "death by misadventure." No inquest is expected. It was established that Grandisson was alone in the elevator at the time of the incident, nor were any other persons in the deceased's penthouse apartments.

Acquaintances could offer no likely motive for suicide, discounting the recent sharp decline in support for Back-to-Earth following the yet-unsolved murder of Starfleet Chief of Staff Marcus van Diemen. Ms. Parker noted that Admiral Douglas T. Shepherd, van Diemen's successor as Chief of Staff, had breakfasted with Grandisson on the morning of the incident. Admiral Shepherd was unavailable for comment.

Grandisson's personal physician, Dr. T. J. McCoy of Emory Medical Center, said, "Mr. Grandisson was a very healthy man, considering that he was nearly one hundred years of age. He'd had some reconstructive surgery that kept him from space travel, but otherwise he was a very well man, a very satisfied man. I can't imagine anything so damaging that satisfaction as to make him take his own life."

Memorial arrangements have not been made public. The Atlanta office of Back-to-Earth Inc. announced that it is seeking contributions for a Grandisson Memorial Fund. . . .

It was almost painful to watch Zharn in action; he moved faster than the eye could comfortably track him. He seemed to flicker between the machines in the Officers' Gym as if transporting, rather than moving; only the rush of air gave away his passage.

Kelly stood up from her seat near the door and walked toward him; Krenn stayed behind. Zharn stopped as she approached, an effect as if a running tape had frozen on a single frame.

"Do not touch me," he said, in a friendly tone. "I have a reflex—"

"The Captain told me."

"Do you have a second mission for me?"

"No. My name is Kelly. I am the Executive Officer aboard this ship."

"Honored, Executive Kelly. I am Zharn . . . I have not seen you, and I have been awake . . . for some days. Though there was the time I spent on my mission."

"I was receiving medical care. My shoulder was badly damaged."

Krenn leaned forward, wondering.

"I was badly hurt once," Zharn said. "I'm told it was many years ago, but I don't know." He moved again, around the Gym and back to Kelly in seconds. Then he bent his head, pulled down his loose training jacket to show the back of his neck. Scars like ropes ran down it. "My nerves were all broken," he said. "But the Thought Master Ankhisek mended them."

"Ankhisek is known for his brilliance."

Zharn smiled broadly. "Yes, brilliant! When he fixed them, they were better than new. The Thought Master says my nerves are four times as fast as they were

232

before. And five times as fast as a Human's. Have you ever seen a Human, Executive . . . "

Kelly replied, "Yes, I have."

"They're slow. Really slow. I did well, this mission . . . but soon they'll freeze me, and I'll forget." He stopped still again. "I don't like to forget, but it's important that I not be wasted. So between missions they freeze me, and I don't get any older."

"You look almost my age," Kelly said.

"Well, I've had a lot of missions. Even if I don't remember them all, others do. And they say my record is glorious." Zharn flew into the boxing ring, triggering a holographic sparring dummy: he knocked down the projection in a moment, punched it three times as it fell, kicked it before it could vanish. Another projected fighter appeared, and Zharn demolished it as well. He did not look back at Kelly. He had forgotten her.

Kelly went back to Krenn, and they left the Gym.

She said, "How fast does he age, when he's warm?"

"Sixty-four times. Like the warp relation, to his nerve impulses."

"Then he must be only . . . a few months older than when we knew him. In his mind, I mean."

"He doesn't know. Or care. Are you sorry you saw him?"

She shook her head. "But I'm glad it was now, after the hospital. Before, I . . . it wouldn't have been good, to meet someone who was happy with not knowing who he was."

Krenn's communicator chimed. "Captain."

"Captain Krenn, the Ambassador is ready to beam up."

"Tell him there'll be a brief delay." He turned to Kelly. "Call Auloh. It's time to put Zharn back in his box."

Krenn pressed the door annunciator.

"Come in," Dr. Tagore said.

Krenn went in. Dr. Tagore was seated in a corner of

233

the front cabin, reading. He put the book down without marking his place. "Hello, Krenn."

"Emanuel. I wondered if you would care for a game."

"My regrets, Krenn . . . I don't feel like playing just now."

"Is the one well? Or . . . does the one ask the wrong question?"

The Human smiled. "The one is well. And is honored by the question. Sit down, if you will, Krenn."

Krenn sat.

Dr. Tagore said, "I've told you about Admiral Yamamoto, have I not?"

"The three-fingered one, who played *pokher* well."

"Yes. Did I tell you how he died?"

"No."

"The Admiral was traveling by flier, alone but for attendants and a few escort fliers. There was a war, and it was a secret flight, but the enemy had broken the codes, and knew of it. And they sent out a squadron of hunters, to destroy the Admiral; which they did."

Krenn nodded.

Dr. Tagore said, "It must be understood that the Humans who ordered this did not . . . hate the Admiral. There were some who did . . . and there had been lies told, that he had no respect for his enemy, that he thought them *kuve;* but in the end, it was not hate that did it, it was the necessity of the war, that had already killed hundred thousands. Next to hundred thousands, what is the one, when none are *kuve?*"

Krenn said, "Did the one die well?"

"In his ship. With his hand on his weapon."

Krenn said, "Then perhaps we will meet. I will tell him of Maktai's three fingers. And another I know, who had only two." He understood the story, what it was supposed to say to him; he wondered if Dr. Tagore had told it to Admiral Shepherd.

Dr. Tagore said, "Diplomacy is the art of the possible. Have I said that?"

"Yes."

"But not the art of the necessary. So why . . . *why* are the deaths necessary, when I know something better is possible?" Dr. Tagore was staring, not at Krenn but past him, tears standing in his eyes.

Krenn said, as gently as he could, "There is death, Emanuel. If you had carried a weapon, if you had ever killed, you would know—"

"What makes you think I haven't?"

Krenn laughed, and said, "You told me, when you told Mak, that for all forty-four of your years . . . oh, I . . . misunderstood, Emanuel. Your ages are not like ours . . . you were older than forty-four."

"I was seventy-three then. I'm seventy-nine now. In three months, two days, six hours . . . you see, this I keep apart from Stardates . . . it will be fifty standard years since I held a weapon."

"You were a warrior, then," Krenn said, satisfied. *Now* he understood—

"Oh, no. Though the state did arm me. They gave me the key, you see."

"Key?"

"I put it in a slot . . . " He mimed the action. ". . . and turned it . . . and my wife was not in pain any longer."

The disease, Krenn thought, that was like the agonizer. He looked at Dr. Tagore: the Human was weeping freely now, bent forward in his chair with his hand still extended, turning the key in the life-support machine. For the first time Krenn saw him as small, helpless; but Krenn did not feel strong by comparison. He felt sick.

"You must," Krenn said, in Federation because *klingonaase* would never do, "you must have loved her very much, to do that."

"Did I? But it wasn't her I killed, you see. She had been dead a long time, her mind was gone . . . all I turned the key on was pain.

"I waited so long, while she suffered," Dr. Tagore

235

said, his voice thin but steady, "because I thought, there must be a resolution, both moral and compassionate . . . it was selfish, literally damnably selfish, if I believed in Hell. Which I don't, any more than a Klingon. What extra purpose would it serve, in a universe already so backwards that death can be an act of love?"

His tears had stopped. He sniffled, a ridiculous sound. He said, "I don't ask you to understand, Krenn."

Krenn said, "I do not know if I do . . . but will you listen to a story of mine, that perhaps you will not understand?"

"Of course."

"Then I will tell you about Kethas epetai-Khemara," Krenn said, "and about Rogaine."

"Serkash II," Navigator Kepool said. "One light-day out from the Disputed Zone."

"Zan Klimor, parking orbit," Krenn said.

"Acting," said the Helmsman.

"Zan Kreg, signal to the surface: prepare to receive a Federation Ambassador."

Dr. Tagore stepped out of the lift. "We're out of warp early, aren't we—*Pardon me?"*

Krenn said, "Grand strategic display."

A large-scale map, on which the Zone was no more than a streak, appeared on the display. Mirror was a white three-armed cross, Serkash II a circle.

Just crossing the Zone were three blue crosses. Annotations read BEST ESTIMATED POSITION.

Dr. Tagore said, "But . . . we've recrossed the Zone. We're in Federation space."

Krenn pointed at the blue marks of ships. "That is a planetary assault squadron," Krenn said. "It will arrive at our present location in approximately two hours. Its assignment is to destroy the colony on this planet's surface: twelve million Federation citizens."

"How do you know that?"

"It was in the Red File," Krenn said. "Section Two. Which was deleted before the File was turned over."

"Van Diemen's war," Dr. Tagore said softly. "How did he arrange *this?*"

"Our Admirals are not different from yours."

"No. I suppose not. And it doesn't matter if Starfleet arrives, does it . . . the result's just the same."

"Starfleet will not arrive, now that our escort has been evaded," Krenn said. He touched the communicator key on his Chair. "Special Communications, is subspace jammed?"

"On all frequencies, Captain," Kelly's voice said.

"You intend," Dr. Tagore said, "to fight them?"

"I intend to defeat their purpose," Krenn said, "by whatever means are necessary."

The bridge crew turned, almost as one, to face Maktai. Mak stood up slowly from the Security console, pointed his hand past Krenn, at the Strategic display. "The Admirals have conspired to throw away Klingon lives as if they were *kuve,*" he said, in the coldest voice Krenn had ever heard him use. "This is no more than mutiny, and less honorable. Security stands with the Captain."

The sound that followed was not so much a cheer as collective relief.

Krenn said "Since there is the possibility that the squadron will attack this ship, I must put you ashore, Emanuel."

Dr. Tagore said, "I . . . "

"You are the Ambassador. With you aboard, I may not unlock my weapons."

"Yes . . . I know. Will you, however, do a thing for me first? Will you open a subspace channel to Earth, for one hour—time for a message and reply?"

Krenn opened link to Kelly, gave the order. "Ready," she said. "Your message?"

"What is the Conference's decision," he said, "on Referendum 72?"

"Transmitted."

Krenn said, "What is Referendum 72?"

"To close the Embassy to Klinzhai, and recall the Ambassador."

"But—" Krenn said. "If they meant to hold such a vote, why wasn't it done while you were still on Earth?"

"Because there was a Klingon ship in orbit above the Earth," Dr. Tagore said, "and its guns were under diplomatic seal. They could not pass 72 until you were a long way off."

"*Kai* the Babel Conference, tower of courage," Maktai said.

"Strange you should call it that," Dr. Tagore said.

Krenn said, "Would we have been any better? And we would not have trusted the diplomatic seal."

"Perhaps you're both right," Dr. Tagore said. "There: that may be my last official diplomatic statement." He went toward the lift. "I'll be in my cabin . . . call me when the reply comes."

Krenn went to him instead, along with Kelly, and Maktai.

Dr. Tagore opened the door, saw the three of them, said, "Oh, my, is it as bad as all that? Please come in, don't mind the mess." The Human had been folding clothes, stacking them on the furniture: his library was already folded into its case and sealed, sitting in the middle of the floor.

Kelly said, "The referendum to recall has passed. The final vote was—"

"Don't tell me that . . . not yet. I'll find it out soon enough. Just tell me—was it close?"

"Neither close nor overwhelming."

Dr. Tagore sighed. "Not even with a bang. Well. Under the circumstances, I don't suppose I will be allowed to travel to Klinzhai; someone else will have to close the Embassy office." He said to Maktai, "Tell them to be careful, disposing of the encryption machine; it's obsolete anyway, and it really does contain a destruction charge."

Krenn said, "The squadron will arrive in seventy minutes. We have made arrangements to put you ashore . . . they'll probably meet you with weapons drawn, but I don't think they'll harm you."

"I'm sure they won't. I'm the most harmless of men."

Krenn said, in the Federation language, "Trouble rather the tiger in his lair than the sage amongst his books. For to you Kingdoms and their armies are things mighty and enduring, but to him they are but toys of the moment, to be overturned by the flicking of a finger."

Dr. Tagore had stopped still, a half-folded shirt draped over his arm. "So now you understand," he said, very quietly, "what it is the books have to say."

"It is a Klingon faith as well."

Dr. Tagore put down the shirt. "Yes . . . you told me. . . ."

Krenn tensed. He had not intended that speech for Kelly or Mak. Yet he had said it, as if he wanted it heard.

". . . that there were no more Thought Admirals."

Krenn relaxed, nodded. "How soon will you be ready to beam down?"

"Oh, everything important is packed," the Human said, indicating the library case. "But I'd like to ask the Captain's permission to remain aboard. Until . . . whatever happens, is over."

"And if there is a combat? I will not be able to lower shields, to transport you to safety." It was only the truth: Antaan's penetration technique would not work through *Mirror*'s shields. Nor anyone else's, soon enough.

"Well, I am no longer an Ambassador, which eliminates that objection. If there is a combat, I will do my best not to interfere. And not to be killed too early . . .

"Our destinies are already interlocked, Krenn. It is too late to separate them."

Krenn nodded slowly. He turned to Kelly. "Have Engineering rig a Flag Commander's Chair on the Bridge."

She said, "Dr. Tagore may use my station; I can control communications from the Special Room."

"Which you cannot leave, if it burns?" Krenn said. Then, more calmly, he said "No. We will all be on the Bridge. Emanuel is right; there are destinies that cannot be separated."

Mirror hung still, shadowed by a planetoid, wrapped in electronic silence.

"Hostile squadron two thousand kilometers and closing," the Helmsman said.

Krenn said, "Subspace is jammed, Communications?"

"On all frequencies, Captain."

"One thousand kilometers and closing."

"Tactical."

The display showed three D4 cruisers in echelon; they filled the screen.

"Five hundred kilometers and closing."

"Weapons?" Krenn said.

"Preheats completed, Captain. All circuits show blue lights."

"Take pre-locks, then. But wait for it. Communications, on my command drop our sensor jamming, and open RF link to the squadron."

"Affirm."

"Range to squadron approaching zero."

The three ships passed over the one, barely twice a cruiser's length away. The tactical display seemed to show every weld and bolt and panel. In a moment they were past, impulse drives glowing. Triangles bracketed them on the display. "Prelocks," the Gunner said.

"Communications . . . action."

The main display showed a cruiser's bridge, the face of a Klingon Captain. The view sparked slightly, radio-frequency communication rather than subspace.

"What ship is that?" the Captain said. He was young, and familiar to Krenn. "This is Kian, of *Fury*, commanding a special attack squadron. If you are a privateer, you may join us—"

"This is Krenn, Captain of *Mirror*. Pleased to know of your advancement, Captain Kian."

Dr. Tagore looked puzzled. Maktai went over to the Human, spoke softly into his ear. Dr. Tagore nodded, sadly.

"Captain Krenn? I . . . was not told you were in this sector. Are you not commanding the . . . diplomatic mission?"

"I was. But no longer."

"Then you may join us," Kian said, excited. "There will be high glory—"

"No," Krenn said, "you are mistaken." He turned to *Mirror*'s Weapons officer, spoke a phrase of Battle Language.

Disruptors flared from *Mirror,* punching through thin rear shields on all three of the cruisers at once.

"This is mutiny!" Kian shouted, his teeth showing to their roots.

"Kelly, countermeasures," Krenn said, and the display picture broke up. "Helm." Krenn sketched course plans, and *Mirror* responded, rolling sidewise, keeping forward shields to the squadron.

"Incoming fire," Antaan said from the Science console, "three-eight, three-five, three-three—" He was almost as cool as Akhil, Krenn thought. The tactical display reappeared in time to flare blue, and *Mirror* shook with damage.

"One impact, two misses," said the Engineer.

"Damage report."

"Acting."

Mirror fired again, slashing across the starboard wing of the center cruiser. The scar glowed yellow, then white as the fuel plant began to burn: but the warp nacelle did not separate. Klingon cruisers were larger, stronger, than Rom Warbirds.

More shots came past. *Mirror* was hit again. "Engineer, that report?"

"Crew's quarters hit. Engineering, some damage."

"Special assemblies?"

"No damage there."

"Keep me informed. Weapons, repeat that last shot, target portside."

Blue light cut into the cruiser's other wing. "Maktai."

"Captain?"

"I call for Security Option Two. Set for automatic destruct if we lose the Bridge."

Maktai pushed buttons, took out his key and inserted it in the board, touched another set of controls. "Option set. Security password entered."

"Kelly?"

"Executive's password entered."

Krenn worked his armrest console. "Captain's password entered. Option in force." There was a sound of weapon-shield harmonics, and curves bent on the Engineer's displays.

The Engineer stood. "I'd better get aft. If we lose any more intercooler capacity, I'll have to switch out a main, or we'll melt."

"Do it," Krenn said, and turned to the Helmsman. *"Zan* Klimor, I want *this."* His finger traced across the board. "Gunner, precision fire."

Mirror rolled again, sideslipped vertically past the lead D4. *"Action."*

Light lanced from each ship to the other. *Mirror* trembled. On the other ship's forward pod, the Bridge deck exploded in a crown of fire. "Hit to our flight deck," Specialist Antaan said. "We were decompressed already: no explosion."

Dr. Tagore said clearly, "And if that ship had been set to destruct as we are?"

"Then we would all go to the Black Fleet together," Krenn said, not annoyed. Humans met Death too late in their lives. In many senses. "Is this not an acceptable outcome? *Zan* Kepool, pressors on the *khex,* before their second Bridge can assume control."

"Acting, Captain," the Navigator said.

The damaged ship began to drift, slowly on pressor thrust, toward the other two. They continued to fire past it, then through it.

"Kai kassai, klingoni," Krenn said. "Gunner, two projections on the far cruiser. Your discretion."

The other Captain broke high, to avoid the drifting hulk. *Mirror*'s disruptors found its ventral surface: there was light, and violent outgassing, and the wound released cargo modules into space, some of them glowing with incident heat. Then the modules began exploding.

"That's bombardment ordnance, Captain," the Gunner said. There was an eruption inside the holed ship, and she shook from wingtip to wingtip.

Maktai said, "You were right. They didn't intend to capture the colony."

"What great glory that would have been, raining bombs," Krenn said, finally angry. "What a prize. I told Kian he was wrong."

"Captain," Antaan said, *"Fury*'s shields are dropping."

"Is he surrendering?" Dr. Tagore said.

Krenn turned. "This one would not. *Boost—"*

The center ship, Kian's torn-winged cruiser, fired all its disruptors at once, six blue lightnings at *Mirror*. The display darkened with light-overload.

Fire arced around *Mirror*'s bridge, and every light went out. Someone cursed, in *klingonaase;* Krenn could not tell who. But it was a male voice.

The consoles lit again, then the dim red emergency lighting. Krenn felt lancing pain in his left leg, looked down: one of the repeater screens in the Chair near his boot had shattered, fragments ripping his trouser leg and the skin beneath. He looked around: there were small cuts and burns, no one seemed seriously hurt. Kelly was injured slightly as well, but that was all right; now they could mend her.

Krenn looked at *Fury,* growing huge on the screen. "What are their shields?"

"Still low," Antaan said, clutching a cut hand. "They're recharging to—"

"Hit the pod!"

The Gunner acted, firing without sensor locks: beams tore crooked paths across the curve of *Fury*'s pod, skipping off metal into space, leaving traces burning red.

Fury did not fire.

In the pause that followed, Dr. Tagore said, "Weren't we supposed to have exploded, a few minutes ago?"

Kelly said, "The verification cycle takes forty seconds. We recovered in thirty-one."

Dr. Tagore said to Maktai, *"Kai* Security checks."

Mak laughed.

Kelly said, *"Fury*'s trying to open link, RF channel."

"Accept," Krenn said.

The enemy Bridge was burning. Captain Kian was slumped in his Chair; it was not apparent what had injured or killed him. The Security Commander came into view, pushed Kian out of the Chair. He sat down.

"Krenn," the Commander said, "Krenn sutai-Mutineer, do you remember who I am?"

"Yes, Commander Merzhan. I remember you."

"Before you claim the victory," Merzhan said, "I have a message for you. It was given to me by General Margon zantai-Demma. Are you listening?"

"Captain," the Navigator said, *"Fury*'s boom is separating."

Without looking away from the screen, Krenn stroked his fingers on the command board. "I am listening, Merzhan."

"General Margon said there would be a time to tell

you this, Cadet. I think this time is good. Listen well: there were no survivors of the line Rustazh. *None.* There was only a lineless one of certain attributes, which zantai-Demma had a use for.

"Do you understand, *tokhe Human-straav'?* Does your crew understand? Does your *kuveleta* consort?" He was screaming.

"Communications," Krenn said, "jam all frequencies. Weapons, action."

The display showed *Fury*'s boom moving forward from the main hull, on its internal impulse engines. Then *Mirror* fired on the vector Krenn had ordered, and cut the boom in two; the impulse unit, running light of load, tumbled and shot past the command pod, and was gone.

Dr. Tagore said, "Can he still execute a destruct? By remote control?"

"You understand well, Emanuel," Krenn said. "But he must do it by laser link; everything else is jammed. And it will take him a little time to think of it. *Zan* Klimor: this course."

The Helmsman looked at his order repeater. "Affirm," he said, not too steadily.

"When I was younger than you," Krenn said, "I did not hesitate."

"Affirm, Captain."

Mirror began to roll, her dorsal side to *Fury*'s hull, ventral toward the slowly tumbling pod, sliding into the gap between them.

"*Kai* the Helm," Krenn said.

"Laser pulse," Kelly said.

"What's the phrase, Emanuel . . . about doors."

Dr. Tagore said, "We make a better door than a window." His voice seemed to come from far away.

Krenn nodded. "Gunner, free fire."

Mirror cut *Fury*'s command pod into scrap.

There was a cheer on the Bridge. Krenn heard Kelly softly singing "Undefeated." He turned around.

Dr. Tagore's chair was empty.

Krenn stood up, too late remembering his leg; but he caught the Chair arm, and did not fall.

Dr. Tagore was sealing the last of his bags. "You're hurt," the Human said, as Krenn limped into the room.

"I am well," Krenn said. Auloh had removed the splinters and sealed the skin. "And you?"

"Well enough."

"Did you find the fight dishonorable? I knew Captain Kian, as Mak must have told you: there could be no talking his prize away from him. He was filled with *klin* . . . I take no pleasure in his death."

"I understand this," Dr. Tagore said. "I am pleased that the colony lives. And I am pleased that you are alive, and the others of the crew. And yes, *yes,* I was thrilled, in the thick of the battle. But the universe is still backwards. Don't ask me to be more pleased than this." He sat down on one of his cases. There was a long, quiet pause.

Krenn said, "You are correct, Emanuel. I destroyed Merzhan in anger, and not for any war that might or might not have been."

Dr. Tagore said, "I did not understand all the one said. But I think the epetai-Khemara would be proud of a student who could defeat three ships with one."

Krenn said nothing.

"I am a man of the Federation," Dr. Tagore said, "not its center, but its fringe, yet still within it. But not all people born in Federation space belong. Some go off to the Pioneer Corps, or alone to mine planetoids. Some find that dark country which is madness, and we cannot bring them back, because they are happier there than ever they were sane.

"When a Klingon is born, Krenn, and the one cannot be a Klingon . . . where can the one go?"

Krenn touched the wall communicator. "Dr. Tagore's baggage is to be taken to the Transporter Room." He released the call key, smiled. *"Pozhalasta prishl'yiti bagazh.* One of the first things I ever learned to say in your language. I have never had the chance to use it."

Dr. Tagore smiled, said in *klingonaase,* " 'Where are the secret military installations?' I never got to use that one, either."

Krenn laughed aloud. He took Dr. Tagore's arm, and led him from the room; he was laughing too hard to speak.

They took the lift down the boom to Engineering; crew were busy making repairs, cleaning up debris and burn marks, moving wounded and dead. Few of the workers even noticed Krenn to salute. Krenn keyed a shielded door, and went through, motioning for Dr. Tagore to follow.

In the large chamber beyond were three cylindrical assemblies of metal and crystal, more than a meter across and several meters long, glowing from within: at the core of each cylinder was an assembly of octahedral crystals, of a deep red-gold color.

"Carter Winston's ring," Dr. Tagore said. *"Dilithium."*

"What you asked to see." Krenn laughed again. *"Mirror* is an intermediate design . . . we're only using our existing equipment at higher power levels. The ship is always on the brink of overload. But there is a new generation coming, the D6, which will make full use of the dilithium focus. And then, everything Admiral Shepherd said, will happen."

"But . . . you had it all along."

"There was a race, who called themselves Willall, who had it. But they were *kuve,* and did not know what they had. So the Empire took it, as was only fitting."

Dr. Tagore said, his voice rather small, "And now you have the report, and know how little we have. I am terribly stupid, Krenn. I still am not able to think as a Klingon."

"No, you do not," Krenn said. "Do you think the Council will believe that Starfleet freely gave them a

247

complete report? They will read the report, and assume the truth is greater by a certain factor, and finally see themselves reflected. And the Federation, for its part, will assume we have stolen its knowledge, and we are equal on its level. And there will not be a war. This is what you wanted: I do not think its achievement makes you stupid."

"Oh, my," the Human said, "oh, my." He seemed quite shocked. "Are you . . . all right?" Krenn said, in Federation. "I should not like . . . for you to die now." He had heard that old Humans sometimes died of shock.

"This one is very well," Dr. Tagore said. "This one is farther from death than in fifty years. I feel like . . . Lancelot, when his miracle came."

They rode forward again. The corridor from the lift door to the Transporter room was lined with ship's officers, all saluting, but with their weapons out of sight; Mak's doing, Krenn knew. Dr. Tagore nodded to them, as he passed; Krenn saluted. Maktai passed the two of them through the door.

Kelly was waiting at the transporter console. Dr. Tagore's bags were stacked neatly on the passenger discs.

"I think it has been an honorable mission," Dr. Tagore said, "even if not a glorious one. You realize, Krenn . . . there won't be any place in history to be written . . . for either of us."

"There are kinds and kinds of glory," Krenn said. "And that which is done before the naked stars—"

"Is remembered," the Human said. "Yes. I think that's history enough to make."

There was a tightness in Dr. Tagore's face: Krenn felt an overpowering ache in his own jaw. "Emanuel—"

The Human stopped just short of the transport stage, turned.

"I would tell you . . . on whatever ship I have, in the White Fleet or the Black . . . there will be a place for you, epetai-Tagore. Even if you do not take it."

Dr. Tagore's voice was very strong, in no way old. "And if I should hear that you have passed from this life, Krenn, I will mourn you . . . even if you do not want it."

Dr. Tagore stepped onto the disc. He held up his hand, palm forward. Krenn saluted, and Kelly. They held the gestures for a moment; then Krenn said "Energize," and there was the click of controls, and the silent, golden light, and then nothing.

Kelly reached to null the controls. Krenn said, "Wait."

"Captain?"

"If I ordered you to gather your gear, including your medical data, and beam down here, for . . . treatment, would you obey?"

"*Mirror* would then depart?"

"You would not be abandoned. You would wait for . . . a ship to return."

Kelly said, "Only the Ship's Surgeon may order medical leave. And the Surgeon may not be ordered in matters of medicine."

Krenn said, "The Security Commander's message from *Fury*—"

"You explained that all of the line were dead, Captain. That the name was free for any founder to take. This was in no way contradicted." She touched the transporter controls. "If I am ordered to beam down, I will obey. But if *Mirror* is to return here . . . I should like to return with it."

"Very well, Commander," Krenn said. He touched the communicator. "Crew to cruise stations. Prepare to get under way."

The atmosphere on the Bridge was foggy and thick, the temperature luxuriously higher than normal. Krenn breathed deeply, smiled, nodded to the Engineer: they had earned it. And there was power to spare.

He sat down in the Command Chair, noticing that the broken display had already been replaced. The main display showed the wreckage of Kian's squadron, some of it still glowing. A bit of the bombardment ordnance exploded, far away.

But it was not just Kian's squadron, of course. It was Kodon's. And Margon's. And others' as well. It was all in Section Two of the Rcd File. And when it was known that the war faction had almost gotten its wish—against a Federation that had dilithium, while almost destroying the Contacts Branch ship carrying that crucial information back to the Empire—

The Intelligence Master said he valued the Empire above all things, certainly above any faction of councillors. And Krenn believed that—though he had also arranged other outlets for Section Two.

And the faction that had brought about the death of Thought Admiral Kethas would themselves die of an Imperial displeasure, killed by their own squadron of ships.

The last move of the Reflective Game.

Krenn wondered if Meth would reward him with the truth about his birth. Certainly they had spent high energies, at an event horizon. Or would Meth keep the information, as he had kept Kelly's pattern, always just out of the reach of those he used as weapons?

Krenn smiled. Three years ago he had begun searching for Kelly's past, and Zharn's; and, almost by accident, he had found his own. Meth was correct: information was power, secrets weapons. Krenn thought how strange it was that this secret, that he was not the son of Rustazh, had made him even more the son of Khemara; given him exactly the weapon with which Kethas had tried to arm him. The weapon of patience, against which Klingons had no defense.

"Ready for orders, Captain," the Helmsman said.

"Course for Klinzhai, direct, *zan* Kepool," Krenn told the Navigator. "*Zan* Klimor, Warp 4 until we're across the Zone . . . then Warp 6."

Krenn looked at the stars on the main display. Federation space, he thought, but the same stars. There

250

was the answer to Dr. Tagore's question: Where could the one go? Anywhere: the naked stars were the same.

Too late now. If they ever met again, in this life or the next, he would have something to tell Emanuel.

The Human had been wrong about one thing, though. Dr. Tagore believed that Klingons kept their pain, their grief, to themselves, never shared it. And of course that was wrong.

Was not revenge, Krenn thought peacefully, the final reflection of sharing?

The stars streaked past, and the ship was gone.

Epilogue

Captain's Personal Log, Stardate 8405.15

I am . . . fascinated, as Spock would say.

I am reminded of something Abraham Lincoln is supposed to have said, when he met the author of *Uncle Tom's Cabin:* "So you are the little lady who started this big war." And I keep thinking of all those log entries I have made, indelible now, that refer to the Klingons as "vicious, heartless murderers," or the like. I did that very casually. Certainly the Klingon record has been far from gentle. But I think I shall be more careful now, in what I say for the record.

I know that most of the crew have read the book, either during leave or since; ship's library has printed nearly two hundred copies. (Spock provided the information . . . one of the few times I can recall having to ask him twice for something.) The response has been very quiet—the non-regulation hairstyles have all gone—but still it is there, and I'd be a poor Captain if I didn't see.

Especially notable has been the lull in the war of words between Spock and Dr. McCoy. I suspect there has been a temporary truce, of sorts: Bones will not bring up Spock's episode in the Embassy game room if Spock will not mention McCoy in diapers.

And though I do not have words to tell them, I think all the more of both my friends for what I have read: and for those small glimpses I am grateful.

And for the reminder that the Federation has never been perfect, and never will be, I am grateful as well.

The book may, as Starfleet officially insists, be almost completely fictional. I should be sorry if that is so: truth is always more interesting. And I speak as a man who once . . . once long ago, in the city of Chicago . . . was tempted almost beyond reason to change history.

I feel a sort of bitterness now, one I am not sure if the author intended. Perhaps it is because I *have* seen how things could be made different, given only small changes: I think of the Klingons I have just read about, all of them now surely dead . . . and I think of how much we have lost, by not knowing them sooner.

End entry.

FACES OF FIRE
by Michael-Jan Friedman

En route to Alpha Malurian to settle a dispute between two religions, the U.S.S. *Enterprise* first stops to do a routine check on the progress of a terraforming colony on Beta Canzandia Three.

While Spock is left behind at the colony to continue his scientific studies, the rest of the crew heads to Alpha Malurian Six to find the dispute has turned to war.

Then a ship piloted by a Klingon faction arrives at the terraforming colony to take control of the facility. And when the colonists are imprisoned, Spock must defeat the Klingons or face certain death...

HOW MUCH FOR JUST THE PLANET?

Dilithium. In crystalline form, the most valuable mineral in the galaxy. It powers the Federation's starships...and the Klingon Empire's battlecruisers. Now on a small, out-of-the-way planet named Direidi, the greatest fortune in Dilithium crystals ever has been found.

Under the terms of the Organian Peace Treaty, the planet will go to the side best able to develop the planet and its resources. Each side will contest the prize with the prime of its fleet. For the Federation - Captain James T. Kirk and the starship *Enterprise*. For the Klingons - Captain Kaden vestai-Oparai and the Fire Blossom.

Only the Direidians are writing their own script for this contest - a script that propels the crew of the *Enterprise* into their strangest adventure yet!

For a complete list of Star Trek publications, T-shirts and badges please send a large SAE to Titan Books Mail Order, 19 Valentine Place, London, SE1 8QH. Please quote reference ST10.